WIDE OPEN

WIDE OPEN

DEBORAH COATES

A TOM DOHERTY ASSOCIATES BOOK   **TOR®**   NEW YORK

This is a work of fiction. All of the characters, organizations, and events portrayed in this novel are either products of the author's imagination or are used fictitiously.

WIDE OPEN

Copyright © 2012 by Deborah Coates

A Tor Book
Published by Tom Doherty Associates, LLC
175 Fifth Avenue
New York, NY 10010

www.tor-forge.com

Tor® is a registered trademark of Tom Doherty Associates, LLC.

ISBN 978-0-7653-2898-4 (hardcover)
ISBN 978-1-4299-8811-7 (e-book)

First Edition: March 2012

Printed in the United States of America

0 9 8 7 6 5 4 3 2 1

To my parents, for my love of reading and of the land

ACKNOWLEDGMENTS

To my terrific editor, Stacy Hague-Hill, and my brilliant agent, Caitlin Blasdell, both of whom made this a better book. To my copy editor, Eliani Torres, and the production team at Tor, thank you.

To Sarah Prineas, for convincing me I could write a novel, for reading countless drafts, and for the best sort of encouragement, critical and enthusiastic. To Sandra McDonald, for reading the entire thing, for figuring out the missing bits that made the whole thing work, and for ensuring that none of the characters were named Cornelius. To Jenn Reese, for reading the full manuscript twice and in particular for the ending, which is better for her comments.

To the rest of the Blue Heaven group, C. C. Finlay (most especially), Sarah K. Castle, Greg van Eekhout, Toby Buckell, Paolo Bacigalupi, Daryl Gregory, and Catherynne Valente. To Stephanie Burgis, Catherine Morrison, and Jen Adam for timely and insightful feedback.

To the Dragons of the Corn both past and present: Sarah Prineas, Lisa Bradley, Dorothy Winsor, Chris East, and Rachel Swirsky, and to my local writer friends for years of writing and encouragement and general friendship: Barbara Haas, Jenny Lowery, Karen Piconi Kerns, Ann Recker, and Sue Stanton.

To my father, I wish you were here for this. To my mother, for all the books over all the years. To my sister, Sue, for reading novels together by the sack, telling stories together, and encouraging my writing with her own, way back. To my brothers, Ed and Marty, and Matt, thanks for being great.

To my dogs, who need do nothing more than be dogs, but who do it very well.

WIDE OPEN

1

When Sergeant Hallie Michaels arrived in Rapid City, South Dakota, she'd been traveling for twenty-four hours straight. She sat on the plane as it taxied to the gate and tried not to jump out of her skin, so ready to be up, to be moving, to put her head down and go. And Lord help anyone who got in her way.

She hadn't been able to reach her father or anyone else by phone since she'd gotten the news, just contact with her commanding officer—*We're sorry, your sister's dead. Here's ten days' compassionate leave. Go home.*

Three sharp bongs, and the seat belt light went out. The plane filled with the sound of seat belts snapping, people moving, overhead doors opening up. The woman in the seat next to Hallie's was still fumbling with her buckle when Hallie stepped past her into the aisle. She felt raw and sharp edged as she walked off the plane and up the Jetway, like rusty barbed wire, like she would snap if someone twisted too hard.

Halfway down the long wide concourse, ready—she was—for South Dakota, for her sister's funeral for—

Goddamnit.

Eddie Serrano's ghost floated directly in front of her, right in the middle of the concourse. She swiped a hand across her eyes, hoped it was an artifact of no sleep and too much coffee, though she knew that it wasn't.

He looked like he'd just stepped out of parade formation—crisp fatigues, pants neatly tucked into his boots, cap stiff and creased and set on his head just exactly perfect. Better than he'd ever looked when he was alive—except for being gray and misty and invisible to everyone but her.

She thought she'd left him in Afghanistan.

She drew a deep breath. This was not happening. She was not seeing a dead soldier in the middle of the Rapid City airport. She wasn't. She squared her shoulders and walked past him like he wasn't there.

Approaching the end of the concourse, she paused and scanned the half-dozen people waiting just past security. She didn't see her father, had almost not expected to see him because—oh for so many reasons—because he wouldn't want to see her for the first time in a public place, because he had the ranch and funeral arrangements to take care of, because he hated the City, as he always referred to Rapid City, and airports, and people in the collective and, less often though sometimes more spectacularly, individually.

She spotted a woman with straight blond hair underneath a cowboy hat standing by the windows. Brett Fowker. Hallie'd known Brett since before kindergarten, since a community barbecue when they were five, where Brett had told Hallie how trucks worked and Hallie had taken them both for what turned out to be a very short ride. Brett was all right. Hallie could deal with that.

She started forward again and walked into a cold so intense, she thought it would stop her heart. It felt like dying all over again, like breath froze in her lungs. She slapped her hand against the nearest wall and concentrated on breathing, on catching her breath, on taking a breath.

She looked up, expecting Eddie.

But it was her sister. Dell.

Shit.

Suddenly, Brett was there, a hand on her arm. "Are you all right?" she asked.

Hallie batted her hand away and leaned heavily against the wall, her breath sharp and quick. "I'm fine!" Her voice sounded rough, even in her own ears.

Dell looked exactly as she had the last time Hallie'd seen her, wearing a dark tailored shirt, jeans with a hole in one knee, and cowboy boots. She was a ghost now and pretty much transparent, but Hallie figured the boots were battered and scuffed because she'd always had a favorite pair that she wore everywhere. Even when she'd dressed up sometimes, like no one would notice the boots if she wore a short black dress and dangly silver earrings. And no one did—because it was Dell and she could carry something like that off, like it was the most natural thing in the world.

Hallie scrubbed a hand across her face. *Goddamnit, Dell.* She wasn't going to cry. She wasn't.

"I'm sorry, Hallie. I'm sorry."

Brett said it over and over, like a mantra, her right hand a tight fist in Hallie's sleeve. In sixth grade after Hallie's mother died, she and Brett had made a no-hugging-ever pledge. Because no one had talked to Hallie that whole week, or looked her in the eye—just hugged her and handed her casserole dishes wrapped in aluminum foil.

Trust Brett to honor a pact made twelve years ago by eleven-year-olds.

"Brett," Hallie said, "I—"

"Hallie!" Suddenly someone *was* hugging her. "Oh god, Hallie! Isn't it awful?"

Lorie Bixby grabbed her around the neck, hugged her so tight,

Hallie thought she might choke. "It can't be right. I know it's not right. Oh, Hallie . . ."

Hallie unwound Lorie's hands from her neck and raised an eyebrow at Brett, because Lorie hadn't been particular friends with Brett or Hallie back in school, though they'd done things together, because they lived close—for certain definitions of *close*—and were the same age. Hallie hadn't seen her since she'd enlisted.

Brett raised her left shoulder in a half shrug, like she didn't know why Lorie was there either, though Hallie suspected it was because Brett hadn't wanted to come alone.

They were at the top of the stairs leading down to the luggage area and the parking lot. To Hallie's left was a gift shop full of Mount Rushmore mugs and treasure maps to gold in the Black Hills. To her right was a café. It beckoned like a haven, like a brief respite from Afghanistan, from twenty-four hours with no sleep, from home.

But really, there was no respite. This was the new reality.

"Tell me," Hallie said to Brett.

Brett hadn't changed one bit since Hallie'd last seen her, hadn't changed since she'd graduated from high school, except for the look on her face, which was grim and dark. She had perfect straight blond hair—cowgirl hair, Hallie and Dell had called it because all the perfect cowgirls in perfect cowgirl calendars had hair like Brett's. She was wearing a bone-colored felt cowboy hat, a pearl-snap Western shirt, and Wranglers. "Tell you?" she said, like she had no idea what Hallie was talking about.

"What happened," Hallie said, the words even and measured, because there were ghosts—Dell's ghost, specifically—in the middle of the airport, and if she didn't hold on tight, she was going to explode.

Brett drew a breath, like a sigh. "You should talk to your daddy about it."

"Look, no one believes it was really suicide." Lorie leaned toward them like this was why she'd come, to be with people, to talk about what had happened.

"What?" No one had mentioned suicide to her—accident, they'd said. *There's been a terrible accident.*

"No one knows what happened yet," Brett said cautiously, giving Lorie a long look.

"Tell me," Hallie said, the words like forged nails, iron hard and sharp enough to draw blood.

Brett didn't look at Hallie, her face obscured by the shadow of her hat. "They say," she began, like it had all happened somewhere far away to people who weren't them. "She was out driving over near Seven Mile Creek that night. Or the morning. I don't *know*." Like that was the worst thing—and for Brett, maybe it was—that she didn't have all the particulars, the whys and wherefores. "She wracked her car up on a tree. There was no one else around. They're saying suicide. But I don't— No one believes that," she added quickly. "They don't." As if to convince herself.

"Dell did not commit suicide," Hallie said.

"Hallie—"

She walked away. This was not a discussion.

She didn't look to see if Brett and Lorie were behind her until she was halfway to the luggage carousel.

Five minutes later, they were crammed into Brett's gray Honda sedan. Hallie felt cramped and small sitting in the passenger seat, crushed under the low roof. Lorie sat in the back, an occasional sniff the only mark of her presence.

Brett turned the key in the ignition, the starter grinding before it caught. Hallie felt cold emanating from Eddie's and Dell's ghosts drifting behind her in the backseat. Though Lorie didn't act as if she could feel them at all.

"She called me," Brett said as she pulled out of the parking lot.

"What?" Because Dell and Brett hadn't been friends.

"Yeah, right out of the blue," Brett said.

"When?"

"Monday morning. *That* morning." Brett swallowed, then continued. "She wanted me to skip classes—I'm working on a master's in psychology, you know—well, you don't know, I guess." It didn't surprise Hallie. Brett had always wanted to know how things worked, even people. She'd been a steady B student in high school, but she worked until she knew what she wanted to know or got where she wanted to get.

"I'm thinking about University of Chicago for—" Brett stopped, cleared her throat, and continued. "She said she wanted to celebrate."

"And she called you?"

"Shit, I don't know, Hallie," Brett said. "She called, said she wanted to celebrate. Suggested horseback riding up along, well, up along Seven Mile Creek. It was weird."

"Maybe she didn't have anyone to ride with anymore."

"She didn't have a horse."

"What?" Because Dell had always been about horses.

"She'd been gone," Brett said, like they didn't have horses outside western South Dakota.

"Did you go?"

Brett was silent while she maneuvered through the sparse late-morning traffic and onto the interstate, headed east. They had an hour, hour and a half depending, to get to Taylor County and the ranch. Or to the funeral home in town. Hallie wasn't looking forward to either one.

"She canceled at the last minute," Brett finally said. "I'd already brought the horses up, was getting ready to load them in the trailer when she called. She said she'd been mistaken."

"Mistaken?"

"Yeah . . . I hadn't seen her but one night at the Bob since she'd been home. She said she wanted to celebrate, I don't know, something. And then she canceled."

Hallie's hand rapped against the underside of her knee until she realized she was doing it and made herself stop. "Did she say anything?"

"When she canceled?" Brett shook her head. "She just said something came up. But that's where they found her, Hallie. Up on the Seven Mile."

Jesus.

Hallie didn't want to be riding in this car, didn't want to be listening to any of this. She wanted to move, to . . . shoot something. Because Dell hadn't killed herself. She hadn't. If no one else would say it, Hallie would.

2

They rode in silence for the next half hour. Hallie'd thought knowing more about how Dell had died would help, would make coming home easier to handle. She hadn't counted on seeing Dell's ghost, on discovering that the fact of how she died—Dell drove her car into a tree—told her pretty much nothing at all.

Lorie put her hand over the back of the seat and let it rest on Hallie's shoulder, like Hallie could make things right. Find out what happened. Beat someone up. Do something.

Dell's right here, Hallie wanted to say. *Can't you see her?*

Lorie began to talk, to tell Hallie about working at some new company in West Prairie City with Dell, about how that was the reason Dell had come back, about how Hallie should have seen her because she had been . . . well, she'd been . . . well . . . yeah.

More silence.

Brett dropped off the interstate onto old State Highway 4, back in Taylor County, finally. Things began to look familiar.

Familiar and different because she had changed and the county had changed. The track up to the Packer ranch, which they'd just passed, had gone to prairie. The Packers had tried to sell up two years before Hallie left, and then they'd just disappeared, left the ranch to the bank, let it all go. Hallie wondered what the buildings were like up there, because things didn't last on the prairie; even things you thought were permanent could disappear in the dry and the cold and the endless wind.

Brett turned off the state highway onto an uneven county road. Hallie looked at her. "Aren't we—?" She stopped. "We're going to the ranch, right?"

Brett bit her bottom lip. "Your daddy says you're going to pick the casket. And . . . the rest of it."

Hallie gave a sharp half laugh and pinched the bridge of her nose. Of course he did. When their mother died, she and Dell had picked out the casket with help from Cass Andersen and, if she remembered right, Lorie's mother. Because her father could wrestle an angry steer and rebuild an old tractor engine and even mend a pair of ripped jeans, but he couldn't face the civilized part of death, when the bodies were cleaned up and laid out and someone had to decide how to dress them and fix their hair and what was going to happen for the rest of eternity.

Brett looked straight ahead. "Yeah," she said. "I hope—"

There was a loud thump from underneath the car. The steering wheel jumped in Brett's hands, and the car veered sharply to the right. Brett had been doing seventy on the flat straight road, and it took long adrenaline-fueled seconds of frantic driving—punctuated by "My god, what's happening!" from Lorie in the backseat—to avoid both ditches and bring the car to a shuddering stop on the graveled shoulder.

Hallie was up and out of the car while the dust was still settling. "Flat tire," she said unnecessarily. No one answered her or got out of the car to join her, either, and after a minute, she stuck her head back in. Brett looked at her, face gone white, then sniffed and poked ineffectually at her seat belt. Lorie was silent in the backseat, her knees pulled up to her chest as if this were the one last thing she'd both been waiting for and dreading. Hallie reached a hand back through the open window, then withdrew.

Jesus!

Brett finally got out of the car, though so slowly, it set Hallie's teeth on edge. Brett had always been the calm one, the one who maintained an even keel, no matter what. She'd had this way of standing, back in high school, with a thumb tucked in her belt and one hip cocked that used to drive the boys wild. Brett hadn't even paid attention to those boys, more interested in barrel racing and the cutting horses her daddy trained and sold to celebrity ranchers for twenty-five thousand dollars apiece.

But now, she was slow, like she'd aged five hundred years, standing by her door for what felt to Hallie like an eternity—get you shot in Afghanistan, standing around like that, get your head blown right completely off. Brett reached back into the car for the keys, knocking her hat against the door frame; her hand shook as she set it straight. She stood for a minute with the keys in her hand, like she couldn't remember what to do with them.

Finally—finally!—she walked to the trunk. Hallie'd already paced around the car and back again. Brett's hand was still shaking as she tried once, twice, three times to slide the key into the keyhole. Hallie couldn't stand it, grabbed the keys, opened the trunk, and flung the lid up so hard, it bounced back and would have shut again if Hallie hadn't caught it with her hand. It wasn't Brett or Lorie sniffling in the backseat or the flat tire or Dell's death or even Dell the ghost hovering off her left shoulder she was pissed at. It was all of that and not enough sleep and twenty-four hours out of Afghanistan and the sun overhead and the way the wind was blowing and the gravel on the shoulder of the road and the feel of her shirt against her skin.

"Hallie—," Brett began.

"I got it," Hallie said. She shifted her duffel to one side and pulled out the spare tire, bounced it on the ground—at least it wasn't flat. *Lucky* it wasn't flat, because in her present state of mind, she could have tossed it into orbit.

Brett didn't say anything, and Hallie didn't know if she was relieved to have one thing she didn't have to take care of or smart enough to know that Hallie just needed one more thing before she lost her shit completely. The sun had dropped behind a band of clouds, and the breeze had shifted around to the northwest. The temperature had dropped maybe seven degrees since they'd left the airport. Hallie had a jacket in her duffel bag, but she was damned if she was going to waste time getting it out. She fitted the jack against the frame and cranked it up until the wheel was six inches or so off the ground.

She realized she didn't have a lug wrench, went back to the trunk to look, tossed out her duffel, an old horse blanket, two pair of boots, and a brand-new hacksaw. She found a crowbar and a socket wrench, but no lug wrench. She could hear the distant sound of a car, though in the big open, the way sound carried, it could have been a mile or five miles away.

She stopped with the crowbar in her hand because she wanted to smash something. She hadn't slept, she hadn't eaten, her sister was dead, and when this was done, she'd still have to go to the funeral parlor and pick out a casket. She was cold and she was hungry. She had a goddamned flat tire in the middle of nowhere, and she couldn't fix it, because there was no. Fucking. Lug wrench.

"Brett!"

"Yeah?" Brett reappeared from wherever she'd been, probably just the other side of the car.

"Where's the lug wrench?"

Brett bit her lip, looked into the trunk, like maybe Hallie had just missed it. She frowned. "Daddy might have taken it last week for his truck."

"Might have? Might have?" Hallie's voice was low and very, very quiet. "Jesus fucking Christ on a stick!" By the time she got to *stick,* she was yelling. Loudly. The useless crowbar gripped so tight in her hand, she'd lost the feeling in the tips of her fingers.

"You live on the god. Damned. Prairie. We haven't seen another car for the last twenty minutes. You're driving through the deadest cell phone dead zone in America. Did it not fucking occur to you that you might need a lug wrench?"

"Need a hand?"

Hallie turned, crowbar raised, pulling it up sharp when she found herself facing a cop—sheriff's deputy to be precise—dressed in khaki and white and so goddamned young looking.

Shit.

He held up a hand. "Whoa." A smile, like quicksilver, crossed his face. He said, "I didn't mean to startle you. I thought maybe you could use some help."

He had dark gray eyes, short dark blond hair cut with painful precision, and was thin, more bone than flesh. His black sports watch rested uncomfortably against his wrist bone. He had an angular face that wasn't, quite, still blurred by youth. He was not so much handsome as pretty—features barely marred by life. *Older than me,* Hallie realized, *but still looking so, so young.*

"We got a flat tire." Suddenly Lorie was scrambling out of the backseat. "Just—pow!—a blowout, you know. Scary! And Hallie's just home from—" Hallie's glare stopped her cold. "—from overseas," she said lamely, then sucked in a breath and went on, like things— Hallie—could slow her down, but not for long. "It's been horrible," she said. "Everything's been horrible. And this just sucks." Then she started to cry and actually looked horrified at herself for crying. Hallie figured she'd been shooting for something normal—flirting with the cute deputy sheriff—and been slammed by the fact that they were all here because someone had actually died.

Hallie was horrified, too, because instead of wanting to put an arm around Lorie and tell her it was all right, that they'd get the tire fixed, that things would get better from here, she still wanted to smash something.

It was Brett who took Lorie's arm and led her away to the front of the car, grabbing a box of tissues from the front seat. The deputy went back to his car and opened the trunk, returning with a lug wrench. He bent down and started loosening the wheel.

"You should really keep a full emergency kit on hand," he said, loosening the nuts—up, down, over, back. "It gets kind of empty out here."

"You *think*?" Hallie's voice sank back into that dangerous quiet register again. She dumped the crowbar back into the trunk because she really was going to hit something if she didn't watch it.

Five minutes later, he was finished, wiping his hands on a starched white handkerchief he'd pulled out of what appeared to be thin air. "That should hold until you can get to the garage," he said. "You'll want to—"

"It's not my car," Hallie said. Who the hell was this guy? He hadn't been around when she'd left; she was sure of it. She'd have remembered him. He was so, well, beautiful, she couldn't stop looking at him, though he was not her type—too clean cut. So fucking earnest, too. It pissed her off.

"Oh," he said. "I'm—"

"Deputy Boyd Davies." Lorie was back, looking more composed, but with red eyes and a blotchy face. "This is Hallie Michaels. We picked her up at the airport. She's home because her sister . . . because she—"

"Oh," the deputy said again. His face thinned down. He looked from Hallie to Lorie to Brett and back to Hallie. "I'm sorry," he said.

Hallie wanted him gone, wanted the world closed back down. "Thanks," she said. "Couldn't have done it without you. But we've got to—" She pointed vaguely at Brett and the car and the entire open prairie north of where they were standing. "—go now."

"I—" The deputy had started talking at the same time she had. He stopped, and when she had finished, he said, "I could follow you to Prairie City. Make sure you get there all right."

"I don't—," Hallie began.

Brett interrupted her. "That'd be good," she said.

"I can drive," Hallie said, like that was the problem.

"I bet he has to go that way anyway," Lorie said.

Though Hallie wanted to argue—wanted an argument—she couldn't think of an actual reason. "Fine," she said. "Fine."

The deputy nodded, and Hallie realized that he'd been going to follow them anyway, no matter what they'd said, which pissed her off again—or, actually, still.

"Who is that guy?" she asked when they were back on the highway.

"He's new," Lorie said. "Well, like, a year. Isn't he cute? I mean, he's really good looking. Everybody thinks he's, like, the best-looking thing ever. And he is. But he's kind of quiet." And that was familiar—finally—something she remembered about Lorie, that she liked to talk about boys. In detail. For hours.

Though whatever today was, it wasn't normal, or familiar. Dell's ghost settled in beside Hallie, drifting cold as winter right up against her shoulder, to remind her.

3

Big Dog's Auto sat on the western edge of Prairie City, a cornfield directly behind and prairie stretching to the west. The near bay held a red pickup on a lift; the far bay, two motorcycles, a car engine on blocks, multicolored fenders, and the hood from a vintage Thunderbird stacked against the wall. Cars were parked three deep along the side of the shop, two with the hoods raised and one jacked up and the right rear tire removed.

Brett came out of the office to the left of the garage bays while Hallie was rummaging in her duffel, digging out a jacket. The temperature had dropped another five degrees during the twenty-minute drive into Prairie City. The deputy—what had Lorie called him—Davies, was sitting in his car out on the road, like he didn't have anything else to do, which he probably didn't, because nothing ever happened in Taylor County. Other than Dell hitting a tree—and where was he then?

"It's going to be at least two hours," Brett said. "He's got to run over to Templeton for a tire."

"Jesus." Hallie rubbed her hand across her eye.

"Sorry," Brett said. She tilted her hat up and stepped back on the heel of her boot. Hallie remembered that Brett liked things to work and to keep on working. Sometimes she convinced herself to ignore

25

things that didn't fit with what she wanted, like that her car was old and parts wore out. "Lorie's getting a ride with Jake when he gets off work," Brett continued, "but that'll be, like, an hour. Maybe your dad can—"

"I can give you a ride."

Hallie turned and looked at the deputy, who had approached as she and Brett were talking. Eddie Serrano was beside him, staring at the left side of his face like it was the most amazing thing he'd ever seen.

"Who *are* you?" she said.

He looked startled, like he thought she should know. And, yeah, there weren't that many people in Prairie City—or the whole county, for that matter—but had he ever seen her before? She didn't think so.

"My name is Davies," he said. "Deputy Davies."

"Yeah, I know that," Hallie said. Was he stupid? Or was she making no sense?

"He's all right." Tom Hauser came out of the little office to the left of the garage bays, wiping his hands on an oily rag, looking so unchanged in a denim shirt, faded khaki pants with grease down the side, and hair cut so short it almost hid the gray that Hallie blinked. "He's not going to leave you in a ditch or anything." Tom stuck out his hand. "I'd say it's good to see you back," he told her, his expression grim, "but, yeah, it's really not. Awful sorry to see you under these circumstances," he said.

She took Tom's hand and he gripped it tight, like the handshake itself meant something more. "How long?" he asked.

"Ten days," Hallie said. "Well, nine now. Then I'm . . . back." Which seemed impossible. When she'd been there, South Dakota had seemed impossible, and now that she was home, it was Afghanistan, her fellow soldiers, dust, and roadside bombs and rifle fire that seemed like an old dream.

She attempted to pull her hand back, but Tom held it fast. He looked at her steadily. "It can be tough," he said. "A trip like this— Hell, the jet lag alone . . . You come on in here if you want to talk. Okay?"

"Yeah," Hallie said, reclaiming her hand. "Okay." Like she would actually ever do that.

He gripped her arm at the shoulder, shook her slightly. "I was sorry to hear about Dell," he told her. "She was a good kid."

Somehow that, the matter-of-fact way he said it, brought Hallie closer to crying than anything else all day. She shrugged his hand away, said, "Okay, I'll see you later," to Brett, pulled her duffel from the trunk, and walked to the sheriff's car, where she had to wait for Deputy Davies to join her because he had, inexplicably, locked his car.

"Seriously?" she said when he unlocked the passenger door. "You could see your car from where you were standing."

He took her duffel and slid it into the backseat. "I have guns," he said.

"You and everybody else."

Inside the car, the dashboard gleamed. The center console, the radio, the steering wheel, even the knobs on the defroster were completely spotless. Deputy Davies adjusted his side mirrors, which clearly didn't need adjusting. Hallie said, "I need to go to Stephens's, the funeral home over in West PC."

He hesitated. "I'm sorry about your sister."

"Yeah." She'd forgotten that everyone knew everyone else's business. Like the army, only with fewer tanks and mortars.

Neither of them spoke as they headed northeast out of Prairie City. Eddie was in the back, staring at Hallie's duffel. Dell ran a ghostly finger along the back of Hallie's neck.

"Dell's—my sister's death," Hallie said abruptly, resisting the urge to swipe at the cold along her spine. She kept expecting these ghosts, these—things—to feel like old spiderwebs or the accumulated dust of a lifetime, something thin and heavy at the same time, but they were just . . . cold. "My sister," she said again, like that couldn't be emphasized enough. "What do you know? Were you there? After?"

He looked at her without turning his head. "That's an ongoing investigation," he said.

"Is it?" Hallie leaned toward him, like getting closer would make what she said more forceful. "I hear they're calling it suicide. I hear it's all been decided."

He ran his thumb along the side of his nose, as if that might help him think. His bright white shirt was buttoned at the cuffs and stiff with knife-sharp creases, like he'd ironed it with a ruler. "She was your sister," he said.

"Yeah," Hallie said, "she was."

"I still can't talk about it," he said.

"I'm going to find out what happened," Hallie told him. "If not from you, then someone. If no one will tell me, I'll figure it out myself."

He looked at her then, something in his eyes she didn't recognize, but he didn't say anything else. Hallie rubbed her eyes. She didn't even know what questions to ask. Didn't even know enough to know where to begin—too many planes, too much bad coffee, and not enough sleep. But it had to be done and done now, because now was all the time she had.

It took a little over fifteen minutes to reach West Prairie City and the Stephens's Funeral Home, the last building on the short main street. It had once been the biggest house in town, built by a railroad man, back in the day. It was a full two stories with a big dormered attic. A rectangular single-story extension had been added twenty or so years ago, with a wheelchair ramp and heavy planter boxes built of brick.

Deputy Davies pulled into the parking lot to the east of the main entrance. Hallie stared at the building, but she made no move to get out of the car.

"Do you want me to come in?" Deputy Davies asked.

His voice was kind, which had the perverse effect of galvanizing Hallie to both action and rudeness. "No! Jesus, no! It's fine." She fumbled with her seat belt, flung open the door, then stuck her head back in. "I won't be long," she said.

"It's not a problem." He reached toward the rearview mirror, then stopped and dropped his hand, as if he'd suddenly realized he was doing it.

Hallie shut the door harder than necessary, went up the wheelchair ramp, and entered through the double glass doors. The entry floor was thickly carpeted, muffling her footsteps. The last time Hallie'd been here, the carpeting was dark green shot through with blues and golds; now it was a red so deep, it looked black, lightened with thin geometric lines of gold and brown. It smelled the same, though: a mix of disinfectant and flowers. A narrow wallpaper border with colors that matched the carpet ran along the upper wall, somehow managing to look both modern and out of date at the same time.

"Can I help you?"

Hallie looked to her left, where a man stood in an open doorway as if he'd been waiting for her. He was maybe thirty, dressed in a dark suit, white shirt, and dark tie. His hair was dark, too, but already turning gray. Hallie remembered his father. She'd been eleven when she met him, and she thought he was ancient because his hair had been completely white. He probably hadn't been more than forty-five.

"You're Art Stephens," she said.

"Arthur, yes." He gave her a thin-lipped smile that was both restrained and sensitive. "You must be Alice Michaels."

"Hallie."

He put a hand near her elbow without actually touching her and steered her down the hall. "Your father's taken care of the initial paperwork, the deposit, everything. But he wouldn't—"

He was extraordinarily calm, sympathetic without being unctuous. Hallie wanted to hit him. Or hit something, punch a hole through the wall. "He doesn't like caskets," she said, the words clipped and quick. "It's a thing."

Which wasn't the truth, but—what the hell. Art Stephens, local mortician, didn't need to know why her father did the things he did. Her father wasn't here. Hallie was.

Art opened the door to the casket display room and waited for her to precede him.

She rubbed her eye fiercely.

Shit.

But this was easy. Right?

Easy as pie.

Eddie floated past her, followed a moment later by Dell. Hallie pressed the heel of her palm hard against the hollow underneath her cheekbone.

Hallie knew something about being dead. She did. She'd died herself three weeks ago, outside Kabul. It had been— Hell, it had been kind of shitty, actually. Not so much don't-walk-into-the-light as big-black-hole and nothing the same after. The medic had told her it took seven minutes to revive her. She'd been sure he was wrong. Until she saw her first ghost.

Yeah, just three weeks, but it was harder and harder to remember normal, to remember a life without death and ghosts and loss.

And now this.

Hallie stepped into the room, pointed to the third casket in the slanted row to her left, and said, "That one."

"Are you—?" For the first time there was a trace of . . . Doubt? Emotion? Something un-mortician-like in Art's voice. "You can take all the time you need," he said.

"That one," Hallie repeated. The casket in question was polished maple with beading along the edge and metal fittings. Not fancy, but not plain either. Dell's ghost stared at the brass on the drop handle like she'd never seen brass or drop handles or possibly even a casket before. Eddie's ghost seemed equally taken with the soft shirred lining.

"Yeah," Hallie said, "that one."

"Let me get my book." Art departed, leaving Hallie alone with her ghosts.

She walked over to the casket she—or the ghosts—had chosen. She gripped the side. Dell's ghost floated beside her, looking at— Okay, Hallie had no idea what she was looking at, which was part of the problem, wasn't it? *Look at me,* she thought desperately. *See me.*

"Do you want to see her?"

Hallie snatched her hand away from the casket and turned to find Deputy Davies behind her. Goddamn. Thick carpet was a bitch.

"What?"

His gaze was steady, professional, but there was something else, too, as if he was waiting for her to do or say something. "I thought maybe you'd want to see her."

"No! Well, yes, but—" Which was pretty accurate, all told. She had seen people die, had seen people she knew after they were dead. They looked cold and empty and . . . gone. She didn't want to see Dell like that, didn't want to look. And yet . . . she needed to, had to see her. Because that's what death was—knowing.

"Yes," she said. "Yes, I do."

He gave a sharp nod, though he didn't move. Eddie's ghost abandoned the casket to drift over and stare at the side of his face again.

Art returned, copied off the coffin number as if he didn't already have all of them memorized, and Hallie realized that maybe the deputy had been waiting for that.

"I'm going to want you to show us the body," he said to Art.

"But—" Art looked at Hallie. "It's not— She's not ready."

Thank god, Hallie thought.

"That's fine," said the deputy.

Art looked from one to the other again. He gave Hallie another thin-lipped smile. "This way," he said.

He led them out of the casket display room and down a short hallway. When they walked through the doorway at the end of the hall, the floor covering changed abruptly from carpet to linoleum, the lighting was harsher—overhead fluorescents—the walls painted a practical institutional off-white.

Hallie liked it.

She could deal with stark, with professional, with suck-it-up and get-it-done. She knew how that worked.

"Please wait," Art said when they'd entered a largish room at the back of the building. He departed through another door to the left and was gone just under five minutes.

He returned with a wheeled steel table containing a body—Dell's, presumably—covered with a sheet. Hallie backed up against the wall and braced herself. It wasn't that she thought she wouldn't be able to bear it.

It was that she knew she could.

4

A rt put his hand on the sheet, looked at Hallie, and said, "You understand that she was in an accident. We've cleaned her up. But, there's damage." He looked pained, as if he wanted kinder, gentler words, but couldn't think of any.

"Yes." Like the word had been bitten off, chewed up, and spit back out. "I understand."

He drew the sheet back slowly. Respectfully, Hallie thought, and she appreciated that.

Hallie could hear herself breathing, and she couldn't figure out if the room was that quiet or if her breathing was that loud. *I've seen dead bodies before,* she told herself over and over and over, like a protection spell, like it would protect her.

Dell looked . . . Well, she looked dead. There was that. Her skin was gray, her features slack. Hallie laid a light hand on her cheek. It was so painful to look at her, to know that they'd never talk or laugh or argue again, that Hallie found herself focusing on the tiniest things, on the three holes in her left earlobe, one of which Hallie had made herself with a sterilized needle when she was eleven and Dell was fifteen, on the long thin scar along her collarbone, where one of the barn cats had jumped on her from the hayloft.

"Why is she so—?"

Art looked at Deputy Davies. Hallie didn't know if he was concerned for her or just didn't want to say it.

"She broke her neck," Davies said.

"Oh."

"She wouldn't have suffered."

You don't know that, Hallie thought.

Dell's ghost drifted closer, like she wanted to see herself, which—if things weren't creepy enough already—

The deputy put his hand on Hallie's arm, startling her. "Thank you," he said. Hallie couldn't figure out what he'd be thanking her for; then she realized he was talking to Art Stephens.

As Art lifted the sheet in preparation to replace it, Dell's ghost drifted *through* her own body.

"Wait!" Hallie lifted her hand.

Art held the sheet, half-raised. Deputy Davies tightened his grip on her arm.

Hallie ignored them. She held her breath, only half-realizing it, because there had been something—

Dell's ghost paused as if Hallie had been speaking directly to her. She drifted back toward Hallie, through the table and Dell's body and—

"What is that?" Hallie asked. In the hollow of Dell's neck—Hallie leaned closer, could feel an icy chill from the proximity of Dell's ghost against her arm and her right cheekbone—there was a symbol or a scar, like a lightning bolt but . . . messier, with undefined edges, like a real bolt of lightning in the middle of a massive thunderstorm.

"I'm sorry?" Art began.

A tattoo? Who would get a tattoo there? She reached out to touch it. Dell's ghost drifted away from the table.

The lightning bolt disappeared.

"Do you—?" Hallie looked at the two men. Art's face was professional, concerned, restrained. Deputy Davies frowned. He looked his age, or more like his age, which she guessed to be about twenty-six. Neither of them were looking at Dell. Davies motioned to Art, who pulled the sheet back over Dell's body.

"Look—," Hallie began.

"We should go." There was something in his eyes that stopped what she'd been going to say. Compassion? Pity? She wanted neither. Who was he to pity her?

Art Stephens accompanied them to the front entryway. He assured her that everything would be tasteful and just as she and her father had requested. He was pleasant, sincere, and she could barely stand to listen to him. What difference did it make? They could have fireworks, floating streamers, and a pony keg at Dell's funeral, and she would still be dead.

And what the hell was the lightning bolt? Or whatever? Had it really appeared and disappeared? Had Art seen it? Had Davies?

Once they were in the car, Davies turned the key in the ignition, backed the car out of the parking space, then sat, facing the road, as if he was waiting for something. He looked straight out the front windshield, squinting slightly, though the sun was lost behind thick gray clouds that looked like winter.

Hallie thought about what she'd seen inside. "Did you see something?" she asked. "On her neck?"

He turned his head and looked at her. Not compassion or pity or *Good Lord, you're crazy*. Just . . . looked at her. "Her neck was broken," he said.

It sounded a little like a question: *Was that what you meant?* So that she said, "Hmmm . . ." because she figured that he hadn't or couldn't or didn't see what she saw. Which . . . she wasn't sure what *that* meant in the greater scheme of things, except that something was going on beyond Dell in a car alone out on Seven Mile Creek.

They headed northeast out of town, Eddie staring at Hallie's duffel in the back seat and Dell— Well, Hallie couldn't actually see her at the moment.

The whole thing was too much to think about—ghosts, Dell's death, invisible lightning bolts.

"There has to be something more you can tell me," she said abruptly, an edge of desperation in her voice that she didn't like. "I need to know," she said. "I just—I need to know."

He tapped his right thumb against the steering wheel. It was almost three o'clock in the afternoon. He'd presumably been working all day, in and out of his car, doing . . . something. But there was nothing out of place about him. Not a wrinkle, not a crease, not a line. "She was your sister," he said, like it hadn't already been said half a dozen times.

"She was." But she wondered if he understood what that meant. Hallie's mother had died when she was eleven. It had been Hallie and Dell after because her father—he didn't know much about girls. Dell had been lots of things Hallie was not—outgoing, expressive, social, but she'd also been hardworking and dedicated to things she considered important. She'd had crap taste in boyfriends, but could pick the right horse for someone, even when they insisted that really, they'd wanted something different. "Trust me, this is the one," she'd say. And she'd be right.

"Look," Deputy Davies said after a minute. "It was a single-car accident. No one else was with her. There was no other vehicle involved."

It was Hallie's turn to stare out the front windshield at the low rolling hills and the big wide open. There was a certain comfort in how familiar it was, in how "right" it felt, the prairie and the big sky and the shifting gray and brown and gold. But that comfort, the release of tension because she was home and she knew what that meant, was canceled out by Dell's death, by knowing that nothing would ever be the same.

"I want to see it," she said suddenly. "Show me where." Like she could tell, just from seeing, what had happened.

He was quiet for a minute, and she thought he'd refuse. He probably *should* refuse. From his perspective, she was nothing but trouble. What was Dell to him? Another body, another report, another trip to someone's house to tell them their sister/daughter/friend was dead.

"All right," he said, like it was the beginning of the conversation, not the end.

The clouds had turned steel gray and were starting to spit rain by the time they pulled onto Seven Mile Creek Road. Hallie was cold, but she couldn't tell if it was because the weather had turned even colder or because there were two ghosts in the car with her. Probably both. They'd come up the county road, turned north, and headed back toward Highway 54.

Hallie thought they'd stop at that intersection, the one between Seven Mile and 54, thought that must have been where it happened because there was a stand of trees right there, between the road and the creek—cottonwoods mostly and a couple of old bur oaks. They did stop, waited for an old black Suburban to cross the intersection, then turned left onto Seven Mile Creek Road past an old garage and a partially collapsed house. The old cracked asphalt crumpled to nearly nothing as they came up on the town of Jasper, or what was left of it after the tornado in '94—a couple of concrete block buildings without roofs or windows, stalky weeds ranged along what was once a road or driveway, a rusted-out car next to a stack of old tires.

Beyond Jasper, Seven Mile dwindled to practically nothing—old asphalt, then gravel, then, abruptly, hard-packed dirt.

Davies turned left again, bounced a little as the car dropped onto a dirt track with dusty brown blades of grass spiking up along the crown.

"This—," Hallie began, then stopped when the deputy looked at her. But this couldn't be right. What would Dell have been doing up here? At night? By herself? "I thought she hit a tree on Seven Mile," Hallie said, eyeing the deputy suspiciously.

"I didn't tell you that," he said.

"You didn't tell me anything."

They headed down a shallow slope toward Seven Mile Creek itself. There were scrub trees along the creek. To the north were two groupings of big old trees seven or eight deep separated by a hundred feet or so, windbreaks for a ranch house that no longer existed.

Deputy Davies stopped the car, and Hallie climbed out while he was still turning off the engine. She thought it was warmer than it had been when they left West Prairie City, but it was hard to tell because Dell and Eddie exited the car with her, like traveling with her own personal blast of arctic air. The clouds broke apart just then, the sun streaking through like the victor of some ancient battle.

"Here?" Hallie said as the deputy came around to her side of the car. "What was she doing here?"

"I don't know," he said. But he thought he knew, Hallie could tell. He thought she'd come out here to kill herself.

She stalked away from him. Between the road and the windbreaks was mostly prairie grass, some still green from summer, but most of it gone dry and brown. Tangled brambles tugged at Hallie's pant leg as she walked. She could see tracks through the hip-high prairie grass, tire tracks that crossed and crisscrossed each other. Dell, the police, an ambulance maybe, but also old tracks—high school kids and hunters, couples and loners looking for someplace no one would find them, at least not for a while.

Hallie and Dell had come down here in the summers when they

were in high school—the creek ran all summer, and there was a tiny watering hole for swimming. No one they knew claimed the land, so it hadn't felt like trespassing, more like a place that was theirs for a while, until they left and someone else—illicit lovers or kids with pellet guns—came in their stead.

They'd even double-dated a couple of times—Dell and Pete Bolluyt and Hallie and whoever. They'd swim in the creek and poke through the old basements in Jasper, maybe build a fire in the evening and roast marshmallows.

The last time had been the summer Hallie graduated from high school, when Dell had been home for three weeks, and it was she and Hallie and Pete and some guy Hallie'd met at the Founders' Day turkey shoot in West Prairie City because he said he liked her gun.

It had been a good day—relaxed. Toward the end, Dell had declared that she would buy the land someday and rebuild the farmhouse that had once stood there and breed the Best Quarter Horses in the World.

Maybe she would come here to kill herself.

Shit. No, she wouldn't. She wouldn't do it. Not Dell.

No.

"Was there a note?" Hallie asked the deputy, who had been following silently behind her.

"I can't—" Then he stopped. "No," he said. "There was no note."

"She didn't kill herself," Hallie said. She turned away, then stopped cold. Because she could see it, right in front of her, the tree Dell had hit. It was a big Ponderosa pine. The nearer trees had died off, leaving it standing alone, separated from the next closest tree by twenty yards. There was a deep gouge where the car had hit, ripping off the bark and leaving a wide swath of clean new wood in its wake.

Hallie'd seen destruction. She'd seen people die. She'd killed a man her first week in Afghanistan, a suicide bomber who'd rushed their convoy. But this was—if not different, then harder. She would never see Dell again. Not alive, anyway.

"Are you okay?"

Deputy Davies's voice was quiet. She was surprised that he'd brought her here. He seemed like a by-the-book sort of guy. Not that she wouldn't have come herself as soon as she'd gotten a vehicle. Maybe he knew that. Maybe she should give him credit for it anyway.

"I'm fine," Hallie said. But she wasn't.

She walked up the road. If she could get some distance, if she could look back, see the whole broad picture, maybe it would make sense. Maybe she'd be able to see how it had happened, what Dell had been doing here, what her death could be called other than suicide. The deputy let her go, stayed back by his car, and she was grateful for that, for giving her the space.

Something metallic flashed sharply in the field to her left, reflecting in the slanting afternoon sun. Hallie stepped off the road to investigate. The field still bore the remains of old fence posts, weathered down to soft gray sticks, warped and cracked. The fencing itself was long gone. Barbed wire probably, and the ranchers would have hated it, cutting access to the creek. The field, once a horse paddock or something similar, had brambles and multiflora rose mixed in with the prairie grasses, marking its proximity to water.

The wind tugged at the back of Hallie's jacket like an old friend pulling her back. Dell's ghost was behind her. Hallie couldn't see her, but she could feel the cold like permanent winter along her spine. Though if that was Dell behind her, then where was Eddie? She looked back, couldn't see Eddie or the deputy, but the field was a foot or so lower than the road. She couldn't see the sheriff's car from where she was either.

She stumbled over a concealed rut. The sun had shifted or her angle had changed enough that she couldn't see the flash of metal that had caught her attention in the first place. She tried to estimate where it had been, maybe twenty yards farther on from where she was standing. But when she reached that point, she didn't see anything—just dirt and brown grass and tangled thorns. Probably didn't matter, probably just something that had been there forever and didn't have anything to do with Dell or her death.

Yeah.

She took a deep breath and turned back.

Suddenly, Dell was *right there*. Eddie, too. Right in front of her, both of them flying at her, like frightened birds. Not like when Dell had gone through her at the airport, neither of them trying to go through her. Just hitting at her, frantic, their insubstantial hands, like winter wind against her face, her neck, her chest. And it was blinding cold—blizzard cold, hopeless cold, desert cold, blind from the sun so cold just stop please stop.

Stop.

5

"Hey."

Hallie opened her eyes. She was lying on the ground, looking up at Deputy Davies. He looked concerned or nervous, she couldn't figure out which, crouched beside her. She sat up and he stood, straightening one trouser leg so the knifelike crease fell straight, the movement so automatic, Hallie didn't even think he knew he'd done it. "You fainted," he said.

Hallie shook him off and scrambled to her feet. "I didn't faint," she said, but even to her, her voice sounded shaky. "I didn't," she said again, as if saying it twice would make it true.

And she hadn't—had she? Fainted? Something had happened with the ghosts. Dell and Eddie had been—there—hammering at her like she was the barn door and they were desperate to get out. She looked around. Neither of them was in sight now, but she was still bone cold; it was all she could do to keep her teeth from chattering, her jaw clenched so tight, her muscles ached.

She scanned the ground, dropped to one knee and pretended to tie her shoe, but with the sun behind a cloud once more, it was impossible to see the bit of metal or whatever it had been that caught the light earlier.

"Are you sure you're all right?"

"Jesus, I'm fine," she said.

"We should go." He touched the sleeve of her jacket. "It'll be okay."

It won't, Hallie wanted to say, but she didn't. She was pretty sure he already knew.

"My name is Boyd," he said as they walked to the car.

It was out of the blue, like they'd become friends somewhere along the way.

"Boyd," she said, testing it out on her tongue. Odd name. But then, he was kind of an odd guy.

And maybe they *had* become friends . . . had become something. He was with her when she'd seen Dell's body. He found her lying on the ground and hadn't said, *Oh my god, don't move!* Or, *Stay right there—I'm calling an ambulance.* Or, any variation of *Sit still, don't think, I'll take care of everything.*

"Thank you, Boyd," she said.

He looked startled.

"For bringing me out here," she added.

He looked at her evenly. "Most people wouldn't thank me for that," he said.

"I'm not most people," she told him because she couldn't, in that moment, think of anything else to say.

Neither of them talked the final half hour drive to the ranch. Hallie because she was exhausted and Boyd because . . . actually she didn't know why, but she was grateful in any case because she didn't have it in her at the moment to make casual small talk.

Halfway there, Eddie reappeared, drifting on the seat next to her. She wasn't sure whether it was a relief or a disappointment.

They turned onto the long drive to the ranch, and Hallie was caught by how much things had and hadn't changed. Big round bales were stacked two high just north of the drive. Farther on, near one of the stock tanks, a small herd of cattle grazed, prepping in their own way for winter, heavier coats, eating the last of the green grass.

Boyd pulled around the last open bend, and Hallie gritted her teeth because they were here. The house, painted in three shades of brown, the big metal tractor barn with the rolling doors wide open, and the horse barn down the lane—all of it just the same as it had been when she'd left. Like nothing ever changed, even though everything had.

She sat in the car for a minute.

"I could come in," Boyd offered.

That galvanized her. "Shit," she said. "No."

She unfastened her seat belt and got out, opened the back door and pulled out her duffel. She leaned back into the front seat. "I mean," she said. "Thanks. For the drive out here. For—"

He raised a hand. His face was serious, as if what he was saying was more important than the words coming out of his mouth. "You take care," he said.

He turned his car around and headed back down the drive. Hallie watched until he was out of sight, his red taillights winking out as he dipped below a low rise. She didn't know why she stood there and watched; he was just a guy. She probably wouldn't see him again.

Shadows slanted long across the yard, just beginning to fade to gray when she finally turned toward the house. Her father was standing on the back porch, waiting.

"Hey, Dad," she said as she approached, because this wasn't going to be emotional; that wasn't how they did things. Her father looked the same as ever—more gray in his sandy hair, thicker in the waist, broad shoulders more rounded. But still the same—red denim shirt faded nearly pink, old jeans, and battered boots.

"Let you come home, did they?" he said.

"I called," Hallie reminded him.

He rubbed a hand roughly across his face. "Yeah," he said, "but I figured something would happen. Hell, it's the army."

They stood like that as shadows lengthened. She couldn't make the first move. She didn't know why. She just couldn't. Then— Shit, this was stupid. She dropped the duffel and took a step forward.

Her father was there in two long strides, caught her up in a hug so fierce, she thought he might suffocate her, hadn't hugged her like that since—well, in a long time.

"Jesus Christ, Hallie," he said, his voice muffled against her hair. "Jesus Christ."

They stood there for what must have been a long time because they would never say this in words. They just—that was how it was.

When she stepped away, he picked up her duffel, hefted it once in his hand like he was weighing it, then gestured for her to precede him into the house.

"Was that the Boy Deputy brought you home?" he asked.

It surprised a quick laugh out of Hallie. "Is that what you call him, the Boy Deputy?"

"Hell, what is he, about two?" her father said. Then he added, "Thought you'd be here before now." Which was his way of asking, *Why did a sheriff's deputy bring you home?*

"Brett got a flat tire," Hallie said.

Her father snorted—all this, better than talking about Dell. "She needs a decent pickup truck," he said. "That ratty little car she's got isn't worth a damn."

"Shit, Dad, I'll tell her," Hallie said. "Bet she runs right out and buys an F-150 just to make you happy." It felt good and painful both at once to talk like this, like nothing had changed.

She opened the door to the brightly lit kitchen, her hand automatically pulling the door up to compensate for the old, loose hinges. The house smelled like she remembered it, like old coffee and saddle leather and wet boots. For a moment, she could almost kid herself. Then Dell and Eddie slid past her, rolling through the open door on a blast of winter cold. *Yeah,* she thought, *that's right, because nothing's changed at all.*

6

Hallie's first night home passed in a blur, sleeping hard, then waking, confused, not quite remembering where she was. When she slept, she dreamed of explosions and fire and blood and fear. Some of it felt real, like she'd been there before. Some of it felt wrong—not her—not her yelling, not her blood, not her death.

The next morning, after almost ten hours of badly needed sleep, Hallie took care of the remaining arrangements for the funeral while her father did ranch chores. She called people she hadn't talked to in years—her father's friends, mostly—and asked them to be pallbearers. One guy called her, someone she'd never heard of before, said he ate breakfast with her daddy every Tuesday down at the Silver Dove. Figured they'd be needing him to help out, said she should tell him the time and the place and he'd be there. Which she did, because it would be one less awkward conversation she'd have to initiate.

In between, people came, like Dell hadn't already been dead three days, like they'd just been waiting for Hallie to get home. It reminded her of the days after her mother died, when Hallie and Dell had sat outside under the spare pin oaks and said mean things to kids from town while women organized the kitchen or the laundry or feed for the horses, and men walked across the fields, looking for her father so they could lean against fences and never say a word.

After her third conversation with Art Stephens about how many people she expected at the funeral, currently scheduled to be graveside at the cemetery, Hallie slammed the kitchen phone down harder than necessary and went outside with no idea in mind except to get out. She'd been home almost exactly twenty-four hours, and it felt both as if she'd never left and as if everything were so foreign, she would never understand it again.

But she had to understand, and she had to do it quickly because she had only seven days. Seven days. Counting today, which was already half gone. Seven fucking days to figure this out. And she didn't even know yet what there was to figure out. Didn't know anything except Dell's ghost and a symbol on her body. And Dell. Because Dell would never kill herself.

The sky was clear when she stepped out the back door, though dark against the western horizon, thunder rumbling in the far distance. She couldn't tell if the storm was headed toward the ranch and didn't much care. *Let it come,* she thought.

The old yellow dog, which her father had gotten from a neighbor ten years ago as a puppy, circled her as if there was an invisible wall circumscribed around her at twenty feet. Eddie's ghost floated beside her, had hardly left her side since she'd gotten to the ranch, had been there so long, the cold hardly even bothered her anymore. Dell's ghost, on the other hand, kept disappearing then reappearing. When she was present, she spent her time alternately staring at Hallie and at the door.

She'd barely reached the lane down to the horse barn when she heard the sound of a vehicle coming up the drive.

Shit.

She recognized the dark blue Suburban immediately. Cass Andersen. Hallie's aunt. Her mother's sister. Double shit. But it had to be faced. Like everything. Because that's what this trip was all about—suck it up and face it, because it was never going away.

Cass pulled into the yard on a swirl of dust from the drive. She was out of the Suburban in a heartbeat, grabbing Hallie into a tight hug without ever saying a word. Hallie hugged her back, even though she hadn't meant to, had to blink back tears—again—because what good was crying, anyway?

They stepped apart.

Cass Andersen was a big woman dressed in old jeans, a flannel shirt with the sleeves rolled up, and a pair of battered lacers. A cowboy hat with a crunched-up brim covered salt-and-pepper hair caught back in a thick braid that ran halfway down her back. "This is a goddamned hell of a thing," she said.

A quick three-stroke flash of ice right through her skull left Hallie feeling like she'd been flash-frozen and left in the arctic sun. Cass grabbed her arm. "Are you all right?" she asked, her gaze sharp and penetrating.

"No, I'm fine." Hallie took a step backwards, shoved her hands in her pockets. She felt stupid and slow and cold to the bone.

"I'm glad you're home," Cass said.

"I'm—" Hallie rocked back on her heels. She wanted to say something, wanted to say the right thing, but she wasn't sure what that was.

Cass clapped her on the shoulder. "Come on," she said. "I've got stuff in the back. Help me carry it up to the house."

"Did you talk to her?" Cass asked when they were halfway across the yard, arms laden with boxes filled with bread and pans and paper towels.

Hallie stopped. "What?"

"Dell," Cass said impatiently, her normal way—brisk, impatient, sharp—also kind, compassionate, and generous. "She said she was going to call you. I told her I didn't see how that'd be possible. But you know Dell."

Hallie wished it were pain all the time instead of the sharp stab like a stiletto every time she thought about Dell here doing whatever it was she'd been doing, about Dell dying. But this—

"She wanted to talk to me?"

"That's what I said. Yes." Like Hallie needed to make more effort to keep up with the conversation. "I don't know," she continued. "Something was bothering her. Wouldn't talk to me about it."

"Shit," said Hallie.

"That's about right," Cass agreed.

Before Hallie could even think about what that meant, that Dell had tried to call her, the phone rang from the kitchen and Hallie went to answer it. It was the funeral home—not Art Stephens but his assistant—with some idiotic question about the program for the service. When she hung up from that, there was a call from the weekly newspaper in West Prairie City wanting to confirm something about something, and Hallie just told them yes even though she wasn't actually sure what they were asking.

When she hung up from *that*, more people had arrived. Cass served them iced tea in red, blue, and yellow plastic glasses that Hallie's mother had gotten as part of a promotion for calf starter twenty years ago at the feed store.

"Sorry."

"Damn sorry."

"Awful shame. Just awful."

They clapped her on the shoulder or shook her hand. Some of them hugged her. Hallie would have escaped to the horse paddock or around the side of the big equipment shed to sit in the weeds and stare at the horizon, except she knew they'd talk about her after she was gone. Which seemed worse, for some reason, than sticking around.

So, she sat at the table and drank too much coffee and listened to them talk about the weather.

"I've never seen anything like it," Tel Sigurdson said. "Five lightning strikes one right after the other. All in the same spot. Or near enough. Burned it black as pitch. And the smell? Holy shit. I tell you what."

"Been a lot of lightning strikes this fall," Sammy Sue Vogt said. "The Lutheran church in Templeton's been struck twice."

"Been a lot of *storms* this fall," Pat Sigurdson said. "I practically got flooded off the road coming out of West PC last Tuesday. When I got home? Dry as a board."

"Was a good summer, though, overall," Cass said as she set another pitcher of iced tea on the table. "Best weather I can remember in—hell—probably twenty years."

Nods around the table.

Pat Sigurdson got up and started cutting pieces of the cherry pie she'd brought and offering them around. Dell had dated Pat and Tel's son Brian for a year in high school, which was a long time for Dell, a whole year with the same guy. Hallie wondered where he was now, what he was doing, if he even knew Dell was dead.

She might have asked, any topic being better than the weather, but someone chose that moment to bang on the back door, which stopped the conversation cold as everyone turned to look.

"I got a . . . delivery." He was younger than Hallie, dressed like a drunken cowboy with his shirt half-untucked and battered boots with worn-down heels. Hallie hoped it wasn't a uniform. "This is the Michaels ranch, right?" he asked, peering around Hallie into the kitchen.

When Hallie told him it was, he said, "Shit, I been looking for you all day. Never had a delivery this far from the City before."

"Huh," Hallie said, signed her name where he pointed on his

sheet, and in return accepted a basket so big, she had to carry it in two hands.

"Good Lord," Cass said when she set it on the kitchen table. She had to pick up her coffee mug to make room. "Who on earth sent that?"

Hallie dug through the colored cellophane wrapping and the oranges, apples, nuts, and chocolate until she found a small envelope, which she opened. The card had a company logo on it. "Uku-Weber," she said. "Who the hell *is* that?"

Cass said, "Uku-Weber. That's why Dell came back. Didn't she tell you?"

Sammy Sue and Pat looked at each other. Tel cleared his throat. "It's a pretty solid deal," he said. He squeezed Pat's shoulder as she settled back into the chair next to his. "New kind of windmills. Super efficient at a third the size. Head of the company's a young fellow, made his start-up money out in Colorado. They've got a setup out north for demonstrations, and the stuff they've got in prototype is pretty damned amazing. Pat and I, we're thinking about investing."

While Tel talked, Hallie flipped open the card that had come with the basket. Inside was a handwritten note.

Most of it was standard stuff: "heartfelt condolences . . . deepest sympathies . . . couldn't be sorrier for your loss." At the end, set off from the rest and written with a slightly different pen,

> *Dell was one of my dearest friends and a valued, valued employee. Without her, neither Uku-Weber nor I would be who we are. Words cannot express my sorrow.*
>
> *I regret that I cannot attend her funeral. As this is also true for some of my staff, I have scheduled a private memorial the day following. She was loved by all, and I know*

that they each want a brief moment to remember her and
what she has meant to them. Please attend if you are able.

Sincerely,

Martin Weber

"Wait," Hallie said. "Martin Weber is Uku-Weber?"

"Yup," Cass said. "He came back with Dell about a year ago. Said he was starting a company and he wanted to do it here. Said there would be jobs. Which," she added, "they're mostly construction jobs so far, but the building isn't finished yet."

"But—," Hallie began, then stopped. Wasn't he that guy? The one from that four-years-gone summer? The guy who'd liked her gun, which had been a joke between them, the three or four times they'd gone out before Hallie left for the army. Because he'd meant *I like you*—at least, that's what Hallie'd figured at the time. Martin Weber. Who'd been from Rapid City, and Dell knew him only because he'd gone out with Hallie.

Martin Weber. He'd been a smart guy; she remembered that about him. Kind of charming, though not exactly her type. She wondered if he'd been Dell's type, if that's why she'd gone to work with him. That was another thing she'd probably never know.

7

By the time everyone finally left, it was almost four o'clock.

Hallie sat down at the kitchen table, pulled out the phone book, and called Uku-Weber. The woman who answered the phone told her to talk to Martin, though she had no idea when he'd be in or how to get in touch with him.

"What do you do there?" Hallie asked.

"What do *I* do?" the woman, who'd identified herself as Miss Roche, asked.

"As a company," Hallie said. "What is it that you do? You must do something."

"Uku-Weber is a research and development company." Miss Roche sounded like she was reading it off a brochure. "When we are fully operational, we will be at the cutting edge of research into weather prediction and control."

"What does that mean?"

"What does it mean?"

"What was Dell's job?" Hallie asked. "And do *not* repeat my question back to me."

"What—?" There was a moment of silence. "Really," Miss Roche finally said, "you need to speak to Mr. Weber."

She called the sheriff's office. They told her what the Boy Deputy had told her: that it was an ongoing investigation.

"I thought it was suicide," she said to the woman who'd answered the phone. She could hear clacking in the background—was she knitting?

"Yes, well, I can't really say." The woman, who Hallie assumed was the dispatcher, had a clipped quick voice that ended on an up-tone, so that everything she said sounded like an order in the form of a question. "That would be for the sheriff to say," she added.

"Can I speak to the sheriff?" Hallie asked.

"He's not in right now."

"Can you leave a message?" Hallie's own words became more and more precise the longer they spoke.

"Yes," the woman said, "but I don't know when he'll be back. He's up to Brookings for the day."

"Thank you." Hallie slammed the phone back into its cradle. *For nothing,* she added under her breath.

She called Lorie.

"I can't really talk right now," Lorie said.

"Was she at work on Monday?" Hallie asked.

"Dell?"

"Yes, Dell. Who the hell else would I be asking about?"

"Hallie . . ." Lorie's voice was low. "Do you really think this is . . . productive? Shouldn't you be helping your dad or . . . or, I don't know, coming to terms?"

"What?"

"What?"

"What the hell are you talking about?"

"Just . . ." Hallie heard voices, someone murmuring right up near the phone, maddeningly, because she couldn't make out what they were saying. "Take care," Lorie said, and disconnected.

Hallie rubbed her forehead. She wished fewer people would tell her to take care and just goddamned answer her questions.

Her father came in, letting the kitchen door slam behind him like a thunder clap.

"Everybody gone?" he said.

Hallie didn't remember whether she was supposed to answer questions like that or let them hang in the air between them, because it was pretty obvious that everyone was gone.

"Yeah, Dad, they're gone," she said.

Her father blew out a breath and looked around anyway, like there might still be someone lurking in a corner. Then he and Hallie stared at each other for a long minute, like, *What the hell do we do now?*

"You want something to eat?" her father said.

"I've been eating all day," Hallie said.

"Hmmph." Her father crossed to the sink, washed his hands, then rummaged in the refrigerator for a beer. He crossed back to the door, stopped as if he knew he should do something, but wasn't sure what. "I'm going out to the tractor shed," he finally said. "Work on the Allis. You—" Hallie figured he didn't know how to finish that sentence. *You okay? You want to come? You want—* Because what they both wanted—Dell back—they were never going to have.

"I'm going out," she said. Decided just like that and realized that, yeah, she had to get out of here.

She wasn't going to—couldn't—spend the night sitting around, staring at doors or walls or the ceiling, waiting for morning and Dell's funeral. Her old pickup truck was outside all gassed up and ready to go. Her father had put in a new battery, changed the oil, and bought new tires, too, which had made her look at him, because he hadn't known when she'd be home again.

"What?" he'd said. "You'd do it for me."

She'd grinned at him, though it was bittersweet. "Join the army and let's find out."

Right now she was more than grateful, because she needed to be out, to talk to people about Dell and what she'd been doing since she got back. And a Friday night in Taylor County? She knew exactly where to go for that.

She went upstairs after her father left and took a quick shower, toweled her hair dry, and combed it out with her fingers.

From the closet, she dug out a pair of black jeans that had been new four years ago. They hung loose on her hips, and she snugged them up a bit with a narrow leather belt. She put on a dark red shirt with silver buttons—blood red, she thought, which almost made her take it off, but then she figured what the hell and tucked it into her jeans. She took a pair of Wolverine work boots she'd never actually worn for work out of the back of the closet and pulled them on.

She picked up a small nylon zippered bag that she'd put on her dresser when she unpacked her duffel. She opened it, and out of the tangled mix of cheap earrings, an old watch with a broken strap, and a silver necklace her mother had given her when she was ten, she extracted a simple bracelet made of lapis lazuli and braided leather. Eddie Serrano had given it to her two weeks before he died to pay off a bet.

"Don't think this means we're going steady or anything," he'd said. "'Cuz I got a gal back home."

It had made Hallie laugh because Eddie talked about Estelle constantly. He always referred to her as "my gal back home," like he was in World War II, though she was in a master's program at NYU, majoring in nineteenth-century American literature.

"Where am I going to wear this?" she'd asked.

He'd bumped her shoulder with his arm. "Ah, you know," he'd said. "We'll be going back pretty soon. Wear it to celebrate."

So she put it on, for Eddie, because he hadn't made it to the celebration.

She tucked forty dollars and her driver's license in her back pocket and headed downstairs.

Her father was waiting for her in the doorway between the dining room and the kitchen. He tossed something at her. She had to back up a half step to catch it.

It was a cell phone.

"It was hers." Her father cleared his throat. "I thought . . . I haven't shut it off or anything. You need one. You're not going to be here that long. And . . . ah, shit, just take it." Like she was arguing with him.

He went on into the kitchen. Hallie turned the cell phone over in her hands. Nothing special about it, probably the free one that came with service. She flipped it open, turned it on, and scrolled to the address book.

Nothing.

No names, no phone numbers, like Dell had never even used it.

Her father was at the kitchen sink, wiping his hands on an old kitchen towel that used to be blue but had faded to a random gray from countless washings. It was almost completely threadbare in spots, and there was an old burn streak along the edge from some ancient kitchen disaster. It still did its job, though, drying wet hands and dishes, and her father never got rid of anything as long as it had some use in it.

"Don't be—," he began, and stopped. Then, "Be careful."

"I'm always careful," she said.

He laughed.

The Bobtail Inn—TRUCKS PARK AROUND BACK—was five miles from the nearest town. Nothing but an open-span pole building surrounded by the biggest gravel parking lot in three counties. It was a little before eight when Hallie pulled up, and the lot was already half-full. Half a dozen young men in cowboy hats and Wranglers were leaning on pickup trucks near the north entrance. They each had a longneck in their hands, and when one of them threw his head back and laughed, his neck showed tan against the bright white of his shirt.

It was so familiar, laughter pouring out open doors, tires crunching on gravel, boys in precision-ironed shirts, girls in denim miniskirts and cowboy boots. Nothing would ever be the way it was. But this place? This was a place Hallie understood.

Dell and Eddie flanked her as she crossed the lot, close enough that she could feel them both. She'd called Brett and Lorie on the way, and though they wouldn't be here yet, she wasn't waiting, wanted that first cool gulp of beer right from the bottle.

She wasn't more than two steps inside when someone grabbed her arm and yanked her sideways.

"Hallie Michaels."

Pete Bolluyt snagged her right up tight against him, his hand gripping her elbow hard enough to bruise. "Imagine running into you here," he said. His voice like molasses, all slow drawl, but the iron grip on her elbow told Hallie he was wound tight as a coil of barbed wire underneath. But then, he always was, even back in high school, like he was always waiting for something that never came.

He wore a big black cowboy hat, a black and silver shirt, and the biggest damn belt buckle—

"Let go of me, Pete," she said.

"Or—?" He grinned at her.

She looked him in the eye and stomped on his instep as hard as she could. A muscle ticced under his left eye. He let go of her arm.

She took a step back.

He looked the same and yet, different, a glittery . . . something in his eyes that Hallie didn't remember from before. His face had thinned down, cheekbones sharp and prominent.

Hallie noticed these things only peripherally. What had captured her attention, drawn it like a missile sensing heat, was Pete's belt buckle, which had exactly—exactly—the same symbol etched in silver that Hallie had seen at the base of Dell's neck. Hallie's breath caught in her throat.

"Heard you been asking questions," Pete said.

"What?" Hallie pulled her attention from the buckle—what was that symbol?

"Asking questions—about Dell, about her death, about the company," Pete said.

"'The Company'? What is that, like a cult?"

"You be careful what you ask," he said. His voice softened when he said it, and for that one moment, she couldn't tell if he was threatening or warning her.

Hallie took another step back. People squeezed past her; it was crowded now, but Hallie held her ground. She wanted to see Pete's face when she talked to him, not some random spot on his shirt halfway between his nose and his crotch.

"You hear me?" he said.

Maybe it would be smart to be subtle, for once.

"What's that thing on your belt buckle, Pete?"

Maybe not.

Pete's hand slapped over the buckle, like he'd been caught in the open. His jaw worked for a moment; then he said, "You don't live here anymore, Hallie. And you don't know what you're messing with."

"She was my sister, Pete."

"I mean it, Hallie."

"So do I."

They stared at each other for a minute, like a standoff. Hallie said, "I thought you loved her."

For a swift second, there was a look on his face, vulnerable and open. Then it was gone, and there was no mistaking the fury that replaced it. "You bitch," he said.

He grabbed at her again, but Hallie was too quick for him, out of range and walking away. She didn't look back, though she felt an itch between her shoulder blades, like she had a target painted there.

Lightning bolts. What the hell?

She had just ordered a beer at the bar when a huge commotion, all whoops and hollers, started at the exact same moment someone dropped a hand on Hallie's shoulder.

"Jesus, Lorie," Hallie said when she turned.

Brett, who was just behind Lorie, stepped up and got a beer for herself and a Coke for Lorie, and they found a table away from the dance floor. Lorie kept up a running monologue, pointing out who'd been here the last time she'd come to the Bob, who'd been in their graduating class in high school, who hadn't graduated from high school, who had a job, who hadn't worked a single day since last July, and who was dating, stepping out on, leaving, or marrying who. At some point, she worked in an apology for brushing Hallie off earlier on the phone. "There were people around," she said, then went right back to talk about who she saw at the post office three weeks ago.

Hallie didn't stop her, knew she did it like a wall between herself and the fact that this wasn't a celebration—more like the way life was going to be from here on out. No more Dell. Ever. Because it was noticeable here, like a black hole, because they'd all been here with Dell at one time or another, because she'd loved it here.

Lorie leaned forward. "Do you remember her?" she asked, pointing at a woman sitting three tables away from them with three other women her age. She wore a tea-stained straw hat with a hondo crown,

tight blue jeans, and a sleeveless top. "Jennie Vagts?" Lorie continued. "She was, like, two years behind us in school. Went to college
over in Brookings, but she's taking a semester off. Or . . . that's what
she told Dell when she interviewed out at the company. I think she
got in trouble or something, and her mother made her come home.

"I saw her over at Cleary's yesterday, because that's where she's
working now. She had a good job—I mean a *good job* out at Uku-
Weber, and she just up and quit last week." Lorie snapped her fingers. "Like that. Who would do that?"

Dell's ghost settled in just behind Hallie. The icy cold of an arctic
winter cut through Hallie's shoulder blade like a knife. Brett tapped
her index finger against her beer glass. Hallie could feel Pete watching her, like an itch she couldn't scratch. She turned around, spotted
him in the growing crowd, and stared back. Pete nodded to the man
across the table from him, a heavyset man in his mid-twenties, who
looked over at Hallie and laughed. Pete smirked, then turned back to
his companions.

You fucker, Hallie thought, *I could take you.* He was bigger than
she was, probably meaner, but she'd learned things in the army, in
Afghanistan. And she wasn't the same girl who'd left.

"Hallie!" The sharpness in Brett's voice told Hallie she'd already
said her name more than once.

"Yeah?" There was another beer in front of her. She picked it up
and took a long swallow.

Brett leaned closer. "Don't mess with Pete," she said. "He's not
like you remember him."

"I thought he left," Hallie said. "After the . . . after that fight."

Several months after Hallie left for Fort Leonard Wood and the
army, Pete had gotten in a fight with two other young men in the parking lot at the Bobtail Inn. The way Hallie heard it later, the other men
started it. But Pete had finished it. Put both men in the hospital, one

of them for two weeks while his jaw was rebuilt with wire and steel plates. The only reason Pete hadn't served time for it was because his father had money and wasn't afraid to use it.

"Oh, he left," Brett said, leaning toward Hallie as the band began to play. "He was gone for two and a half years. But he came back last fall, bringing in men, buying purebred cattle—Charolais and Simmental, some weird Chinese breed. We thought he was actually going to make a go of the ranch.

"Not make money," Brett added after a moment. "Because you don't on purebred cattle—not around here. But we thought he was going to run it like a ranch, make it a showplace or something."

"Yeah," Lorie said. "Then he brought in the lions."

"No one knows if that's true or not," Brett said.

"Oh, it's totally true," Lorie said. "Maggie Torvall's mother told her, and she told me. Her mother used to work out there. For Pete's father, not Pete, because who would want to work for Pete? Except I suppose people do, though not always local people, although—"

"Lorie!" Both Brett and Hallie said it at the same time, and it seemed so normal, it took Hallie's breath.

"Sorry," Lorie said. "Anyway, the lions are real."

"Seriously? Lions? Why?"

Brett shrugged. "Who knows."

"We think Pete has a meth lab up there," Lorie said confidentially.

"Lorie!" Brett said.

"Well, don't we?"

"A meth lab?" asked Hallie, because that didn't sound like Pete, except . . . well, there had always been a streak in him of recklessness and desperation.

Dell had always been a little in love with Pete from back as far as sixth grade. He *was* handsome—dark hair just long enough in back that it curled a little along his neck in summer heat, tall, and lean—Hallie'd always thought he was mean, always looking for a way to get something over on people. "He's good with horses," Dell had said, which settled it in her mind, because how bad could he be if he could handle horses? Hallie remembered once when their father was gone and one of the horses had gotten tangled in fence wire. It was Pete whom Dell had called when neither she nor Hallie could get close. He'd walked right up to that horse like it was easy and talked calm and quiet while Dell had cut it free.

But that was before. Now, he had a lightning bolt on his belt buckle, just like the one on Dell's neck. And he'd threatened her. "Do you think he had something to do with Dell's death?" she asked.

Brett looked at her sharp from underneath her cowboy hat. "Dell's death was an accident or . . . an accident," she repeated. "Why do you think anyone had anything to do with it?"

"C'mon, Brett. Is that what you really think?" Hallie asked. *Is that what you really think of Dell?* what she meant.

Brett rubbed a hand across her nose, unconsciously tracing an old scar. The band was playing; Lorie had just departed for the dance floor. "Sometimes shit happens, Hallie." She looked bleak for a minute. "Sometimes it just does."

"Like I don't know that," Hallie said with a flash of anger. Like she'd just been playing at being a soldier, like she hadn't been in Afghanistan, like bombs never exploded, like no one ever died. "But why was she on Seven Mile Creek? Why did she run into that tree? There's hardly a road. And she'd been coming back up, not headed down. Why? How did it happen? That's what I want to know."

Brett looked at her, steady and quiet. Then, she blinked. "Maybe because it really was suicide," she said quietly.

"Fuck that," Hallie said just as quietly. She shoved her chair back so hard that it almost toppled right over onto the floor. "Fuck. That." She walked away.

8

Someone grabbed Hallie's arm as she made her way through the growing crowds. She shook it off, realized after she'd done it that it was Jennie Vagts. Hallie held up a hand—*just leave me alone*—and kept going, so angry. Just—angry. Not at Brett for saying what everyone else was saying. Not even angry at Dell for dying like she had. Just so . . . damn . . . angry. At the army for sending her to Afghanistan. At herself for dying and coming back. At the ghosts for being dead.

She reached the women's restroom. It was quieter, the music reduced to a bass vibration. And warm. Until Eddie drifted in behind her. "Goddamnit," she said. The other two women in the room looked at her in the mirror as they stood at the sink. She rubbed her hands across her face.

Suck it up, Hallie, she told herself for the umpteenth time.

When she left the restroom a few minutes later, the band had switched to seventies country music, Gatlin Brothers and Emmylou Harris. Eddie slid casually through her arm, and though she should have been prepared for it—he'd done it enough times before—it made her gasp.

She hadn't taken two full steps from the restroom door, was turning sideways to let a broad-shouldered woman with close-cropped ginger hair pass by, when someone grabbed her hard and shoved her against the wall.

"Pete says you's a real good time." Hot breath against her neck, and she almost flipped out right there—too much, too close, made her gag. She turned her head. It was the guy who'd been sitting with Pete at his table earlier.

Goddamnit.

She tried to break his grip on her arm, and he shoved up closer to her, pressing against her and jamming his knee between her legs.

"Let me go, you son of a bitch," she growled.

"Pete says you'll go with anyone," he whispered low in her ear. "Says you like it rough. That right, honey?"

"Let go of me now," she said, each word enunciated like a school-teacher with a brand-new certificate. Tried to make it sound like she had ice in her veins, though she didn't, was furious and frightened and so, so tired.

"Oh, I don't think so," he said. He grabbed the front of her shirt and—shit—he had a knife, right here, right in front of everyone—which told her a lot about Pete and his friends and what kind of crazy he was mixed up in now.

Hell.

She'd faced a man with a knife one other time, in an alley in Germany. She'd trained for it, before that, but training was different. You didn't die in training, were facing blunted weapons. In the alley, she'd heaved a half-full trash can at the guy and run like hell.

She couldn't run here. She had no place to run.

The band struck up "Tennessee Waltz," and half the Bob gave a whoop of recognition. People who hadn't danced all night got up from their tables and moved toward the dance floor. In another minute, it would be packed. A couple pushed past them. The grip on Hallie's shirt tightened, snugging her up even closer. He smelled like Jack Daniel's, old hay, and stale tobacco.

The knife lay flat along her ribs. He shoved her sideways half a step. "Come on," he said, wheedling. Jesus! Was he trying to persuade her? "I'll show you things you ain't never seen."

Everything went white. All the anger, all the fear she'd carried every day in Afghanistan, bubbled up inside her like lava. "No!" she shouted. "Fuck, no! Get off me."

She shoved him so hard, the knife caught in her shirt, sliced it clean like paper. He stumbled and tried to catch himself, tangled with the legs of a couple of Sigurdson hands, knocking them forward into the girls they'd been dancing with. One of them shoved back, managing to elbow a tall ropy cowboy in the chest, who came back with a quick rap to the other guy's head.

Hallie dived across a table and landed on top of her assailant before he could get his legs back under him, hit him solid in the mouth hard enough that it numbed her ring finger. "Goddamn you!" she yelled, and hit him again.

Someone dragged her off, and she kicked him. He cursed and grabbed her by her shirt, and she kicked him again, knocking him into one of the tables by the dance floor. One of the men who'd been sitting there shoved himself backwards and knocked over a waitress carrying two pitchers of beer. She came back up quick and whacked him on the shoulder with the empty pitcher, then slipped on the wet floor and went down again. Someone at another table laughed, threw his hat to a friend, and dived into the middle of the mess with a big grin, as if this was the thing he'd been waiting all night for.

Someone grabbed Hallie's arm.

She swung as she turned and almost hit him before she realized it was Boyd, dressed in his sheriff's uniform, all khaki and white and looking like a choirboy. Jesus!

She dropped her fist. Boyd started to drop her arm, but then he stopped, just stood there like a statue and stared at her as if something he saw had surprised him.

"Hey—," Hallie started to say. Then, "Shit!" She grabbed him by his shirtfront.

He had enough time to say, "What the—?"

Just as she said, "Look out!" and shoved him sideways out of the path of a descending barstool.

One of the stool's legs caught Hallie a sharp glancing blow on her arm, knocking her down, her arm numb to the elbow.

"Stay down!" Boyd shouted at her. Or at least that's what she thought he said before he dived back into the crowd.

She would have gotten up anyway—because who the hell was he?—except Eddie and Dell chose that moment to descend on her. They were practically on top of her, as if to protect her—as if they could. She felt like she was frozen to the floor.

"Goddamnit!" If she were the sort of person who cried, she'd be crying. Instead, she was the sort of person who got crazy-pissed, and crazy-pissed got her to her feet even though all the blood in her veins felt as if it had been replaced with water cold as ice.

Somebody hip-checked her into a table.

Then it was done.

The lights came on, which someone probably should have done first thing, because it was always harder to have a really ripping tear-down fight under the harsh glare of fluorescent lighting.

Dell was floating in the exact same spot Sandy Oliver was standing, though Sandy didn't give any sign that she noticed. It made Hallie dizzy to look at them, Sandy's face blurring into Dell's then slowly blurring back again. She closed her eyes and turned away, shaking her arm to force feeling back into it.

Lorie came up behind her, eyes sparking from the excitement. "Are you okay?" she asked Hallie. "What happened, anyway?"

Two deputy sheriffs had four men, plus the waitress who'd been wielding the pitcher, lined up against the far wall. Brett joined Lorie and Hallie. "First time in the Bob in how long?" she asked Hallie. "And you had to start a fight."

"Shh," Lorie said. "She'll go to jail."

"I didn't start it," Hallie said.

"Nobody's going to jail," Brett said.

"How did they get here?"

Brett looked at Hallie. "What?"

Hallie tucked her arm, all pins and needles, against her side. "The deputies," she said. "How did they get here?"

Brett frowned. "In cars, I'm thinking."

Hallie tilted her head to look at her. "Yeah, okay. What I meant was, how did they get here so fast? Usually everybody's standing in the parking lot laughing by the time they arrive."

"Maybe they were already out this way for something else."

"Yeah. Three of them?"

Brett shrugged.

One of the deputies, a short stocky man in his forties, who had arrested Hallie's father once for breaking six windows in the county courthouse after Hallie's mother died, walked to the center of the room. "Anyone want to tell me who started this?" He waited long enough to sweep his eyes across most of the patrons, including plenty of people far enough from the dance floor that they hadn't even known there was a fight before the lights came on. The deputy—Hallie couldn't remember his name—put his hands on his hips and said, "Why doesn't that surprise me."

It went quickly after that—not like most of them hadn't done this before. The Bobtail was all loud music, beer, quick sprawling brawls, and sex in the back of pickup trucks that smelled like motor oil and wheat straw. The owner's license had been suspended at least twice that Hallie knew, but it didn't matter. The Bobtail always came back. It was what it was, and everyone came here.

Two men and a woman who were actually, literally, falling down drunk were hauled off to one of the sheriff's cars. A few people drifted back to the bar, but most folks figured it was time to go. Things never looked as easy to escape from or to with the lights on.

The Boy Deputy approached them.

"You know what happened?" he asked her, revealing that quicksilver smile again. He dropped his gaze right after, staring at the bracelet Eddie had given her, then looked up and waited for her answer.

Before Hallie could open her mouth, however, Lorie stepped up. "She doesn't know anything. Why would she know anything?"

"Lorie—"

"We just wanted a quiet beer, just wanted to sit and talk and—"

"Lorie, I—"

"We didn't ask for trouble. She wasn't—"

"Lorie!"

"What?"

"Shut up."

Lorie huffed, halfway between a snort and a mutter, which would have made Hallie laugh if she didn't feel spun all thin, like wire. Eddie had drifted away again, but Dell was there, running an ice-cold finger up and down her arm.

She rubbed her left eye. "What do you want me to tell you?"

Boyd blinked. "What happened."

He was so serious. It made her tired.

"Nothing happened," she said.

"Davies!" One of the other deputies called to him from the other side of the dance floor. He left, sparing one quick look back.

She looked around. God, she was tired. "Are they still serving beer?" she asked no one in particular. "Because I need one."

At the bar, she picked up a stool, righted it, and sat down. The bartender grinned at her. "What'll you have?" he asked.

"Anything," Hallie said.

She sat there for most of an hour, drinking less than half a beer. The deputies left. Pete Bolluyt and the man who'd jumped her both left, the latter sporting a black eye and limping. Pete looked at her across the wide expanse of floor and winked, like a promise.

Hallie gave him the finger. He could threaten her all he liked, but he couldn't stop her.

At some point, she remembered the rip in her shirt, mostly because he'd actually cut her a little. She went into the bathroom, cleaned it, and left her shirt untucked so it wouldn't rub. She didn't care that it hurt, figured she deserved it in some way she couldn't fathom.

Lorie and Brett were waiting for her when she came out. "We're going to run up to the city for fries or something," Brett said. "You want to come?"

Hallie shook her head. "I'm tired," she said. "I'll head out in a few minutes." Other than Pete and Pete's belt buckle, she hadn't learned anything new about Dell or Martin Weber or his company. Today was over, or as good as. Tomorrow was the funeral, another day gone. They ticked over in her head, like slamming doors. She owed Dell more than bar fights and beer. Hallie and Dell's ghost both knew it.

Brett pulled her head back and arched an eyebrow, as if that would allow her to see Hallie more clearly. *You don't see anything, Brett,* Hallie thought, *because you can't see ghosts following me around.*

Brett gave a small laugh as if she knew exactly what Hallie was thinking, which was decidedly unlikely. Lorie hugged her, and then they were gone. Hallie got coffee from the bartender and sat in one of the badly lit corners at the end of the bar for another hour. While she sat, she made lists in her head of things she knew or wanted to know, lists of lightning bolts and Uku-Weber and what Pete Bolluyt had been doing since he'd come home to Taylor County.

9

When Hallie finally left the Bobtail, the parking lot was mostly empty. The night air was cool, but not cold, a light breeze blowing out of the west, fresh air that didn't smell of stale beer and electric lights. A couple of boys in tight jeans and battered boots sat on a pickup tailgate in the south corner of the lot, underneath a flickering light with a twelve-pack between them. One of them raised his can of beer at her, an invitation. And maybe if it had been another time, maybe if Dell hadn't died, she'd have done it.

Because sometimes beer and boys and stupid conversations were enough to get you by.

She waved at them and continued across the lot to her truck, when she heard the slow crunch of tires on gravel behind her.

Shit.

"Everything all right?" It was the Boy Deputy. Again.

His left arm rested on the car door, his index finger tapping against the frame. He was looking at the bracelet on her wrist again. She shoved her hand into her pocket.

"You all right?" he asked. "Need a ride?"

Because that would be the topper to a perfect evening, she thought, showing up at home in the sheriff's car again. "No." She looked at him sideways. "You want to test my breath?"

"You're not drunk," he said. She couldn't stop looking at him, which was annoying, though not actually his fault. Only his short precision haircut saved him from being too pretty. It was why he looked so young—because he was so pretty. "I just thought," he continued. "That you might be, you know . . . shaken up."

"I've been in fights before."

The light was good enough right there that, though it shaded everything in blues and grays, she could see him raise an eyebrow. "Really?" he said. "And you look so innocent."

Yeah, fuck you, she thought.

"You don't always come to the fight," she said. "Sometimes the fight comes to you." And, shit, if that wasn't the dorkiest thing she'd said out loud in a long time. Because she could have said, *I don't go looking for trouble,* which would have been a lie, but concise. She cleared her throat and looked up, but she couldn't see the stars past the parking lot lighting.

A car, or a pickup truck, Hallie couldn't tell, pulled into the parking lot. It idled near the entrance for several seconds like it was waiting for someone, then backed around and drove away.

Boyd got out of his car, left the motor running, and leaned against the side. There was a ghost right behind him. Hallie blinked. She didn't recognize her—a woman with short blond hair, dressed in a long dark skirt and jacket. Was she going to start collecting them? Like charms on a bracelet? First Eddie and Dell, then random ghosts of perfect strangers?

"Where did you get that bracelet?" he asked.

"What?"

His shoulders hunched, suddenly awkward, like that wasn't what he'd meant to say at all. "Sorry," he said. Then, after a minute, "This isn't official, you understand."

"Okay . . . ," Hallie said with a frown because she didn't understand. What the hell was he talking about?

He took a step toward her but kept one hand on his car, like it grounded him. "Are you sure you didn't talk to Dell before she died?"

"Pretty sure," Hallie said, like *Are you kidding me with this?*

"We have her phone records." He looked up. A crow, its black feathers gleaming blue in the parking lot light, dropped onto a battered green pickup truck twenty feet from where they were standing. It tipped its beak, cocked its head, and looked at them. "She'd called a lot of places." He continued. "Turkey. Germany. New York. Missouri. Like she was looking for someone."

"She knew I was in Afghanistan," she said. Had Dell hoped she was coming home? Had she asked her to? Sent her a message that Hallie never received? Wasn't like Hallie could have picked up and gone. Maybe Dell had wanted help so badly, she'd made herself believe that Hallie could.

"If you talked to her or she left a message somewhere, it might help me figure out what happened."

"Us."

"What?"

"Us. The sheriff's department. That's what you meant, right? It might help the *sheriff's department* figure out what happened."

"Us."

"I didn't talk to her," Hallie said.

They looked at each other.

"You need to be careful," he finally said.

Hallie drew herself up, her bones vibrating. "I need to be *careful*? Dell killed herself, right? Or it was an accident? Right? Right? That's what you told me. That's what everyone tells me. So don't tell me now that I need to be careful unless you're also planning to tell me what's going on."

His right index finger tapped against his thumb. Hallie was pretty sure he'd stop if he knew he was doing it.

"I don't know," he said.

It sounded like the army: *I don't know* meaning *You don't need to know.*

"Fuck you," she said, digging in her pocket for her keys. "I don't need—"

Dell's ghost hit her from behind like an insubstantial freight train, straight through her—*blood, scream, fire, ohmygod, pain pain pain-painpain, ohmygod, makeitmakeitstop!*

She dropped her keys, one hand on the gravel of the parking lot; the sharp point of a rock jabbing her knee. It hurt, like ice crystals in her lungs. It was . . . just to breathe. She felt as if she'd been standing outside at the South Pole in a blizzard. Cold like fire, like the Arctic Ocean, like death.

"Hey."

Boyd touched her elbow, and it startled her so badly that she almost hit him, scrambling to her feet because she wouldn't be vulnerable. Not in front of him. Not again.

"Whoa." He took a step back, his hip touching the passenger door of his car. "Are you okay?"

Before she could answer, Boyd's radio crackled to life, the sound a hundred times too loud. As he bent his head to answer it, Dell drifted back. She reached out her hand and laid it on Hallie's face. Hallie flinched from the sudden, sharp cold and drew her breath in sharply.

Boyd looked at her. "Hold on," he said into the mike. He put his hand on her arm again and even through her shirtsleeve it felt warm, like the only warm thing ever. "Are you okay?" he asked again.

"Stop asking me that," Hallie said. "Jesus!" Anger as an antidote to pain.

76

Boyd's frown deepened. "I—"

"Do you want to fuck me or something? Is that it? Because it's not going to happen. And you don't— Maybe I should file a complaint."

Bitch.

She wanted him to call her a bitch or sputter about how he wouldn't, couldn't, never meant— She wanted him to be stupid about it, to be uptight and embarrassed and to go away. Just for fuck almighty's sake, leave her alone.

"If you need anything," he finally said. "If you need help. You can call me."

Hallie stared at him. *Take a hint,* she thought. *Go away.*

And, finally, he did.

Hallie rubbed a hand across her face, standing there like an idiot for several minutes, watching where he'd gone.

She walked back to her truck. It was going on one thirty in the morning, and she was tired. She didn't realize her hands were shaking until she tried to open the pickup truck door.

She leaned her head against the steering wheel for a minute. As she was putting the key into the ignition, Eddie drifted in and settled, waiting for a ride home.

"What are you doing here, Eddie?" she asked as she started the truck and finally pulled out of the parking lot. She seriously wished she knew, wished she didn't dream about him dying every night, all messy and crying and begging her to tell his girl back home— Yeah, even in her dreams.

Hallie and Eddie had been together her whole tour in Afghanistan. He'd been a math geek, had joined the army to get money for college, wanted to teach math to kids who hated it.

"Do you know what math is?" he'd asked her the first day they met, like a quiz.

"Math defines the world," she'd said. She'd been stacking boxes all day. She was hot and tired, and they were shipping out at the end of the week. She was not interested in discussing mathematics with some geeky kid she'd never met before.

He'd looked put out at her answer, as if he'd been expecting her to talk about two plus two and four. She'd grinned at him and showed her teeth. *Go away and leave me alone, asshole,* she'd thought.

But he came back the next day with a game board and a battered set of plastic chess pieces. "You probably don't know how to play," he'd said.

"Oh for god's sake, set them up," because she'd never liked being underestimated. She hadn't realized until their third or fourth game that *he'd* probably set *her* up.

Eddie had been incredibly tough in his own way and utterly unsuited for the army and for Afghanistan. He'd talked about theorems and proofs and traffic patterns in downtown San Diego. People would look at him as if he'd lost his mind. He and Hallie played chess all the time, every chance they got, like it was the only thing standing between paradise and hell. Eddie had been precise and detailed, always thinking six moves ahead. Hallie'd been all big picture messy, knowing what was coming, but unable to say how or even exactly what she knew. He won more than she did, but her victories always blindsided him.

They memorized the board and played in the Humvee on convoy making moves in their head or with *x*'s on scrap paper until the rest of the team began offering feedback—like each piece was real. It'd been Hollowman, griping about grunts and weather and weapons, who'd inspired them to invent Soldier's Chess, where the pawns got semiautomatic rifles and mortars because, by god, they were soldiers and were doing all the work, and why should they die so easy? All of it culminating in a glorious day when they'd scraped out a giant chessboard in the dirt and convinced a bunch of bored American,

British, and Mongolian soldiers to be pawns and knights and bishops. For a moment or two that day, Hallie'd forgotten guns and war and the constant threat of death.

A week later, Eddie died.

And she'd killed him, hadn't she? Because not only had she volunteered them for that detail, being pissed off at something she couldn't even remember anymore, but she'd also convinced them to take the trail that got them killed. Because it was more direct and they needed to get there fast and no one had said not to take it, it had been cleared, after all.

Maybe that was why she was carrying him around with her now.

She pulled into the yard at the ranch. The yard light shaded everything in blue and white, chasing shadows back to the barn. There were no lights on in the house, not surprising, since it was almost two in the morning. Hallie turned off the truck and sat, listening to the engine tick over.

She didn't think about it, didn't think about what time it was or what she was going to say. She pulled Dell's cell phone out of her back pocket and dialed the number from memory, because she'd been looking at it for days, looking at it and not calling.

The chaplain had given her the number. "It's his fiancée," he said. "Sometimes it's good to hear from someone they served with. It helps a little. And as you're going back . . ." Eddie's ghost had stared at him when he'd said it, like he'd stared at Boyd at Big Dog's Auto. But then, Eddie stared at a lot of things.

"Hello?" The voice at the other end of the phone was scratchy with sleep, worried because it was—hell—four in the morning in New York.

"I'm sorry," Hallie said. She cleared her throat. "Is this Estelle? Estelle, uhm, Chase?"

"Who is this?" The voice suspicious now, about to hang up.

"I'm . . . Hallie. Hallie Michaels. I knew Eddie. Over there. In Afghanistan."

There was silence. "Oh."

"I thought . . . I don't know." This was stupid. What was she supposed to say? "I'm sorry," she said. "This is—"

"No, no. It's okay. Just . . . I don't know either." Hallie could hear tears in Estelle's voice. "Just talk about him. It doesn't have to be good. He wasn't perfect. Just talk. Okay?"

Hallie gripped the cell phone hard enough that the edge bit into her fingers. What was she supposed to say? "He played chess."

Stupid thing to say. He played chess? She was his fiancée; she knew that. But Estelle gave a watery laugh. "Yeah. Our first date, he dragged me to a chess club. Can you believe it? He . . . he loved it."

"There was this soldier in our squad," Hallie said. Eddie was right beside her. Right *there*. Cold along her elbow and the right side of her face. "Mark Swift. We called him Swiftie. Eddie asked him that question he asks—asked."

"About math? He asked my mother that question! First time he met her, he—"

She stopped so abruptly that Hallie would have stumbled over the silence if they'd been walking somewhere. She rushed in with words, any words, just to fill the gap. "He—we played a lot. It was all— He was good."

"Yeah," Estelle said. "He was. He wanted to be a teacher, you know. Because he had this one teacher—" She started crying.

Hallie didn't want to listen to this. She didn't. Wanted to be someplace cold and frozen and alone, north of the arctic circle maybe, where the permafrost went down thirteen stories deep and the ocean froze in wintertime. Somewhere without ghosts or dead soldiers' fiancées or anyone who would make her feel anything ever again. "He talked about you all the time," she said.

"He did not," Estelle said, like she wanted to believe it, but she wasn't going to, because that was what people said at times like this, whether it was true or not. "He was the only guy I ever dated," she said. "Because I'm not— No one ever— I'm not pretty," she stated flatly. "It was a blind date that first time. My cousin fixed us up. And it was so embarrassing and kind of awful, but he was sweet about it, you know? I didn't think he'd call, but he did—the next day, even. And I liked him. I—he was the best guy. But I never knew, I couldn't ask him, because why? Why would he go out with me? I don't understand."

Jesus.

Hallie knew what she was supposed to say, not just what was expected, but what was true, but she hadn't ever said it. And now she was saying it for a ghost who couldn't say it for himself. Shit. She pressed the heel of her hand against her cheekbone just under her right eye, sucked in a breath, and said, "He loved you. He did. He told me that you read books all the time and he couldn't get over that—how many books you read, that you talked about them like they were real—the characters in them and the things they did. He told me before he met you, he only cared about math, that he didn't think anyone needed any of that other stuff—English and other languages and history. He said you made him see the world. He told me he didn't even know he wanted someone until he met you."

Estelle was crying hard now; Hallie rubbed a finger over her eye. "Look," she said. "I'm sorry. I'm—it was stupid to call. I shouldn't have—"

"No! It's all right! It's—" She drew in a breath. "Thank you. Just for a minute, I could see him again, like he was here."

Hallie felt cold like frozen iron down her arm, then a rush of air, warm and smelling faintly like pine. When she looked over, Eddie was gone.

10

Hallie finally got to bed around two thirty. She had meant, when she came inside, to sit down and list off the things she knew about Dell or her death one more time, but she didn't manage to stay awake past lightning bolts and belt buckles. She woke once, shivering, and dug another blanket out of the hall closet like it was the middle of winter and the wind was rattling the windows in their frames.

When she woke again, it was morning. She spent half a second wishing she could stay in bed, then tossed the covers aside and got up. Dell's funeral was going to be graveside at eleven o'clock, and the forecast had said it would be sunny and sixty degrees.

Hallie considered for about five seconds whether she should wear a dress and decided that since she didn't have one, then no, she didn't have to wear one. She did have a pair of black dress pants, a white button-down shirt, a black and silver belt, and polished boots. She added a hip-length leather jacket and stuffed a pair of gloves in her pocket because it was South Dakota and the weather could do anything at any time.

Though Dell followed her to the bathroom and back, there was no sign of Eddie. Hallie knew he was gone, had known since she finished talking to Estelle. She wasn't sure how she knew, or what it meant that she knew, but she'd been certain from the moment she felt warm air like spring breezes on her arm.

Hallie's father didn't protest when she offered to drive to the funeral. He was wearing his only suit, which he'd had for as long as Hallie'd known him, dark gray, single button, still fit him pretty good. He wore a white shirt that had hung in his closet forever, a string tie with a silver pull, his best cowboy boots, and a black felt hat with a silver band.

They left the ranch at ten and drove down past Prairie City, turned off onto an old county road, past Cass's ranch, and crossed the one-lane bridge over dried-up Thorsen's Creek. Hallie took the next right, drove less than a quarter mile, right down close to Bear Creek, and pulled in next to a dozen pickup trucks and Suburbans.

The small cemetery just beyond the gravel parking area was filled mostly with Severaids and Andersens. It was less than a mile out of Thorsen, but since Thorsen now consisted of three people and a mule, it was pretty much the same as the middle of nowhere.

"Your mother was an Andersen," her father had told Hallie yesterday. "She'd have been okay with it."

She wouldn't have been okay with Dell dying, Hallie'd thought, but she didn't say that because who *was* okay with it? Not her father. Not her either.

Hallie and her father got out of the pickup, her father tipping the brim of his hat to a couple of ranchers who owned land just south of them.

More trucks and Suburbans and a few sedans pulled in. The tiny graveled lot filled, and people parked along the side of the road, backed up nearly to the crossroads. Cattle grazed a quarter mile east, but close in there was just the cemetery, the narrow parking lot, the creek, and a vast stretch of knee-high grass that moved with the rhythm of the wind. People lingered by their vehicles, talking to neighbors they rarely saw before making their way across the cemetery.

Boyd was there, which surprised Hallie, in a dark suit with a bright white shirt and narrow tie. There were a bunch of people she recognized and others she almost recognized, couples she remembered from high school, teachers who'd gotten old while she'd been gone. Everything so familiar, except Dell was dead and someone, maybe right here in the parking lot talking to Hallie or her father, knew why and how it had happened.

Brett found her. She was wearing a navy blue skirt, dark brown cowboy boots polished like she used them for a mirror, a dark red shirt, and a denim jacket. She took Hallie's arm like it was a lifeline.

"I hate this," she said.

"You hate that Dell is dead," Hallie said.

"Yeah." Brett grimaced. "I keep thinking there was something I could have or should have done."

"Yeah," Hallie said, "oh, yeah."

There was no wind, but it was damp, tiny wisps of fog, like haze along the edges of the cemetery. Hallie let half a dozen people go on ahead of them; then she and Brett started down the central drive.

They were halfway across the cemetery when she stopped cold. Ghosts rose from their graves—dozens of them. They rose straight through the ground fog, so that at first she'd thought the fog was thickening. Then she could see them, the curve of a skull, the suggestion of an arm, a body—far, far less substantial than Dell or Eddie. Dell looked practically alive in comparison, but they were distinctly and definitely there, all the same.

Shit.

"Hallie?" Brett tugged on her jacket sleeve.

The ghosts rose higher. Did they expect something from her, as

Eddie had? Clear up loose ends they'd left behind? Because she couldn't do it, not all of them.

Then, the ghosts stopped. They floated in the air for a long frigid moment until, like a held breath slowly released, they slipped back into their graves and were gone.

"Hallie!" Brett's face creased in a worried frown. "Are you all right?" she asked.

"Yeah, come on, let's go," Hallie said, because these ghosts weren't like Eddie and Dell after all, right? They were more like the memory of ghosts, though cold like winter, all the same. "We'll be late," she said to Brett, like she hadn't just been standing in the middle of a cemetery staring at things no one else could see.

Dell's grave had been dug under a tree, separated by the trunk of that tree from their mother's grave. Hallie's father had wanted to bury their mother on the ranch, somewhere quiet where he could sit and talk to her and no one would see him or know. Cass had talked him out of it, though Hallie and Dell both thought he should have done it because she'd loved the ranch as much as he did, because she'd died there or close enough. But maybe this had been better. Hallie knew he came to visit her, on his way back from town or Rapid City. Probably got him off the ranch more than anything else.

When they finally reached the grave site, Hallie couldn't stop looking at the casket. It was beautiful—she'd picked it out, of course . . . or Dell had, because she wanted to pretend that the ghost and Dell were the same. And yet, she didn't want that, didn't want them to be the same. She wanted Dell not to be trapped, wanted her not to be dead, wanted . . . She wanted this not to be happening, is what she wanted—Dell and ghosts and cemeteries—nothing good from any of it, that was the bottom line.

Dell's ghost drifted past her, frosting Hallie's right elbow, staring at her own casket—at least, Hallie thought she was staring at her casket. Cemetery ghosts ranged behind her, most of them simply rising from the grave and falling back, but at least a dozen of them right there, right behind her. It made her feel slightly sick—dizzy and a little nauseated. She licked her lips.

The service was short. The minister, who served three tiny prairie churches spread out over fifty miles, spoke for less than five minutes—how he'd known Dell when she was three and when she was fifteen and when she was twenty, how she'd always been the same, like lightning in a bottle. "Burned too fast," he said, which made Hallie sad and angry at the same time.

Another minister from one of the four churches right in West Prairie City, though Hallie couldn't remember which one, said a prayer. Some guy she didn't know stood up and talked for five minutes about something, though she couldn't have said afterwards anything he'd said. The ground mist thickened, climbing up her legs, up everyone's legs, though none of them knew it. She tried not to look as if she was freezing—tried not to shiver, tried to keep her teeth from chattering—but she was *cold*.

She was afraid when her turn came, she wouldn't be able to talk, afraid she'd just stand there, hunched into herself, chattering. Someone put their hand on her elbow, and it was so . . . warm, even through her jacket, that she almost fell, pushing herself toward that warmth, clinging to it, holding the ghosts at bay.

"You look cold," a voice said quietly in her ear. It was the Boy Deputy. Boyd. She pulled away from his touch and hoped he didn't notice how reluctantly she did it. "I'm fine," she said.

"I have an extra coat in the car."

She shook her head. It would be her turn in a minute. To make people understand who Dell had been and why she had mattered.

And yet she wanted to say to him, *Stand right there, right at my back,* because when someone stood there, just behind her, she couldn't feel them, the ghosts, the full pressure of the graveyard.

When he stood behind her, she could breathe.

11

Afterwards, she could not have said what words she spoke when it was her turn. She knew what she'd planned to say, how everyone knew Dell and no one knew her. How they were all standing there remembering her, and every one of them remembered someone different. And that was all right. Because Dell was all those things—good and bad—what everyone remembered about her was what made her real.

But afterwards, she didn't know whether she'd actually said the words she planned to say, whether she'd talked about the good things, whether she'd cried. All she'd been able to think about was keeping the cold from showing, her teeth from chattering, her shoulders from shaking.

She went back to the truck right after, letting the others trail behind. They were going back to Cass's—ostensibly because it was closer. Going to eat a dozen different kinds of casserole, drink cheap red wine, and talk about things Dell had done or would have done or never did.

Unknown ghosts lingered at the edge of the cemetery, like they wanted to come with her, but didn't want to leave their graves behind. It was too much to hope that Dell's ghost had seen her grave and her in it and decided that maybe she belonged there instead of following Hallie around. No, she'd turn up later. Hallie was becoming at least certain of that.

The day had been low and overcast, and now Hallie could hear the distant rumble of thunder. There was a brief splatter of rain, large hard drops; then it stopped, not even enough to wet the ground.

Lorie came up and grabbed her arm, tight. "I'll be there. Okay? I'll be there," she said fiercely, as if Hallie might have spent hours wondering what Lorie was doing after the funeral. "I have to run a quick errand. Drop off— I'll be there. You don't have to face this alone."

Hallie nodded, paying only partial attention. Sure, they'd been in school together, but Lorie had been Dell's friend most recently. So, yeah, Hallie expected her to be here, to come to Cass's afterwards. But she didn't worry about it.

Her father stood twenty feet away, at the edge of the parking area, talking to several other men, all of them with their suit coats shoved up and their hands stuck in their pockets.

Jennie Vagts, whom Lorie had pointed out last night at the Bob, approached her. Her medium-length brown hair was pulled back with a clip, and she was wearing a navy blue dress with a silver concho belt.

"Hey," she said. She was gripping the strap on her purse hard, twisting it so that Hallie wondered how it stood the strain. "I'm sorry about Dell. We worked together."

"Lorie said you left." No sense beating around the bush.

"I mean—" Jennie scanned the crowd. "—I did work there. And I left." She twisted the purse strap harder. "I might be going back, though. Not because Dell died." She looked horrified for a minute that Hallie might think she was moving into the empty space Dell had left behind. "Because I thought—I saw something there one day and—well, I was wrong, that's all. I was wrong."

"What are you talking about?" Hallie asked.

Jennie continued to scan the crowd. "I haven't seen Mr. Weber," she said. "I thought he'd be here."

Hallie frowned. "He had something else going on."

"Oh no, he—" She looked in a startled way at something over Hallie's left shoulder, then said in an oddly formal tone, "I'm sorry, I have to be going now," turned abruptly, and walked away.

"It was a good service."

Hallie turned to find Boyd just behind her. "It was—" She stopped. She didn't want to say it was a good service, because what was good about burying Dell? And yet it was the sort of thing people said, a way to make conversation in an awkward, painful time.

"I thought—" Boyd looked stiff and uncomfortable. Dell's ghost hung over his right shoulder like she was listening. "—I've been thinking about what you said about . . ." He hesitated as if he couldn't figure out what he wanted to say next, or maybe how to say it. "What you said about Dell, about how she wouldn't have killed herself."

Hallie was struck again by how *exact* everything about him was, even the way he spoke. "I don't want to engage in a conversation about an ongoing investigation, but Dell came into the sheriff's office last Monday. Wanted to talk to the sheriff, and when he wasn't there, she left. Do you have any idea what she might have wanted?" He leaned forward as he said it, intense, like he knew more than he was telling her or thought she knew more than she was telling him.

"Why does everyone think I know anything?" she said sharply. "I was in fucking Afghanistan. I didn't have a cell phone. I didn't have e-mail. Nobody talked to me. Nobody told me anything."

Boyd blinked.

"Are we ready to go here?" Hallie's father approached with a quick ground-eating stride. Hallie realized that the parking area was already mostly empty. Everyone else had gone home, back to work, or on to Cass's.

"Oh, I think so," Hallie said brightly.

She was opening the truck door when Boyd laid a hand on her arm. She was reminded—like she could forget things like that—that people were warm and ghosts were cold like the north pole. Maybe she should spend more time with people.

"I don't know," she said quietly. "I'd tell you if I did."

He removed his hand and took a step back, allowing Hallie to climb into the pickup.

"You should watch that guy," her father said as Hallie turned the truck and headed away from the cemetery.

Hallie laughed. "Seriously?"

"He's an operator," her father said.

Hallie looked at him.

"I've seen him with a girl or two," her father said.

"I'm not dating him," Hallie told him.

"Huh," her father said. Then, "We going home?" he asked hopefully.

"No," Hallie said. "We're going to Cass's. Suck it up."

Brett was in Cass's kitchen when Hallie arrived, reheating casseroles and making pots of coffee. Her motions were smooth and serene as she pulled dishes out of the microwave and the oven, tracked down hot pads, poured water and dumped grounds and stacked coffee mugs on trays. Not like she belonged in a kitchen, more like she belonged in the middle of things, smooth, unhurried, calm. Hallie realized how much she'd missed this Brett, the one who never got ruffled.

"Was that Jennie Vagts at the funeral?" she asked Hallie.

"I don't even know her," Hallie said.

"We were in school," Brett reminded her.

"She wasn't in our class." Like Hallie knew no one outside her old high school class and the army, which was actually pretty much true.

"What did she want?" Brett handed Hallie two oven mitts and a casserole. Hallie looked around—was she supposed to know what to do with this? "Take it in the dining room," Brett said with a hint of exasperation.

When she came back, which took about five minutes because at least seven people stopped and shook her hand and told her "Welcome back" and "Isn't this a hell of a thing," she said to Brett, "Was she friends with Dell or something?"

Brett looked blank, then realized Hallie was talking about Jennie Vagts. She frowned. "I don't think so. Well, Dell never talked about her. But . . ." She hesitated. Lorie came into the kitchen, returned from whatever errand she'd been running, demanded napkins and clean glasses, and left again. "Nobody gets together like we used to," Brett said. "I'm in Rapid City all week. In grad school," she added helpfully, in case Hallie had forgotten. "I help Daddy with the horses most weekends. We just . . ." She trailed off.

Dell's ghost drifted over, staring at a particular dirty glass on the counter—an old jelly jar with a cartoon character that had been old before Hallie'd been born—like it was the most interesting thing in the kitchen.

"What do you know about Martin Weber?" Hallie asked.

Brett looked startled. "What do you mean?"

"I mean, what do you know about him?"

"What do you want me to say? He came back about a year ago."

"With Dell?"

Brett shrugged. "I didn't pay much attention. Dell was here first, maybe a month before, making arrangements for the land. But she was always a part of it. Uku-Weber, you know. It's why she came back."

"Didn't you think that was strange? That she was hooked up with him?"

Brett frowned. "They were business partners."

It was Hallie's turn to frown. "I dated him the summer we graduated from high school, Brett. Don't you remember?"

"I was gone that summer."

Which Hallie had forgotten, that Brett had been gone most of that June and all of July, down in New Mexico, taking care of her grandmother after hip surgery. "Dell never said anything?"

"About how she hooked up with Uku-Weber?" Brett shook her head. "But really, Hallie, we didn't talk."

"Did Pete work there?"

"At Uku-Weber?"

"Yes."

"Pete Bolluyt?" Lorie said, coming into the kitchen with a quartet of empty glasses pinched between her fingers. "You know, I'm surprised he's not here," she said.

"Really?" Hallie had to admit, despite his behavior last night at the Bob, she was a little surprised herself, although given the way things were and—no kidding—a meth lab, maybe she shouldn't be.

"He's the one who called everyone—all the Uku-Weber folks—after."

"So Pete does work there," Hallie said. "I thought he was running cattle."

"Oh, he doesn't work there," Lorie said. She took a tray of cold cuts out of the refrigerator and started unwrapping them. "He's, like, an investor or something. Plus the company's putting up a demonstration site in that field of his out by the road. Something about cold fronts or wind power or, you know . . ." Lorie shrugged like it was all beyond her. "He and Martin—Mr. Weber—are like this." Lorie crossed her fingers.

Hallie shook her head. It didn't make sense.

"What does Uku-Weber do, exactly?" she asked Lorie.

"Well, the new wind turbines, of course, and that . . . *thing* out at the demo plot." Lorie waved her hand in a broad gesture. "There's this big lab in the back, although it's not finished yet. Really, things are just getting started." She looked at Hallie hopefully, as if aware that she hadn't explained anything, but confident that an earnest expression and a general perky cuteness would carry the day.

"What do you do there, Lorie?" Brett asked as she finished putting a dozen glasses into a side cupboard.

"Everything," Lorie said. "I answer phones and do invoices and take inventory on new shipments. I—"

She was interrupted by a loud crash of thunder followed by a rumble so low, Hallie could feel it in her chest. It went on for what seemed like forever. A brief rattle of hail on the roof, then rain, slashing down like they were suddenly in the middle of a rain forest in monsoon season. Hallie went to the kitchen door and opened it. People who'd been in the yard talking or getting ready to leave ran for the barn or the porch or their cars. Lightning struck in the field not more than two hundred yards away.

Then it was done. Water dripping off trees and the porch roof, droplets glistening in the sun, which had already reemerged.

"Jesus," Hallie said.

"That's the way it's been," Lorie said. "Weather all the time."

After the rain stopped, Hallie went outside to look for her father—she was ready to be gone, had had enough of people and shaking hands and hugging. None of it brought her any closer to understanding how Dell had died or what she'd been doing out on the Seven Mile. And another day was nearly gone.

Down by the barn, she found Tel Sigurdson and Tom Hauser

looking at an old Farmall tractor that probably hadn't been moved in thirty years, grass tall around it and the dried vines of morning glories winding through the steering wheel.

"Those turbines are twice as efficient for their size," Tel was saying. "I've seen the data. And the demo, with that machine he's got? It's way beyond cloud seeding. He can bring the rain. He can—" He stopped at Hallie's approach.

"Are you talking about Uku-Weber?" Hallie asked.

There was a moment of guilty silence. Then Tel said, "It's a hell of a thing. They're planning another demonstration next week, split a storm front. If you're around, you should—" He broke off as if he'd remembered exactly why Hallie was around. "I mean—"

"Yeah," she said.

"What do you think about Martin Weber?" she asked. "Have you met him?"

Tel shrugged. "He seems sincere. Not like a lot of these guys you see coming here because they think we're dumber than shit and we'll work cheap. You see him around, too. He comes to town meetings and he'll come into the Dove, you know, for breakfast. He listens to what people say, doesn't just try to tell us what we ought to think. He seems all right."

Hallie looked at Tom, but he didn't add anything to what Tel had already said, just looked across the field like the answer was out there somewhere.

"Have you seen my dad?" Hallie asked, letting him off the hook a bit.

Tom looked at her then, waved a hand toward the road. "Headed up that way, last I saw," he said.

"Thanks." Hallie walked back toward the vehicles parked along the lane; it was completely possible that her father was sitting in the pickup truck, waiting for her to show.

She was thinking about what Tel had said, about weather and Uku-Weber, when Jennie Vagts fell into step beside her. Neither of them said anything right away. Dell drifted backwards in front of Hallie as she walked.

Hallie stopped. "Did you want something?" she said.

Jennie looked startled. "I was heading out." She gestured up the lane, presumably toward her car.

"Oh."

"It was—" Jennie shifted from one foot to the other.

Dell laid a ghostly hand on Jennie's face. The sun emerged from clouds in that same moment, and in the bright afternoon light, Hallie almost missed it. Along Jennie's jaw was the same lightning bolt configuration she'd seen on Dell's neck.

She grabbed Jennie's wrist. "What's going on?" she asked. "What does that mean?"

"What are you talking about?" Jennie tried to jerk her arm away.

It looked like a faded tattoo, like a watermark.

Dell drifted away. The mark disappeared. What the hell?

"There's a mark," Hallie gestured. "On your face."

Jennie rubbed her hand along her jawline, like she had dirt on there or something.

Hallie heard a truck coming up the lane fast, oblivious of the vehicles parked all down the narrow drive. She grabbed Jennie by the wrist and pulled her out of the way. A swirl of dust, clatter of gravel, and the truck—big and dark and shiny—spun to a stop on the corner of the lawn.

The engine was still pinging over when the door opened and Pete Bolluyt dropped out of the cab.

Perfect.

He saw Hallie immediately, an expression on his face that Hallie couldn't read. She smelled alcohol on his breath when he was still half a dozen feet away.

As Pete came toward them, Jenny retreated to the line of cars along the driveway. Hallie stepped up.

"Where were you?" she said by way of greeting, because she'd expected him at the funeral, even after last night, after sending a guy with a knife after her, she'd thought he was dumb enough or arrogant enough or cared enough to be there. "Wasn't she worth it?"

She'd expected it to make him angry, wanted to make him angry. And his face darkened, but when he spoke, his tone was almost mild. "He said we shouldn't come."

"What?"

"I told him . . . I told him we needed to be there." Pete's hands were shoved in his pockets, and he was leaning forward as he spoke, shifting his weight from one leg to the other, and Hallie thought he might fall on her, which, if there was anything left to piss her off about this day? That would be it. "I tried to get him to at least come here." He hauled a hand out of his pocket and pointed at the lawn directly underneath their feet, as if Hallie might not understand which particular *here* he was referring to. Dell drifted across the narrow gap between them, staring at Pete's face as if it contained the world.

"Here," he repeated. "Because he wouldn't come to the cemetery. Said he *couldn't.* But I think it's because of—" He stopped abruptly, collected himself, and took a step back before continuing. "But, I knew her. . . ." He nodded, like he and Hallie were having a conversation. "Before. And whatever happened—whatever hap—" He stopped, caught his breath up sharp, and took another quick step backwards, as if he'd almost fallen over. "Whatever. That counts for something. Doesn't it? That matters."

"What the hell are you talking about?"

Pete frowned, as if he'd just realized whom he was talking to. He leaned toward her. "It's important, *that's* what I'm saying," he told her. "What we do is important. And you—you need to stay out of it. Go back to the war."

"Fuck you," Hallie said, said it low, because she didn't want to be angry today. Not today.

Pete cocked his head to the side. "No one wants you here, Hallie."

"Yeah?" Enough was enough. "Did they want Dell to die? Is that what they wanted? Who killed her, Pete?"

"No one wanted her to die! I didn't want her to die." He was shouting now, leaning in on Hallie, and she was going to punch him in a minute.

"She died anyway, Pete. Where were you?"

Silence stretched taut between them. A half-dozen expressions flickered across Pete's face—sadness, fear, rage, and something darker than any of those, something Hallie couldn't name, something secret and base. He leaned close until his lips were right next to her ear.

"Where were *you*?" he said.

Hallie punched him hard in the chest with the flat of her hands. He stumbled back and fell with a jarring thump. She was ready for him when he scrambled back to his feet, wanted him to come, but Boyd was there and Tom Hauser, grabbing Pete's arms, dragging him away from her.

Boyd gave her a look, like, *What did you do?* She would have punched him, too, if he'd said it out loud.

Boyd dragged Pete to his truck, where they stood for several minutes, talking. Boyd talking anyway and Pete listening, which surprised Hallie, that Pete would listen to him.

Tom Hauser was saying something to her. "Fine. I'm fine," she said, because that seemed like what he expected, but she was thinking about what Pete had said about Martin and the things they'd done.

Boyd reached out a hand and Pete shook him off, reached for the door to his pickup truck, and Boyd stood and looked at him and shook his head. Immovable object. Jennie Vagts stepped up and said something to both of them.

Pete stepped back, threw his keys on the ground, and flung himself around to the passenger seat. Boyd picked up the keys and handed them to Jennie. He laid his hand over hers and said something. She shook her head, got in the truck, backed it around, and drove away. Dell drifted halfway up the lane after them, then turned around and drifted slowly back.

Hallie's father came up to her, working his way through the small crowd that had formed halfway up the drive. "If the show's over," he said to her, "I guess I'm ready to go."

12

allie slept badly again that night, dreaming of Dell and Afghanistan and someone chasing them through the mountains in a driving snowstorm. She finally gave up on sleeping shortly after six and took a long hot shower, which felt good while she was in it, but her teeth started to chatter as soon as she was back in her bedroom again. She pulled on long underwear, Dell right next to her.

"I'm doing the best I can," she said to Dell's ghost. Maybe she didn't have much in the way of answers yet, but she had a direction. She had questions. It was more than she'd started with. And for at least a moment, at least while she was pulling on her work boots, the five days remaining seemed like almost enough time.

"Why are you dressed like that?" her father said when she came downstairs.

"Like what?"

"Like it's twenty below zero."

"You're a noticing man, Dad," she said as she went into the kitchen and poured herself some coffee.

Her father grunted in reply.

When she came back, she picked up the local newspaper and sat down. The phone rang.

Her father didn't even look up. "Get that, would you?"

"Phones don't bite, Dad," Hallie said, but she got up and went into the kitchen.

There was no one on the other end of the line, and after she said hello a couple of times, Hallie shrugged, hung up, and went back into the dining room.

"You need help today?" she asked her father as she sat back down and picked up the paper, though she already had a list, now that the funeral and all it entailed was finally finished. She intended to find out more about Uku-Weber and Martin and what Pete had been up to while she'd been gone. She wanted to track down Jennie Vagts, too, find out more about that mark or tattoo or whatever it really was. She had five days left, and she knew she had to make the most of them. But she asked anyway, the old tug of ranch work and obligation.

Her father shook his head. "Norman wants me to look at some land he's thinking about, over near Templeton. Be back after that, probably around noon."

The phone rang again.

"Jesus!" her father said.

"I'll get it," Hallie said.

"Hallie?" It was Brett.

"Did you just call here?" Hallie asked.

"No." There was a pause. "I wanted to see how you . . . were doing." Her voice faded on the last words, as if she realized the futility of asking Hallie anything about her feelings.

"I'm fine," Hallie said.

"Yeah," Brett said. Hallie could hear *sure you are,* without her actually having to say it. "When are you going back?"

Hallie counted up in her head. "Friday morning." Christ. It was already Sunday. And what did she know? Nothing.

"We should go for a ride," Brett was saying. "Or something."

"We should figure out what happened to Dell," Hallie said.

"You should leave that to the sheriff."

"Really? Pretty sure he thinks she killed herself."

"Hallie . . ."

"No." She closed her eyes because she didn't want to fight with Brett about this. Because Hallie was going to find out. Even if . . .

"I'll see you before I go." She hung up before Brett could say anything more.

While she'd been on the phone, her father had finished clearing the table, wiped everything down, and left. When she looked out the front window, she saw the back of his pickup disappearing down the drive.

Hallie turned out the lights in the kitchen and dining room and went down to her father's office, part of an addition from the sixties that was darker than the rest of the house and always cold. It looked as if no one had ever worked there, the computer hidden, three file cabinets in the closet behind closed doors. The desk clear of everything except a monitor, a desk lamp, and two pens lined up perpendicular to the wall.

Outwardly, her father didn't act like he'd ever organized anything in his life, had a coffee table in the living room with a dozen magazines and newspapers from six months to a year ago. But there was something about cupboards and cabinets and, apparently, his desktop, some compulsion to put them in order and keep them that way. It had started when Hallie's mother died, as if keeping the cupboards and closets perfect meant she wasn't really gone, meant things would someday be okay.

Hallie fired up the computer—a powerhouse of a desktop that loaded up in nothing flat. She searched on Pete Bolluyt, on Martin Weber, and Uku-Weber.

There were three items on Pete—that his father had died three years ago in an automobile accident in Texas, that he'd been arrested in San Francisco a year and a half ago for breaking into an antique store, and a picture from the West Prairie City newspaper of Pete at a local rodeo with a girl Hallie didn't recognize. The girl was holding a trophy half as big as she was. Pete had his arm around her, and they looked . . . happy. Hallie clicked back to the search page.

There were plenty more items on Martin Weber, clear back to when he'd graduated from high school in Rapid City. There were pictures at the groundbreaking for his new company. Excerpts from a speech he'd given about how pleased he was to be bringing jobs to his "spiritual home" in Taylor County, how he hoped that making profits and saving the world would never be mutually exclusive in the Uku-Weber lexicon, and a lot more in the same vein that Hallie didn't bother reading. There was a picture from two years ago, of Martin at a county literacy fair in Colorado, presenting a check to the librarian in charge. The librarian, Karen Olsen, the caption said, looked at him with clear delight, and maybe something more. The article said a bunch of stuff about fund-raising and giving back and a life dedicated to making the world a better place.

Uku-Weber had a website, but there wasn't much on it—all marketing-speak, which said a lot of nothing without ever specifying what exactly the company did or was going to do once construction was completed. Though there was a small section titled "Research" that might have been interesting if Hallie'd had the patience to sift through a dozen sets of spreadsheets and graphs of power outputs and blade rotations and production efficiencies, which basically seemed to say what Tel had already told her, that Uku-Weber turbines were more efficient than other turbines the same size. Finally, she found three articles in the anemic business section of the local weekly paper and one long article with half a dozen pictures in the Rapid City paper, which managed to say almost nothing as well.

She did a search on Dell and found two newspaper photographs and a Facebook page she hadn't known Dell had.

Before she shut down the computer, she paused, pulled the search engine back up, and typed in, "Davies Boyd South Dakota."

Just to see.

Nothing much came up except a short article from the local paper back in March when he'd arrested someone named Yancy McDowd for simple assault out at the Bobtail Inn.

Hallie shut down the computer, stood, and stretched. No one said this would be simple. But shit. Shit. She'd be back in Afghanistan and nothing to show for it if she didn't start finding answers soon. She went upstairs, grabbed keys, wallet, cell phone, and left the house.

When she walked out the back door, her father's truck was back in its usual place, under one of the pin oaks in the yard. Hallie figured he was in the equipment shed, working on the Allis again. It was raining and apparently had been raining for a while, though she hadn't noticed. A sharp jolt of lightning, followed by a loud clap of thunder, and she ducked back under the low porch roof.

Goddamnit.

Because she wanted to be out of there, to be doing something, even though it was Sunday—anything. The Uku-Weber memorial service started in an hour. And that would be something productive, at least. She could get a quick look at the place Dell had worked, talk to people she'd worked with.

She ran for her truck and was soaked through before she got there, slid into the seat, jeans clinging to the soft cloth upholstery. Rain slanted sideways in the weak light from the headlights. The truck's tires slipped on the gravel as she turned around. Two sharp cracks of thunder so close, there was no difference between the sound and the stark white arc of lightning that lit the sky. Water ran down the drive like a river, cutting deep tracks in the mud.

Hallie turned the engine off and cut the lights. She couldn't drive in this; she'd get stuck in the mud halfway down the drive and be worse off than she was now. She sat there as rain pounded on the roof of the pickup, her hands clenched tight on the steering wheel. Dell's ghost drifted beside her in the passenger seat. Water dripped from Hallie's hair and ran along her cheekbone.

She'd never wanted to hide in her life, but she wanted to hide now, because Dell was dead and she'd never said good-bye and her ghost never spoke or responded or did anything. It was just there, just looking like Dell, just reminding her, like she needed reminding.

She pulled the keys from the ignition, gave Dell's ghost one last long look, and shoved open the door, the rain slashing in and soaking the seat even in the few seconds it took for her to jump out and shove it closed again.

Back inside, she showered, changed her clothes, dumped the soaked clothes in the washing machine, and wiped up the water she trailed through the house when she'd come in. When she finished, it was still raining and there wasn't even a ghost of a chance she'd get off the ranch before morning—maybe not even then if it didn't stop by nightfall. But she didn't waste time thinking about that. She'd walk out tomorrow if she had to.

She wandered back upstairs, still barefoot, aimless for the first time in a long time. She picked up Dell's cell phone, stared at it, put it back on the table by her bed, left the bedroom, and stood for another long minute in the hallway before she walked to the end and did what she'd known she was going to do all along—opened the door to Dell's bedroom.

Dell hadn't been living at the ranch, but she'd been out sometimes—liked to work at the desk in her old bedroom, her father had said. Because she'd liked the view, that's what she told him, which was bullshit, but maybe she'd left something there.

Over the course of the next two hours, while rain pounded against the windows, she filled two bags with trash from the back of the closet, things Dell had probably even forgotten were there—six years' worth of wall calendars, paperbacks with ripped covers, and an uncountable number of unmatched socks. She found half a dozen crumpled certificates from high school awards ceremonies, and those she flattened carefully and left on the desk.

She threw a bunch of clothes that had been hanging in the closet for who knew how long in a laundry basket and shoved it into the hall.

In a box on a shelf above Dell's clothes, she found Dell's old journals, all red spiral notebooks she got cheap at the Walmart in Rapid City. She'd written in them religiously every day between fifth grade and August of her junior year. That was when she'd lost her virginity to Brian Sigurdson at the county fair. "It's the end of history," she'd said to Hallie. "What's left to write about after that?"

But Hallie knew there was one more notebook, a blue spiral one that Dell had started her last summer home.

She found it in the center desk drawer, along with half a box of condoms, a dozen old gas receipts, a broken hair clip, two leaky ball-point pens, and a notepad with running horses across the top. The notepad had been buried under the receipts and condoms, and there were only three sheets left on the pad, the adhesive at the top curling up and away like a streamer.

There were three lines in Dell's handwriting on the top sheet: Colorado, Jasper, and a Minnesota phone number.

Shit.

She stuffed the blue notebook and the notepad into a box with the red spiral notebooks and carried it and the trash bags downstairs.

When she walked into the kitchen, her father was sitting at the table, his hands clenched, staring at nothing. His jeans were wet and splashed with mud to the knees, but otherwise he was reasonably dry, which Hallie took to mean the rain had stopped by the time he'd crossed the yard to the house.

Hallie put the trash bags by the door, carried the box with the spiral notebooks and the notepad with her, and sat at the table across from him.

"You been in her room?" he said after a moment.

"Yeah."

"Okay," he said. He unclenched his hands, then clenched them again, the knuckles showing white. "Do you think I could have done anything?" he said.

"What?"

He was looking at his hands, at the grease worn like grooves into his fingers. "She came out here every Sunday since she came back," he said at last. "We had dinner and she'd spend some time up in her room. Said she needed a little space of her own if it was okay with me. Which—it was always her space. Always. Just like yours."

"Dad," Hallie said.

"I know things were hard after your mother. And I'm no good with . . . with girl things." He looked up from the table. "But we did all right, didn't we? I mean—"

"She didn't kill herself." Hallie interrupted him. Because she needed him not to be like this.

He looked at her for a long moment. Finally, he pulled the box she'd set on the table toward him. Hallie lifted the blue notebook and the notepad from the top and let him look inside at the rest.

"These hers?"

Hallie nodded.

He fingered one of the spirals. "I won't read them," he said. "That wouldn't be . . . fair."

She knew he meant the whole thing wasn't fair, that Dell was dead, that Hallie herself would leave again in a few more days, that people died and he couldn't change that.

"I'd like to keep them, though," he said.

"I think that'd be fine," Hallie told him.

13

The next morning, Hallie was determined to be up and out early. Her leave was more than half gone, and she still didn't know what Dell had been doing or why she'd died. But first, she sat down at the dining room table with Dell's notepad in front of her and dialed the phone number written there.

"Bill Stuart."

"My name is Hallie Michaels," she said. "My sister had your phone number."

"Okay." More a question than a statement.

"Dell Michaels." Hallie said, "That's my sister's name."

"Nope." The word drawn out, almost like a drawl. "Where you from?"

"Prairie City, South Dakota."

"Well, I talked to an Addy Temple from, I think, Pierre a week or so ago."

Hallie caught her breath because Dell's full name was Adelle. Her middle name was Temple, after their grandmother's side of the family. "Why did she call?"

"Who did you say you were?"

"Look, my sister died, okay? She died, and I'm trying to figure out why, and she had your phone number."

There was silence for a long time on the other end of the line. "There was nothing in what I told her that was dangerous or even secret," he finally said. "She sent me some specs for wind turbines. I'm a wind energy consultant, do a lot of work with small farms start-ing up—what turbines, how big, that sort of thing. Anyway, she sent me some specs, and I looked at them for her. No big deal."

"The specs," Hallie said. "What did you tell her?"

"Wasn't much to tell her, except she must have run the numbers wrong. Told her to check the measurements again and get back to me."

"Okay," Hallie said. "Thanks." Then. "Wait. Could there be some kind of tech you've never heard of, something brand-new and super efficient?"

"Wind is wind," he said. "You can't squeeze more energy out of it than it's got."

The day was crisp and clear when she finally left the house, as if yesterday's rain had never happened. The long drive to the road was still muddy and the back end of the truck slid once with the wheels spinning, but she muscled through and was soon out of the drive and more or less dry gravel road and heading down the county road to-ward West Prairie City. She saw only three vehicles on the road, an old white Bonneville, a gray Suburban, and a red three-quarter-ton pickup hauling a trailer stacked with hundred-pound bales of hay. The pickup truck driver waved when he passed her, and she waved back, though she didn't recognize him.

She slowed as she approached Uku-Weber. It sat on open prairie ground, a long drive to approach and a parking lot in front. No creeks or brushland or even windbreaks around it. No way to sneak in, though Hallie wasn't much for sneaking, especially at nine o'clock in the morning.

There were maybe half a dozen vehicles parked directly in front of the building, but otherwise the lot was empty. Right up near the front entry was a row of spaces with rectangular green and white signs that read VISITOR. Hallie parked in one, turned off her truck, and sat for a moment, looking at the building.

The entrance comprised huge panels of glass looking onto what appeared from the outside to be a two-story atrium. There was hardly any mown grass lawn, maybe a ten-foot strip around the building before it all turned back into short-grass prairie. Along the southeast edge of the parking lot, there were signs of construction—a mound of dirt, chunks of broken concrete, a bulldozer, a small crane, and a front-end loader.

Dried stalks of old grass rattled together in the rising breeze as she got out of the pickup and headed toward the entrance. Dell floated just behind her left shoulder. The double-width walk spread out into a broad patio with seasonal grasses in large pots. There was a fountain in the middle with no water, symbols carved along the bottom like petroglyphs.

Hallie stopped.

A ghost floated in the middle of the fountain.

"Well, hell."

She said it out loud and didn't care whether anyone heard her or not. Eddie's ghost had been gone for two full days, since Hallie'd talked to Estelle.

But now, here was another one.

It was a woman, maybe Hallie's age. It was difficult to tell because—yeah, she was a ghost. She had long dark hair and a strongly defined face. She wore a midriff-skimming T-shirt, short denim skirt, a half-dozen loose bracelets on her left arm, and sturdy closed-toe sandals, the kind people wore to hike in.

For a moment, the two ghosts—Dell and the girl in the fountain—floated there, more or less facing each other. Hallie wished they'd talk each other out of her sight, though it didn't matter, because, ghosts or not, Dell and, presumably, the woman in the fountain, were still dead. And Hallie still intended to find out why.

The two ghosts drifted over to Hallie and seemed to follow her as she continued on to the building. When she entered, she was hit with a sharp blast of warm air, which ruffled her hair and made her stop. Dell and the ghost from the fountain floated sharply backwards, as if the downblast had knocked them out the door. There was something . . . substantial about it, the blast of air. It felt . . . gritty. Hallie looked up, but it was two stories to the ceiling and she couldn't see anything. She looked down. There was a narrow grate in the floor running the width of the building, where the sand or grit or whatever it was that had struck her when she walked inside appeared to be sucked in and disappear.

"It's a barrier."

Hallie turned. The atrium was large. Staircases curved up on either side, though there couldn't be more than three or four offices up there. A large reception desk occupied the center space.

"An air barrier," the woman at the reception desk repeated. "It's so we can open the big doors in good weather and still keep . . . things out. So we're not completely dependent on, you know, air handling."

"Things?" Because she couldn't mean ghosts.

"Prairie things," the woman said. She was wearing a tailored suit, but she'd taken the jacket off, revealing a cream-colored tank top. Her hair was short, dyed two different colors, and she looked about fourteen. "Rodents and, I don't know, snakes. Mr. Weber says it can be a problem."

"Huh," said Hallie. Was that what Uku-Weber did? When they talked about the weather of the future or whatever? Bring the outdoors inside? Hadn't Tel talked about wind turbines? About splitting storm fronts? Maybe it was all just talk, the whole thing. "Is Lorie Bixby here?" she asked.

"Would you like me to get her for you?"

"That'd be swell," Hallie said.

It took Lorie a good ten minutes to come out and meet her. Hallie paced the atrium. The ghosts knocked silently against the glass outside, as if they wanted in but couldn't figure out how to accomplish it. The flooring in the atrium was concrete cut to look like twenty-four-inch tile with some sort of giant mosaic pattern picked in subtle shades of brown and tan. The walls were glass, with narrow strips between that appeared to be constructed of sandstone, though they probably weren't. They were etched with petroglyphs like those Hallie had seen on the fountain outside, though now that she was able to study them, she realized that though some of the symbols were Native American, not all of them were.

She occupied herself identifying them, etched so thinly, most people wouldn't even notice them. She'd spotted a stag, a buffalo, something she thought might be a fu dog, a Celtic knot, a pentacle, and on the very centermost strip, a hammer, ax, and sword laid one across the other.

"Hallie! What are you doing here!" Lorie didn't sound particularly happy as she crossed the atrium.

"Dell had an office here, right?"

Lorie cocked her head and looked at her. "Yeah."

"I thought she might have . . . things," Hallie said.

"Oh . . . wow." Like it hadn't occurred to her. "Okay, then," she said. "Come on upstairs."

She led Hallie up one of the curving staircases, talking as they went. "I was just so surprised to see you. Here, I mean. Because, well . . . I thought you were going back?" She said the last like a question, like, *Why aren't you gone?*

Because I'm going to find out what happened to Dell. What she said was, "Not until Friday."

At the top of the stairs, they paused.

"Holy shit," Hallie said.

Because it was the same pattern—the *same pattern*—she'd seen on Dell's body, on Jennie Vagts, on Pete's belt buckle, etched into the atrium floor. A jagged lightning bolt striking the earth from deep in a roiling cloud.

"What—?" Hallie cleared her throat. She felt as if something had crawled up her spine. "What is that?"

Lorie looked over the balcony railing. "Oh . . . yeah. Isn't it awesome! Martin designed that himself. It's so . . . subtle, but distinct, don't you think? You can't even really tell what it is unless you're up here on the executive floor."

"But . . ." *Think, Hallie, think.* Outside, Dell and the fountain girl continued to bump up against the atrium glass. "I mean, what does it mean?"

Lorie looked at her curiously. "It's . . . weather," she said.

"Storms." Death, destruction, power.

"It's pretty cool, huh. It's like, well, it's not exactly the company logo. There's a . . . more stylized version. But it's the . . . heart. That's what Martin says. If we keep that in mind, that it's about how powerful and destructive and awesome weather can be, then we won't . . . we'll respect it. And it won't be like the atom bomb or something."

"The atom bomb?"

"Or something."

She tugged at Hallie's sleeve. Hallie took a last look at the atrium floor, then allowed Lorie to lead her back to Dell's office. It had already been completely cleaned out except for two cardboard boxes sitting on the otherwise empty desk.

"Dell worked here?" Hallie asked, because this didn't look like Dell at all.

"She was mostly . . . You need investors to get something like this off the ground. That's what Dell did. Especially local investors, because you want people to 'buy in.' And local people, they'll support you no matter what if they've got a stake."

Hallie looked at her, and after a minute, Lorie shrugged and added, "That's what Martin says, and he's, you know, he's pretty brilliant. It's been rough, Dell's death. I mean, because, of course, Dell's dead, which is awful. But for the company, too. People aren't sure what's going to happen now. Because she was, like, the local face, you know, someone people recognized."

Hallie opened one of the unsealed cardboard boxes and poked through the meager contents. It hurt, like poking at a wound, the small number of things that made up a life. The box held a wooden pencil holder with three pens, a mechanical pencil and a fine-point marker still inside, a calendar with pictures of cowboys on horseback, a book titled *Leadership and Teams,* which Hallie couldn't believe Dell had ever opened in her life, half a dozen molded plastic toy soldiers, and a handheld anemometer.

She started to open the second box, when Lorie said, "So, you're all good here, right? I mean, I don't want to rush you, but Martin's out to Cleary's half the day, meeting with those local investors I was talking about, and I'm supposed to be with the construction guys because they screw things up. You wouldn't believe— And I'm not really all that good at it, because you know me, I get along with everyone and people—my mom used to say that people—"

"All right, Lorie."

"—take advantage of me, but I don't know that that's true, I mean, I like people." She was chewing on a fingernail as she talked, nervous and excited at the same time. An adventure, Hallie figured, that Lorie had never expected in her life, being part of a startup company with enough money for modern construction and hiring people from out of state. ". . . and so, you know, I have to go."

"I'm fine, Lorie." Hallie finished opening the second box as she spoke.

Staring up at her from a two-week-old newspaper was a picture of the ghost from the fountain.

14

Lorie!"

"What?" Lorie's tone was wary, as if she could feel the change in the room, just from that one word.

"Why did Dell have this?"

The article was about someone named Sarah Hale, who'd apparently been missing for six months. There were conflicting reports about where she'd been last seen—either in a mall in Rapid City or somewhere up around Seven Mile Creek.

Lorie looked into the box, still chewing on her fingernail. "Well, it's the newspaper," she said.

"No, this . . . this . . . this disappearance. What do you know?"

Lorie shook her head. "She was from Rapid City?" Like it was a quiz. "It was kind of a big deal at the time, but, you know, no one knew her."

"This was after Dell came back?"

"Uh, yeah?" Lorie edged back toward the door. "Are you okay?"

"It's fine." Hallie took a deep breath. "Go."

She reread the article. Then she stacked the boxes one on top of the other, carried them out, and stood for several minutes with the boxes leaning against the balcony railing as she studied the lightning bolt mosaic on the floor. She watched the ghosts outside, floating against glass panes they couldn't penetrate.

Two construction workers burst through a small outside door on the west side of the atrium. One of the men held his arm, palm up, while the other man hustled him along.

"Accident," Hallie heard the second man say to the receptionist. "Cut his hand."

The receptionist, young as she was, didn't waste time on, *Oh!* or *Gosh!* or *What should I do?* She jumped up and headed to the back of the building. The man who'd cut his hand shook his head, like it wasn't so bad. He held his right hand—the one that wasn't injured—underneath the other. Blood seeped through his fingers onto the floor.

A flash, as if the lights had gone off and come back on, and Hallie saw something dark run along the lightning bolt etched into the floor, like an electric current or water, flowing faster and faster until it was spreading in several directions at once, until it covered the floor. Until—

A second flash, the lightning bolt on the floor and the symbols on the sandstone strips between the windows lit up like Christmas lights, followed by a *whump* like a compression blast that Hallie could feel in her chest. She took a step back, but it was done, everything back to normal, the lightning bolt, the symbols along the windows. She looked down. The receptionist had returned, was opening a first aid kit. The two men waited patiently for bandages and antiseptic.

Like nothing had happened.

Shit.

It was here—right here. She had no idea what it was. But it was sure as hell something. Something no one else saw. Jesus.

Was this what Dell had known—? But she couldn't have seen it. So how had she known?

And what was it?

Double shit.

She set the boxes down and slipped along the short upper hallway. There were four doors: The first one led back to Dell's office. The next was a conference room with high-backed leather chairs and a glass and iron table. The third was another office half again as big as Dell's, modern yet relaxed, leather chairs, wood floor instead of carpet, wool rugs, an old oak desk, and one entire wall of bookshelves.

Martin's office.

Hallie stepped inside. There was a faint odor of smoke and something else Hallie couldn't immediately identify. The desk was clear except for a computer monitor and a leather desk blotter.

On one of the lower bookshelves, just below eye level, Hallie spotted a roughly carved bowl of polished caramel-colored hardwood. Closer inspection revealed the same lightning bolt design carved on the inside, along with a half-dozen crudely drawn symbols. Hallie scraped at one of the symbols and it flaked off—dark red. Paint? Or blood?

Beside the bowl were a dozen handkerchiefs, pressed and neatly folded, each one with lightning bolts embroidered at the corners.

Blood and lightning bolts? Again. What did it mean?

She crossed to the desk. The monitor was off, and she didn't bother to turn it on. There were three notes tucked into the blotter—an out-of-state phone number, something that looked like a recipe, and Dell's name. Hallie looked at the third note for a long minute. She had worked there, right? They'd worked together. But there was something about the way it was written, just her name, just that, traced and retraced, underlined a dozen times.

Dell.

Maybe it was well past time to talk to Martin Weber.

Hallie left the office and grabbed the boxes in the hallway, took the steps at a quick trot, passed the receptionist without a word, and was out the door. The ghosts—Dell and Sarah Hale—fell in behind her, like waves in her wake.

The wind rose as she wound the pickup up to seventy along the county road. Dark clouds had moved steadily up from the south all morning, low against the horizon. From the corner of her eye, Hallie could see Dell, flickering in and out over the passenger seat. Sarah Hale never flickered at all, steady against Hallie's elbow, a cold so deep, it burned.

She took the corner at the Bear Tree Gas 'Em Up too fast, bumping onto the shoulder and sliding back out onto the road. Someone honked at her from the oncoming lane; she didn't even look at them. It was like she couldn't drive fast enough, like she'd finally found her anger or her heart was finally pumping, like the trip home and the funeral and maybe even Dell's death had been not quite real, like she'd kept expecting to wake up. Hadn't she been in Afghanistan? Shouldn't she be the one who'd died?

She stopped at the four-way and waited as a loaded grain truck rumbled through the intersection. She rubbed at her cheekbone just below her right eye.

Dell had tried to call her; that's what Cass had said, and Boyd—hadn't he said the same thing? Dell had wanted to talk before . . . before she died. And Hallie didn't know why, hadn't known anything, still didn't know anything, but she knew where to start.

Martin Weber.

Because Uku-Weber had lightning bolts and Dell and a ghost in the fountain. And Jennie Vagts . . . Hallie had her phone off the seat, flipped open and starting to dial before she realized that she didn't have Jennie's number.

She tossed the phone with a loud, "Fuck!" Then regretted it because Lorie might know.

"It's not all on you," Eddie had told her once. But if you saw what needed doing, you had to do it. Right? She wanted Eddie back—Eddie's ghost—wanted him here to remind her. Of what, she wasn't sure. Of war. Or fighting. Of going down.

Hallie pulled into the parking lot of Cleary's Downhome Diner and Lounge. She parked next to a rusted yellow pickup with a home-built camper on the back. Pete Bolluyt's midnight blue, dual rear-axle pickup sat right up near the door, shining like it just came off the showroom floor despite the late-morning gloom.

She reached into the pickup bed and closed her hand around an eighteen-inch prybar. It felt light, like it weighed nothing. She toyed with the idea of smashing Pete's windshield. Could feel it, like a vibration in her fingertips, the satisfaction that would come from swinging and smashing, from the sound of shattering glass. But she didn't. Because satisfaction—at least Hallie's personal momentary satisfaction—was not the point right now. She turned away from Pete's truck and headed in.

It took her a minute to adjust to the light inside the bar, even though it had been gray and gloomy outside. To her left, she heard the ping and clang of a pinball machine. Hallie hadn't been in Cleary's since ninth grade, when she'd come—driving the old red farm truck, though she hadn't even had a permit yet—looking for her father, who hadn't been home in two days. The bartender was still Prue Stalking Horse, just hanging up the phone and turning toward the door as Hallie entered. Her face was expressionless, like she could see clean through a person—and maybe she could. Hallie's father had once told her that Prue knew everyone's secrets, knew their weaknesses just by looking at them.

"Does she know yours?" Hallie'd asked him.

"That's why I go there," her father had said.

Hallie'd always thought Prue was Norwegian, despite her name, because everyone was, but her father said she was from Iceland, and she looked like an Ice Queen, white-blond hair, pale blue eyes, unblemished ivory skin.

Shit. Why was she thinking about this now?

She saw Pete at a round table across the room, underneath a window with a neon MILLER sign hanging from it. Tel Sigurdson and some retired West Prairie City banker Hallie recognized but couldn't name were also at the table. Next to Pete, facing Hallie, but with his gaze fixed on the papers in front of him, was Martin Weber.

She hadn't seen him in four years, and he hadn't changed. Seriously, hadn't changed one hair on his head. Exactly the same—red-blond hair cut long, thin gold wire-framed glasses, sharp features like a rabbit or an aristocrat, Hallie had never been sure which. Four years ago, when Hallie first knew him, Martin had been attractive more for what he said and did than for how he looked. He'd talked about the history of South Dakota as if it were a story anyone would want to know, about the latest gadgets from Japan, about Eastern philosophy and how to build a better generator. But it wasn't just lectures about things he knew; he asked her questions like he really cared about the answers. He'd been the only person she told—back then—about wanting to see the world and make a difference. Stupid because she'd sounded like an army recruiter, but he never acted like it was stupid or like she shouldn't want what she wanted. Sometimes, though, she'd noticed a look in his eye, flat and distant, as if in that moment, nothing—none of them—mattered.

The place was almost empty. Hallie skirted a couple of tables as she crossed the room. The prybar burned like dry ice in her hand. She glanced to her right. Dell was holding the prybar, too, ghost-cold sucking the heat right out of the metal.

Pete's eyes narrowed as she approached them. Then his lips twitched up into a grin. He nudged Martin, whose head popped up. He didn't smile, just looked at her, a sheaf of papers in his hand.

"Martin," Hallie said.

"Do you think you'll need that?" he asked, his head tilting toward the prybar in her hand.

Hallie took a step backwards, set the bar carefully on an empty table. "I want to talk," she said, which wasn't entirely true, because she really wanted to hit something. She didn't care if it was Martin Weber or Pete Bolluyt or one of the glass entry doors.

"You want to talk to me?" Martin said. He said it like a question, like he didn't know who she was. And maybe he didn't, because Pete leaned over and whispered something in his ear. One eyebrow raised. "I—," he began.

"Don't—" She held up the index finger on her right hand. Because she couldn't stand it right now, listening to him say how sorry he was, how great Dell was. "I'm going to ask questions," she said. "You're going to answer them."

He managed to look both amused and sympathetic. Tel Sigurdson rose from his chair. "Hallie."

"You can go, Tel," Hallie said.

Tel looked at her for a long moment, looked at Martin, who nodded toward the restaurant door. "It's fine," he said. "She's upset."

Tel considered that, tapped the retired banker on the shoulder, and the two of them got up from the table and left through the door to the restaurant side.

Once they were both gone, Pete scraped his chair back from the table. "I'm going to get me a beer," he said. "If that's all right with you, Hallie?" He made a mocking gesture, like the sweep of a hat.

"A little early, isn't it?" Hallie said.

"It's never too early," Pete said.

While he was gone, Hallie looked at Martin. He waited, his hands flat on the table, straight backed but relaxed.

"Did you kill her?" Hallie asked. She'd meant to ask him first

123

about the symbols and the lightning bolt and the flash when blood touched the floor, but she had to know, had to see what he did when she asked. Pete was returning from the bar with a long-necked beer, and he stopped, looked from one of them to the other.

"Your sister was . . . incredible," Martin said. "She was smart and funny, and it's horrible—I know—to imagine a world without her. It's horrible that you were so far away." He crossed his hands. "I can't imagine how you feel," he said. "I wouldn't presume. But I understand that you want to feel that there's an explanation for—"

"Oh, there's an explanation," Hallie said. She backed up a step. Her leg hit the back of the table behind her. "I don't know what that explanation is," she said, "but I know there's something going on. And I'm going to find out what it is."

"You don't know shit, Hallie," Pete said. He took a long draw on his beer and instead of crossing behind Martin and sitting back down, he took a step away from the table and faced Hallie directly.

"What's that thing you've got on your belt buckle there, Pete?" Hallie said.

Pete actually looked down at his belt, as if he might have forgotten what he was wearing. When he looked back up, his lips had thinned down and his eyes looked mean and hard. "What's it look like?"

"I gave that to him," Martin said smoothly. "It's representative of what Uku-Weber is all about. And Pete is one of my earliest local investors."

"Is that right, Pete? You've got money to invest?"

Pete smiled at her, hooked a thumb in a belt loop.

"Is that from the meth lab or because your father died before he had a chance to change his will?"

Pete slammed his beer bottle onto the table and took two long strides toward her. "You shut up," he said.

"Oh, bring it on, Pete."

"Pete." Martin was halfway out of his chair.

You, too, Hallie thought. It wouldn't settle anything, wouldn't get her one step closer to finding out what had happened to Dell. And she didn't care. She'd been good for days, and it had gotten her nowhere.

She stepped sideways to get clear of the table behind her. "You want to know what I know?" she said to Martin, leaning slightly to her left to talk around Pete.

"This isn't right, Hallie," Martin said. "This isn't what Dell would have—"

"Don't you—don't you dare!"

She started forward. Pete shoved her hard. She stumbled back, recovered, and started forward again. She knew where her prybar was. She could reach it if she had to. And she hoped she'd have to. Hoped—

"Hallie, stop."

The voice was quiet, but it carried over her harsh breathing, over Pete's curses, over the sound of a door closing. Hallie closed her eyes. An ache as big as the South Dakota short-grass prairie spun the breath out of her lungs.

"Boyd." She turned.

"It's not worth it," he said, his voice still quiet, but firm.

"You don't know that," she said. She wanted to cry and hit someone at the same time.

"I do," he said. Against her will, she was impressed by the way he looked at her, as if she were the only person in the room. Even when she knew it was a tactic—get them to focus on you and not the object—it was compelling.

"It's fine, Officer," Martin said, his hands up, palms outward, warding Hallie off like an evil spirit. "Just . . . let's call it a misunder-standing, emotions running high." His lips twitched up in a rueful half smile. "You know."

Boyd didn't smile back at him. He put his hand on Hallie's arm. "Let's go outside," he said.

Hallie clenched and unclenched her fist.

Pete said, "Aw, Hallie, the Boy Deputy going to save you from yourself?"

Hallie would have been all the way over the table if Boyd hadn't grabbed her around the waist and hauled her back. He shoved him-self between her and Pete.

"Get out," he said.

"Goddamnit!" Hallie said, "Let go of me."

"Out," he repeated.

His voice was no louder, but now there was a thin band of steel underneath. If she wanted Pete, she'd have to go through him. "God-damn you," she said, and wasn't sure which one of them she meant.

15

Hallie was leaning against her pickup truck, her arms crossed over her chest when Boyd walked down the steps and across the parking lot toward her. He was carrying the prybar she'd left inside.

"No one's pressing charges," Boyd said as he approached.

His shirt was as crisp and clean and brightly white as the one he'd had on the first time she met him. His khaki pants were ironed with millimetric precision. The buttons on his shirt and his narrow brass belt buckle gleamed dully in the gray late-morning light.

Hallie snorted. "What charges, exactly? Walking with intent?"

There was something in the way he looked right then, something that made him seem not just young, but vulnerable. Like, despite the perfect haircut and spit-shined shoes, he didn't actually know what to do. She blinked and it was gone, that feeling, and he was just . . . the Boy Deputy, just some guy.

"Yeah." Boyd raised the prybar, slapped it into this right palm. It made a dull, heavy sound. "You were just carrying this in case the door stuck?"

"That's right," she said.

"You want to tell me what's going on?" he said after a moment.

"What do you think is going on?" she said.

He sighed.

The glass front door of Cleary's creaked open, like it was exhausted—opening and closing and closing and opening for twenty years and more. Pete stepped out, followed closely by Martin. Sarah Hale drifted out behind them, slid right past them and into the parking lot. Martin stumbled on the steps as she passed. Pete grabbed his arm.

A sharp shaft of light slanted across the parking lot. It glinted off the lenses in Martin's glasses, and for a moment the red in his hair shone like fire. He turned and looked at Hallie squarely. A dark ring on his finger flashed gold. He pointed his finger at her, thumb raised, like a gun.

She didn't realize she'd taken a step until Boyd grabbed her by the wrist. But that wasn't what stopped her. It was the warmth of his hand on her arm, like, of the two of them, he was the one who was real.

Hallie could hear thunder, pitched so low, it was almost inaudible, like a rumble in her own chest. No rain, though, as the low clouds continued to scatter. Martin's head came up, looked to the north, though the storm, wherever it was, had to be miles from town. Pete watched her, his dark gaze flickering down to Boyd's hand on Hallie's arm, flickering back up to stare directly at her as he opened his pickup truck door and got inside.

After they were gone, Boyd let go of her arm and stepped back. "You don't have to talk to me," he said.

"Dell's death," she said. "You want to talk about that?"

He blinked. "She died," he said.

"Yeah. And?"

"And it's an ongoing investigation."

"Jesus!"

A muscle twitched underneath his cheekbone. "Look," he said. "I don't want to get called out like this again. I'll arrest you if I have to. I mean, if you make trouble, or . . . get into a fight. But I just . . ."

He rubbed a hand across his face. "I'm saying that if you want to talk, you can talk to me."

"Yeah." Hallie laughed at him. "You want to tell me about your 'ongoing investigation,' we'll talk. Otherwise, forget it." Deep down, in a place she was never admitting to him, she desperately wanted to talk, wanted someone to talk to. But if he wasn't talking, then neither was she.

He half turned away from her, toward his car.

"Wait."

He looked back.

"Give me my prybar," she said.

He looked at the steel bar in his hands, like he'd forgotten it was there.

"Thanks," she said as he handed it to her, though she wasn't sure what she was thanking him for. She didn't need him. If he wouldn't talk to her about Dell, there had to be people who would. She tossed the prybar into the pickup bed and wrenched open the driver's door. She climbed into the cab, stuck the key in the ignition, and cranked the engine. It caught, coughed, and died.

Shit.

She cranked it again. Then, a third time.

Boyd had opened his car door and started to climb in, but stopped with a hand on the window, waiting. *Go away,* she thought. She rubbed her left eye and cranked the engine again.

Nothing.

With a half-uttered curse, she popped the hood and climbed out of the truck.

"Problem?" Boyd asked.

She looked at him and didn't say anything, just lifted the hood and propped it into place. The battery was new. The leads were all tight. She checked the belts and the wiring. It all looked fine.

"I can jump you." Boyd hadn't said anything while she'd been pottering under the hood, and despite herself, despite how annoying the whole thing was, she liked that, that he didn't step right up to solve the problem, that he acted like she could, you know, do some damn thing herself.

She straightened, looked at him, and shrugged. "Yeah," she said. "Fine."

Twenty minutes later and it still hadn't started. Hallie called Big Dog's Auto—pacing in front of her truck because she did not have *time* for this. Both trucks were out, and Tom Hauser told her it would be at least a couple of hours. Boyd offered to drive her home.

Hallie tried to think of someone else to call. "Don't you have—I don't know—work?"

"It's my job, ma'am." His mouth quirked up in a twisted half smile, and she couldn't tell if he was making fun of her or of himself.

"It's almost noon," she said. "I'll let you give me a ride home, if you let me buy you lunch." Wasn't at all sure she wanted to spend more time with him, but she didn't want to owe him either, and there wasn't anything else she could do right now without a truck.

He stared at her. "All right," he said, slowly. Then, a quick nod, as if he were talking himself into it. "All right. I'll call it in."

Hallie reached back into the pickup and grabbed a twenty she kept in the glove box for emergencies.

She chose the bar side of Cleary's, which served burgers and fries because she thought she'd be more comfortable. The only customers were two men slouched at the bar and a middle-aged woman and her daughter at a round table near the door.

Prue Stalking Horse looked up sharply when they came in, but when she came to the table to take their orders, she looked as cool and imperturbable as ever.

Boyd went to the restroom to wash up. While he was gone, Prue brought their drinks. She said, "I didn't expect that."

Hallie's right hand tapped against the table's edge like a metronome, or the ticking of a time bomb. She forced herself to stop. "Expect what?" she asked Prue.

But Prue didn't hear her—didn't answer her, at any rate—just went back behind the bar, where she frowned and made notes with a pen she stuck behind her ear when she wasn't using it.

Hallie was beginning to regret the impulse that had led her to offer Boyd lunch. What were they going to talk about?

He came back to the table, and she caught him staring at the bracelet Eddie had given her again. She started to put her hand under the table, then thought, *You've got to be kidding me.*

"Why do you do that?" she asked him.

He startled, then settled back into himself, like a horse on a windy day. He reached across the table and took her wrist, turning it so he could look at the bracelet more closely.

"I saw this once," he said. He fingered one of the lapis lazuli beads, then let it go. "It was . . ." He hesitated. "It was on someone who died."

Well.

Maybe they shouldn't talk about anything.

The sun emerged briefly from behind a bank of clouds; light slanted through the window near their table, striking the wooden floor and highlighting an old gouge laid crosswise to the grain. Hallie studied it and hoped their food would come soon.

"You lived here all your life?" Boyd asked, causing Hallie to blink.

"I was born here," she finally said.

Prue brought their food—burger and fries for Hallie, BLT with lettuce on the side for Boyd—and left without saying anything, though she looked at Hallie for a long second, as though she was trying to pass her a message.

"You know her?" Boyd asked when she'd left.

"Prue? Kind of. My dad does."

Things were quiet after that as they concentrated on eating. Hallie thought about what to do next. Tackling Pete or Martin directly now seemed out of the question, and she didn't have a truck—probably wouldn't until tomorrow morning

"You're not from the West River, are you?" she asked Boyd suddenly.

"What?"

"West of the Missouri. Western South Dakota. We call it the West River."

He shook his head. "Maquoketa." Then, because she just looked at him. "Iowa. Eastern Iowa."

"Huh." She said, "Did you ever see the world's largest popcorn ball?"

"No." He laughed. It made him look young, but then everything did.

They talked about other offbeat places that one of them had either seen or not. The Corn Palace, which Hallie had been to twice—once with her parents before her mother died and once by herself, just to do it. Boyd said he'd been to the Iowa State Fair ten times, had seen the butter cow and the world's largest pig.

Neither one of them had ever been to Mount Rushmore. "Although you see it sometimes," Hallie said, "like, you come around a corner, and you can't help it. It's right there, like someday it'll take over the whole sky."

"What about the Badlands?" Boyd brushed crumbs off the table into his hand and dropped them on his plate.

"Almost went once, but . . . something happened," she finished lamely. *My mother died.* "You?"

"Once. Wouldn't go back. It's like . . . chaos, like chaos given form."

And you sure as shit wouldn't like that, Hallie thought, looking at his immaculate uniform, wondering what it took to be that neat all the time.

She had to snatch the bill out from under Boyd's hand in order to pay it, but he gave in with grace, which she appreciated.

Hallie heard the rumble of distant thunder again as she and Boyd walked out of Cleary's to his car. The sky above them had cleared, however. The wind was brisk and cool, but the sun took some of the edge off. West, toward the ranch, Hallie could still see clouds, like a line between daylight and twilight.

16

Twenty minutes later, they crested the slow rise just east of the ranch. Their conversation had lagged again, but Hallie found the silence companionable. As it stretched, though, she started to wonder what it was about him. What had Prue been trying to tell her, anyway? Something about Boyd? That he was an "operator," like her dad had said? Because he was always showing up, always helpful. What did he want?

Then—

"Shit." Smoke, a dark band of it, rose straight up into the sky, muted against the flat gray of the clouds, but clearly smoke from something burning.

Boyd's hands tightened on the wheel. "Is that—?"

"Shit," Hallie said again.

Boyd flipped on the lights and the siren and stomped on the gas so that they flew over a couple of small dips in the road, the car thunking once and then smoothing as the road did. Boyd reached for the radio, but Hallie stayed him. "No," she said. "Wait. It'll take them an hour to get here. We might as well see what's—if it's, you know, worth it."

He spared a glance at her, then concentrated on the road. Hallie didn't think. It could be a tractor fire or a trash fire. It wouldn't be a prairie fire with the rain they'd had lately. It could be—

Don't think.

Boyd entered the yard in a swirl of dust and gravel. The smoke wasn't coming from the house or the big equipment shed or the horse barn set farther down the lane. Hallie was out of the car and headed around the tractor shed, not sure what she'd find. She stopped at the corner of the building. The old toolshed, the one where her father stored broken fence posts and unused cattle chains and old hafts from axes, picks, and shovels was spectacularly on fire.

"Dad!" Hallie's father was throwing dirt on the flames or digging a break around the shed or—probably—both at once. He looked at her, his eyes wide, then waved her to his right.

"Over there!" he shouted. Something exploded in the center of the shed with a loud crack! Hallie's father ducked his head and went right on pitching dirt.

Jesus.

Hallie turned away to find a shovel, but Boyd was already there, handing her one of the two in his hand and running down to the shed. He shouted something into the radio mike attached to his shirt, but Hallie couldn't make out what he was saying.

The wind was from the west, which was not good because the big tractor shed and the house were both downwind. Boyd and her father were already working between the toolshed and the tractor shed. There was a narrow lane between the two as well, and if the wind stayed low, it might slow the fire down. There was moisture in the air, moisture in the clouds above them. Be damned nice if it rained.

Forty minutes later, they had the fire almost under control and, coincidentally, the firefighters arrived. Hallie's father pitched a final shovelful of dirt on the smoldering wreckage of the old toolshed and stepped back for the volunteer firefighters—most of them men and women Hallie and her father had known all their lives—to drag the big hose from the truck. Hallie's father tipped his hat off his head and wiped his face with the same hand, leaving a shallow gray streak through the dark soot covering most of his face.

"What the hell, Dad? What happened?" Hallie asked as she followed him back to the big open door of the tractor shed.

Her father hawked and spit, wiped at his eyes, and gestured her farther upwind of the smoke and away from the loud roar of the fire truck engine as the firefighters started up the pump.

"I was working in the tractor shed when I smelled the smoke."

"What started it?"

"Hell, if I know."

The fire chief, Haxton Blake, who was also the mayor of Old Prairie City—mostly referred to by the locals as Old PC—and who owned the Silver Dove, a diner that pretty much got by serving coffee, beer, and the best fried doughnuts in six counties, approached. "It's pretty much done," he said to Hallie's father, "but we'll leave the little truck here and a couple of folks to watch things for you."

"'Preciate it, Hack," her father said. He and Haxton nodded to each other, and Hallie's father watched as the fire chief walked back down to talk to the others, then stared for a few minutes longer at the pile of charred timber that marked the remains of the old toolshed, a shed, Hallie knew, that he'd been threatening to pull down for ten years.

"Where you been?" he asked without actually looking over at her.

Hallie gestured vaguely. "Up to town. Truck wouldn't start." She looked around for Boyd, having lost track of him in the chaos of the fire trucks and the smoke and everything else. He came around the far corner of the smoldering shed, stopped to talk to Kate Wannamaker, who was raking out the dirt and then headed back toward Hallie and her father. His crisp white shirt was crumpled and streaked with gray and brown.

Hallie's father cleared his throat, the sound harsh and rough.

"I'm going to go head down and water the bison," he said. "You want to make sure the yearlings up the south pasture get fed?" He was walking away before he finished, didn't even wait for an answer, busy getting away.

"You okay?" Boyd asked as he approached.

"Yeah." She would have said more, quite possibly something regretful, because she was getting damned tired of him asking her that question, but Haxton returned and said, "Your daddy gone?"

Hallie scrubbed at her scalp. She felt as if she were coated in grease and gritty at the same time. "Yeah, he went to the back field to—"

"There's no electric to that shed, is there?" Hack interrupted her. Her whole life, she didn't remember him ever letting her finish a whole sentence.

"No, never has been," she said.

"Yeah. Huh."

"Is there a problem?" Boyd asked.

Hallie looked at him, was this any of his business? Then—oh yeah, he was a deputy sheriff.

"It looks funny is all," Hack said, looking back over his shoulder at the shed.

"Like it was deliberate?" Boyd asked.

"Jesus! Watch where you're swinging that thing!" Hack yelled at one of the firefighters who was hauling a second length of hose from one of the trucks to the smoldering fire. He turned back to Boyd. "No accelerants. At least I'm not smelling gas or kerosene. And the burn patterns . . . well, it's just odd is all."

"Could it be lightning?" she asked. "I heard thunder earlier." Although it didn't look like it had rained.

Hack scratched the back of his head. Boyd looked at her and frowned. Like he was—what?—worried? She could take care of herself.

"I don't see how it could have been lightning. Though, I got to admit—" He shook his head as though trying to remember something lurking just out of reach. "I'll check with the weather service. Hey—," he began as if he was going to ask a question, only to be interrupted.

"Everyone okay?" It was Cass Andersen. Hallie looked back through the tractor shed to see that besides Cass's big old Suburban, there were three trucks and a car, all pulled up into the yard. Not that they'd come together—they'd probably seen the smoke or heard the call on the scanner.

"We're fine," Hallie said. She hated that question, always had.

Cass stepped back and looked at her. She looked at Hack. "You all right?" she said to him.

Hack waved a hand toward the shed. "It's all good. Thank everyone for coming out, but we got it."

Hack walked away without saying, *See you* or *Stay away from that shit, it's hot,* or even *Hey* to Cass or Hallie. He was already shouting at someone down by the shed. Boyd put a hand on her shoulder, squeezed it once, then walked away, too, back to his car to write up a report or down to help with cleanup or . . . well, Hallie didn't know what.

"Come up to the house with me," Cass said briskly.

Hallie considered arguing with her, wanted to go hide in the back fields herself, but it wasn't worth it. Up at the house, she busied herself getting out pitchers and plastic cups and told Cass where to find the lemonade and iced tea mixes. Cass talked the whole time.

"My god, what does he do? Alphabetize everything? This isn't a kitchen, it's a filing system. You ought to just mess things up once in a while, see what he'd do."

"Yeah, I'll get right on that," Hallie said. She filled a mug with water, drank half of it in an attempt to ease the raw dryness in her throat from the smoke. She rubbed the corner of her brow with the back of her hand. Her hands, probably her face, too, were covered with soot and grime. She left the kitchen while Cass was talking about something that had happened to someone two towns over some month and a half ago and went into the downstairs bathroom.

It took a lot of scrubbing to get the dirt off and beat back the stink of smoke from her hands. When she was finished, her hair was sticking up in front in short damp spikes. She walked out of the bathroom, still wiping her hands with a towel, and almost ran into Boyd.

"Jesus!" she said. "What are you doing?"

He spread his hands, as if that would make him nonthreatening—as if he was threatening, which he wasn't—just dangerous in some way Hallie hadn't figured out yet. His hands were clean; he must have washed them in the kitchen or the utility sink in the tractor shed. His shirt, which had been so crisp and bright an hour ago, looked beyond salvage. There was a long streak of gray black soot down the left front, rucking up the button-down pocket and ending in a large damp splotch, like he'd wiped his hand, or someone had grabbed him there. The hem of his shirt cuffs had turned completely black, so that it looked as if they'd always been that color. Though he'd washed his face, he still had a dark smudge just underneath his right cheekbone, and it made him look like a kid who'd been playing by the creek.

"I came to see if you were all right," he said.

"Yeah," she said dryly. "I'm swell. I started a fight, almost got arrested, my truck doesn't run, and I just put out a fire. All in all, it's been a pretty good day so far. How about you?"

His lips twitched. "All right," he said. Hallie wanted to look him in the eye, but her gaze kept being drawn back to his watch. It was clunky and black and too big for his wrist, and it seemed important, like it would tell her secrets if only she knew the right questions.

"Look," he said, "I think—" He stopped talking so abruptly that Hallie looked up. He was stock-still, staring at the dining room wall.

Hallie followed his gaze, but there wasn't anything shocking there—an old sideboard badly in need of refinishing with a couple of framed posters that her mother had bought a long time ago: a mountain lion and a panther, the latter a Major Felten print, sleek black cat crawling through tall grass, and the former a mountain lion in nearly the same pose, climbing straight down a rocky outcropping deep in the Badlands. Three art deco lead glass vases sat in a neat row underneath the posters. When her mother was alive, they'd been filled with wildflowers or tulips or daffodils, depending on the season, with silk flowers in the winter, with river rocks or Christmas candy a couple of memorable times. They'd been empty for years.

"Boyd?" Hallie said after a minute.

"I—" His gaze drifted back to the sideboard. "I have to get back to town," he said. He started toward the kitchen, but turned back at the doorway. There was something stark about his features, about the look in his eye. "Be careful," he said. "Don't—" He raised his watch hand, and she thought he was going to point at her or at the pictures on the wall, but his radio crackled to life right then, the dispatcher asking him to radio in his status.

When his radio conversation was finished, he said, "See you around."

Then he was gone.

"Okay," Hallie said to the empty room. "You bet."

17

"They all gone?"

It was dark by the time her father came down out of the fields, the sun long gone behind thick clouds and the light fading out of the sky like it just couldn't hold itself up any longer.

"You see anybody?"

"Don't be pissed at me," he said, rubbing degreaser on his hands at the kitchen sink while cold water ran from the faucet.

Hallie pulled a glass dish covered with plastic wrap from the refrigerator, took a sniff, and decided that the meat loaf was still good. She removed the plastic wrap and stuck the meat loaf in the microwave. "Don't worry, Dad," she said. "I got a whole list."

Their supper consisted of the meat loaf, some warmed-over potatoes, and a dubious tomato that Hallie sliced and put on a plate, but neither of them ate. For the first time since she'd been home, the dining room table seemed empty, the whole room spare and lean, though it held the dining room table, six straight-backed chairs, the sideboard with her mother's posters above it, and two small side tables underneath the windows. Maybe it was the light, she thought, that made it seem old and empty. Or maybe it was just the mood. Her father cleaned his plate, cleared the dishes, and came back to the table with a bottle of beer in his hand.

"That dessert?" Hallie asked.

He didn't answer, just sat and stared at the label on the bottle. "Weirdest thing," he finally said. "That shed going up. Just went up like . . . nothing."

Hallie nodded. "I know. Hack said—"

"Shit, Hallie," her father interrupted her. "Listen, would you?"

"What? What are you saying?"

"I'm saying what I'm saying!" He took a long drag from his beer. Hallie waited.

"You know," he finally said, "no one'd been in there for a while. There could have been oily rags or old blasting caps or a bit of paint or grease or, oh, hell anything. But that's— There was this sound, right before I smelled smoke, a sharp crack."

"Like an explosion?"

"Like—" Hallie couldn't tell if he didn't know how to describe it or he didn't want to. "Like thunder." He paused. "Only more . . . contained. Like if you bottled lightning, pared it down about seventy-five percent, then fired it off in a big arena. Like that would sound."

Hallie didn't know what to say. It couldn't have been Pete—he couldn't have done it in broad daylight, with her father in the equipment shed and the big door open. So, it didn't make any sense, to ask if someone had started it, not even to her.

She asked anyway. "Do you think someone started it?"

He looked at her like she'd lost her mind. "Why would someone set that old shed on fire?"

"I don't know," Hallie said. *To warn me off*, she thought.

The phone rang. Hallie didn't wait for her father to say anything, just got up and answered it.

"Hallie?" It was Pete Bolluyt.

"Shit, Pete. Why are you calling here?"

"I heard about the fire." His voice was soft, like Hallie remembered it from eons ago, before the army and Afghanistan and Dell dying.

"Yeah, we're fine."

"I wanted . . ." Long pause and then, "This isn't how I wanted things, Hallie. I just . . . things get out of hand."

"Really, Pete? Things get out of hand? Is that what happened way back when you put two guys in the hospital, when you robbed a store in California, when your father died? When *Dell* died?"

She could hear him breathing. She knew he was still there.

"Yeah," he finally said. "It really is too late, isn't it?"

"Yes," Hallie said, "it is."

She stared at the phone after Pete had hung up. *What the hell?* But it served to remind her of something she needed to do. She looked through the printed directory, but couldn't find a listing for Vagts. She dialed Lorie's number. No answer. She left a message: "Lorie, I'm looking for Jennie Vagts's phone number. Have you got it? Call me. Or, if you see her, get her to call me. Thanks."

When she walked back into the dining room, her father was nowhere in sight. She looked out the kitchen window. His truck was still there and the lights in the equipment shed were on; an easy man to find if she'd been inclined to find him.

Hallie turned out all the lights in the kitchen except the one over the stove and headed back to the office. Sarah Hale drifted along behind her, though she paused briefly in the dining room to stare at the pictures above the sideboard.

"Yeah," Hallie said, "I don't know what he was staring at either." Every time she thought she had a handle on Boyd, he did or said something that made her think that, no, she really didn't. Not unlike the ghosts, really, because every time she thought she had a handle on them, that some specific action—like Eddie and Dell staring at Dell's coffin—meant something important, there would be something else, something like the way Eddie had stared at Boyd, for instance, that convinced her nothing they did meant anything at all.

Back in the office, Hallie fired up the computer again. Despite everything, she had made some progress today. Now, she had to figure out what it meant.

Sarah Hale disappeared six months ago—which Hallie already knew—maybe up near the Seven Mile, though someone, the newspaper article had said, supposedly saw her later at a mall in Rapid City.

According to news reports, she'd had a fight with her boyfriend and eventually they wrote her disappearance off as suicide, though they'd never recovered a body. The news articles all read pretty much the same: twenty-year-old Sarah Hale, missing since . . . No new information after about two months, though there had been a couple of follow-up articles, one of them the one Hallie'd seen in Dell's office, marking the sixth month since she'd disappeared.

About five links down, Hallie found a website: *The REAL STORY about Sarah Hale*. It turned out to be one big long page of text written in a dark blue font on a lavender background. It appeared to have been written by her sister, Mina Hale, who claimed that she'd been with Sarah.

"I don't remember exactly what happened," Mina wrote fifteen paragraphs in, "but Sarah didn't kill herself."

Yeah, Hallie thought, *that's convincing.*

"We were supposed to meet some people," the sister wrote. "I'm not going to mention names because the police know and they weren't there, but is that what people do who are going to commit suicide? Arrange to meet people for a picnic?"

Who the hell knows? Hallie thought. Though she liked to think she did know, at least in Dell's case, if no one else's. She read on, started skimming when Mina wrote a dozen long paragraphs about Sarah in high school and auditioning for the band.

At the end, there was a question in bold and centered:

What Happened?

"I don't know—okay? Seriously, I don't know. I remember screaming. I remember red and pain and blood and— Someone took her. That's what I'm saying. That's the real story. She was bleeding. I remember that. But I don't think—she wasn't dead."

Below that there was a section called "Notes," which said, "Some of you have written to me and said, 'You're crazy.' And, yeah, I've spent some time in a behavioral unit. But you want to know why? It's because people DON'T BELIeVE ME!!! Everything that's on this page is true. And that's all I have to say about that."

Well, shit.

Hallie stared at the computer. What was she supposed to do now?

She spent a few more minutes trying to track down Mina Hale, but there were at least thirty listings for *Hale* in Rapid City, and none of them were for *Mina* or *M*.

She shut down the computer and sat for several minutes with her head in her hands. She grabbed paper out of the printer and a pen out of the drawer and made a list:

— Dell dead on the Seven Mile
— Sarah Hale dead, disappeared on the Seven Mile—maybe. Probably.
— Ghosts
— Lightning bolts: Dell, Jennie Vagts, Pete Bolluyt, Uku-Weber
— Dell's list: Colorado, Jasper, checking on turbine specs?

She paused, then added:

— Toolshed fire
— Flash of light in the atrium—from blood on the floor?
— Ghosts can't enter building
— Uku-Weber

She underlined the name three times because it was the key, had to be the key; she just didn't know how or why.

She fired up the computer again and did a second search on *Weber,* which found tons of information, Weber being a fairly common name. She searched on *Uku*—music, someone's name, nothing interesting. Nothing useful. She did a second search on *Uku-Weber,* which turned up nothing except the company website, which she'd already seen.

Damnit.

Something had happened at Uku-Weber this morning. She'd seen it, even if no one else had. A bright flash, like lightning without thunder, without sound.

She stood and stretched. It was quiet in the house. All this sitting around was not only getting her nowhere, it was also eating up time. Dell had died a week ago. Hallie would be leaving in three and a half days. She went out to the kitchen, grabbed a jacket and a big flashlight, and was outside and halfway across the yard when she remembered her truck was still in Prairie City at Big Dog's Auto.

Shit.

She changed direction and headed toward the big equipment shed. The night was clear and bright, as if the heavy clouds had scattered with the sun. It was cold, maybe close to freezing. She could smell dirty water and charred wood and the bitter stench of melted plastic, but they were already fading scents, the night breeze light and indirect. The big doors on the shed were open, light pouring out like it was lit up for New Year's. She stood in the open doorway and watched her father, who was bent over the engine of an old Allis tractor from the fifties.

"Hey," she said after a moment when he hadn't noticed her.

He straightened, grabbed an old rag, and wiped his hands. "Yeah?" He stepped down off the short stepladder he'd been standing on.

"I need to go—somewhere," she said, which was both vague and amazingly accurate, all things considered. "Can I borrow your truck?"

He waved a hand in the general direction of the shed door. "Keys are in it," he said. "Gas it up, would you?"

It took her a minute to adjust the seat, which probably hadn't been moved in the ten-year life of the vehicle. There was a thin coat of dust on the dashboard, a coil of rope, a half-full box of finishing nails, and a couple of bright yellow ear tags in the passenger seat. The tags and nails could have gone in the glove compartment, but Hallie knew without looking that the only items in there were the original owner's manual and a pocket-sized spiral notebook with the date and mileage and the amount of gas for each fillup. She turned the key, backed around, and headed down the lane and onto the road.

Everyone talked about Uku-Weber and the future of weather, about weather research and control. Both Lorie and Tel Sigurdson had mentioned a demo site. What had Tel said, that they could bring rain? And that would include lightning, right? Lightning on the floor of the atrium. The sound her father had heard right before the toolshed caught on fire—like the crack of a lightning bolt. Lightning and phenomenal wind turbines. Maybe they had made a breakthrough.

But if they had, it was science. It was getting out ahead, right? What did Dell's death or Sarah Hale's ghost have to do with that? What did blood have to do with any of it? And why, if all that were true, had Dell been checking specs with an independent consultant over in Minnesota?

It took Hallie less than twenty minutes to reach the turn-off for the Bolluyt ranch. The moon wasn't quite full, but the sky was clear and she could see the pale white of the wind turbines as she approached. No fence. No security guard, because who would steal a whole windmill?

She pulled off the road onto the grass and gravel access lane and sat in the truck, studying the site. There was a laminated sign at the edge of the field with a picture of the Uku-Weber building in winter, fall, and summer. In slanted white lettering underneath, it read: *UKU-WEBER WEATHER DEMONSTRATION.*

She got out of the truck, not at all certain what she expected to find. Dell's and Sarah Hale's ghosts drifted along behind her, cold at her back like a sharp breath of winter. The field held maybe three dozen windmills, the breeze turning the blades on several of them lazily, the sound a combination of a creak and a whirr. In the southeast corner was a shed with windows along one side, like the concrete bunker at a missile site. Directly opposite the shed, not quite halfway across the field, was a raised platform, looming black in the night. When she got closer, she could see that it held an apparatus that more or less resembled a cannon. Hallie crossed to it and hopped up onto the platform.

At the rear of the machine, she found a small access panel, padlocked, but the lock was so pathetic, Hallie had it open in less than two minutes. She turned her flashlight on, kept it pointed low, though Pete's ranch house was a half mile away, up a long dirt lane with a creek and a rising swell of open land between. It looked like a typical power panel, though nothing was labeled: a lever on the left, a cramped keyboard, and a small LED display.

She flipped the lever, and the display lit up with a quiet thunk.

She tapped the small keyboard, didn't expect anything to happen, but the panel shifted with each letter, like it wasn't fully seated. She ran her fingers around the edges, found a narrow gap, and pulled. The entire panel came loose in her hands. Underneath, a ribbon wire connected the display to a small twelve-volt battery. No other wires. Nothing to attach the display panel or the keyboard or even the power lever to.

Huh.

She replaced the panel and explored the rest of the machine carefully. On the rear of the machine was the housing for an engine, and there was an actual engine inside, but again, it didn't connect to anything, like it was just there for show. Hallie kicked the housing back into place and stepped back. Dell drifted toward her and stopped. Sarah Hale's ghost pushed at her from behind like the coldest winter breeze. Hallie took three steps forward along the base of the raised platform. Low on the side of the machine, something glinted in the flashlight beam. She angled the beam and bent forward for a closer look. Thinly etched were the symbols she'd seen earlier in the center of the Uku-Weber atrium—a hammer, an ax, and a sword laid one across the other.

Tel said he had seen this machine—this machine right in front of her—pull rain out of the sky. He'd seen it. But this machine did nothing. It was smoke and mirrors. Uku-Weber was smoke and mirrors.

Was that what Dell had known? Was that what got her killed?

She sat in the pickup in the dark for a long time, staring at the windmills and the machine on the platform, all of it looking spectacularly ghostly in the rising moonlight. She felt like she finally knew something.

She wished she understood what it was.

18

When she finally returned to the ranch, all the lights were out except the blue white glow of the big yard light. There was a hint of frost on the air as she crossed the yard. It was completely silent this time of night, the house dark, the only sounds a truck shifting gears on the highway and the wind rising in the east. It was the end of day six, day six of Hallie's ten-day leave. More than half the time gone. And she still didn't have the answers she wanted.

Too restless to sleep, she spent the next several hours in her father's cold office, while Dell and Sarah Hale drifted behind her, looking online for anything on any weather site anywhere in the world that could explain what Uku-Weber was doing. Because there had to be an explanation. No one made rain out of nothing. Or caused a fire that sounded like lightning striking.

She called a guy from her high school graduating class, majoring in meteorology in graduate school at Colorado State, who was incredibly pissy about being woken up at one o' clock in the morning.

"What the hell are you talking about?" he said when he finally understood that this wasn't a crank phone call.

"Lightning," she said. "Could someone control lightning? Could they cause a fire?"

"Lightning can cause fire." Said it slow like he was talking to an idiot. Which maybe he was.

"No, I mean specifically. Cause a specific fire."

"No."

"Advanced research? Like weather control research?"

"Unless it's secret government research I don't know about. And it's not. Then, no. Look," he added, "lightning is an electrical discharge. You need something huge. You'd have to be able to make thunderheads, to control the moisture and the temperature change. You'd have to control everything. No one can do that."

"Okay, thanks."

"Yeah, don't call me again."

She fell asleep at some point, sitting at the desk, and woke, shivering, as night edged into day.

She sucked in a breath and wiped her hand across her face. *Desk, ranch, home.* Because for a moment, she'd thought she was back in Kabul, because she'd been cold there, too.

It had been familiar at first, the cold. She'd grown up with that, with bright clear mornings, cold dry air, sunlight so thin, it didn't seem real. Getting up in the pitch black? Yeah, that had been familiar, too. But the people, the way they looked at her, the constant alien, never-let-your-guard-down, this-is-what-it's-like-in-a-war wore her down, wore them all down.

She jumped up and down a few times, trying to warm up. The only clock in the office had a dead battery or something, because it had read 4:45 since Hallie'd been home. It had to be at least six thirty, though. Her father was probably already sitting down to breakfast. Maybe he wouldn't say anything, wouldn't ask her what she'd been doing sleeping in his office.

Yeah, and maybe pigs would fly today, too.

But her father wasn't at the kitchen table or anywhere else. The only sign he'd been there was a note on the kitchen counter—half a grocery list, actually, and Hallie wasn't sure whether it meant she should go to town for groceries or he had.

She checked for messages on the main phone and the cell phone—nothing. She was about to grab coffee out of the cupboard when she heard a vehicle coming up the drive.

Great.

She tucked in her shirt and scrubbed her fingers through her hair. As she stepped out onto the back porch, the old yellow dog got up from where he was lying by the battered wooden table, wagged his tail slowly at her, then retreated to the tree at the south corner of the yard.

A red older-model Jeep Cherokee pulled into the yard. It had dirt backwards from the front tires in a widening vee, but otherwise it was spotless. The engine died, the door opened, and Boyd stepped out.

"Do you live here now?" she asked.

He wore blue jeans with the hint of a crease down the center, a green plaid cotton shirt ironed with what was by now a familiar knifelike precision. He wore a plain brown leather belt, the same black watch he'd been wearing yesterday, and boots that looked freshly polished except for a scuff mark on the right toe.

"I'm off today," he said. "I thought you might want a ride into Prairie City." He stuck his right hand halfway into the pocket of his jeans, hunched his shoulder slightly forward, and suddenly he looked like every good-looking farm boy Hallie had ever known—fit, but lean, half-grown, and too pretty for the flat, harsh prairie.

"Shit," she said. "I never called Tom back, not with—" She waved a hand. "—all that yesterday."

Boyd shrugged. "Come on," he said. "I'll buy you breakfast." He seemed an odd combination of more relaxed out of uniform and desperate in some deeply hidden way, visible only in how he looked at her and the way a single muscle twitched along his jawline.

"Shit," she repeated. "Come on in the house a minute."

He followed her as she went up the back steps. "You know it's, like, six thirty in the morning?" she said.

"Seven." He held the screen door open as he walked in behind her. "Saw your father over to Sally Jean's when I stopped in for a paper."

"In West PC?" Hallie pulled the tail of her shirt out of her jeans and started unbuttoning it. "I didn't even know that place was still open."

"He's worried about you," Boyd said.

Hallie stopped with her shirt half-unbuttoned, the ivory of her long undershirt showing at the chest and cuffs. "He told you that? Why?" *Why is he worried? And why would he tell you?*

Boyd twisted the watch on his wrist. He looked out the kitchen window, as if he expected something out there to save him from this conversation. "Because he cares about you?" he said.

Hallie rolled her eyes. "Yeah, I bet that's it. I bet he tells random people he's 'worried' about me because he thinks somehow it'll get back to me, and then suddenly life will be gumdrops and fairy tales."

His lip quirked. "Gumdrops and fairy tales?"

"Whatever."

She left him in the kitchen, didn't even offer him coffee, which would have been the nice, polite country thing to do. But she didn't feel polite. Could just imagine Boyd and her father having *poor Hallie, what should we do with her?* conversations. And she didn't need it. Didn't need them. That was what she told herself as she stripped off her clothes and stepped into the shower. Water pounded her head and shoulders and eased her tension.

Fire hot burn me burn me don't kill me Jesus. A thin whisper, like the sound of a blade on stone.

Shit.

Hallie grabbed the shower curtain and pulled so hard, she yanked it loose from two of its rings.

What was that?

But she knew what it was—the same images, the same words she'd seen in her dreams, seen once before, when Dell's ghost had drifted through her. Fire, screaming, sunlight and moonlight. A single image lingered—Dell laughing with a bonfire behind her.

The water had turned cold, and Hallie realized that she was shivering. Again. She stepped out of the shower. The lingering wisps of a ghost drifted out the closed bathroom door. Hallie reached out and almost touched it before it disappeared completely, but drew back her hand, because she didn't want to see that again, couldn't get it out of her mind anyway—pain and fire. She dried herself off and went back to the bedroom, pulling random clothes from the closet.

Those images . . . they weren't just images; they were fear and panic and stop ohmygod stop, as if she were inside someone's head, as if they were the last memories of a beating heart.

And then, there was Boyd.

She should have told him to leave, should have told him she'd get her own damned truck and her own damned breakfast.

But he was so . . . earnest. And, in some way, both out of his depth and not. As if he knew what was coming, was braced for it, wasn't sure he could handle it, but wasn't going to run, all the same.

When she walked downstairs, Boyd was leaning on the sideboard, looking at the Major Felten poster, which—all right—big cats were an odd choice for dining room artwork, but they'd always been there.

"Hey," she said.

He didn't smile, but something relaxed around his eyes, as if he liked seeing her. Which shouldn't have made her feel anything, shouldn't have made her feel warmer inside. But it did.

Damn him.

They didn't talk on the drive into town. Hallie felt the occasional chill across the back of her neck, though she hadn't seen Dell or Sarah Hale since they'd left the house. She welcomed them, though, welcomed their icy-dry coldness. Because she finally understood, though she ought to have known when Eddie left, that they were there—had to be there—to tell her something. And she wanted it to be important, what they were telling her, wanted it to be a weapon or an answer. She didn't have any reason to believe they were or could be a weapon, but she wanted it so badly, it felt like an ache across her breastbone. If the ghosts could just mean something, if there were a reason they were here, a reason she could see them—she could live with that.

She could.

Boyd took her straight in to Big Dog's. Her truck was out front, all washed and shiny. Tom, the station owner, came out the open bay door, wiping his hands on a greasy rag as Hallie stepped out of Boyd's Jeep.

"There wasn't anything wrong with it," he said.

"Except it wouldn't start," Hallie said.

Tom shook his head. "Started right up. Engine turned over just as pretty as you please. Coupla wires looked like they'd gotten a little hot and maybe that was it, maybe they shorted temporarily." He shrugged, his big shoulders sliding easy under his loose gray T-shirt. "Come on in." He waved his hand with the rag in it, and Hallie followed him into his cramped and tiny office. On the cluttered wall was every Valvoline Oil calendar since 1973. The invoice was already half filled out with Hallie's name and the license plate of the truck. He jotted down the charges, added the tax in his head, tore the finished copy off, and handed it to her.

"Ten dollars?" Hallie looked at him. "Jesus, Tom, how do you stay in business?"

"Ah, we didn't even have to tow it," Tom said. "Drove over here, tested a few things, and had Jake wash it. Didn't take but fifteen minutes. Besides—" His gaze flickered over to the 1990 calendar. "—you've been . . . over there." He cleared his throat. "Maybe it's different for you gals—people keep telling me it is—but I can't see why it would be. And I've been there." He shrugged again.

Hallie didn't know what to say, wasn't sure she ever would. "Thanks," she finally said. "I mean—well, thanks."

She'd turned to leave, when he said, "Hey, you going out with—" He gestured toward the flyspecked front window. "That deputy kid. You dating him or something?"

Hallie frowned. "Why?"

"Heard things."

"Things?" she asked. "I'm not dating him," she added.

"Oh, not bad things," Tom said. "Just . . . you know he's from Iowa, right?"

Hallie laughed.

"Yeah, but why is he here?" Tom asked, his voice pitched low, as if to suggest that the mere fact of Iowa was reason enough for suspicion.

"Because he wanted to leave home? Strike out on his own? Make a difference? Because the job was here?"

"Hey, I'm just saying," Tom said.

"Yeah," Hallie said. "I know. Thanks for taking care of my truck."

19

Boyd was talking to one of the mechanics when Hallie came back outside. The mechanic was a tall, skeletally thin man with shoulder-length hair, scraggly at the ends. He looked familiar to Hallie, but she didn't know or couldn't remember who he was. Boyd and the mechanic stood in a narrow slice of shade cast by the propane storage, and Hallie could see a ghost—turned away from her so that she couldn't see its face—hovering at the mechanic's elbow. As Hallie watched, the ghost stretched a finger out and touched the man's arm just below his rolled-up sleeve. The mechanic shrugged, like flicking off a fly. It was the first time Hallie had seen anyone but herself respond to a ghost. She approached, intrigued.

"Hey." The mechanic greeted her, two fingers tapping his temple, like a half-assed salute. That gesture was familiar, too, a reminder of rodeos or cattle auctions or some completely different context from grease and cars and gasoline. The ghost drifted between them, its face still turned away.

"Never expected to see you again, Hallie Michaels," the mechanic said. "Sorry it had to be under the present circumstances."

Good Lord, his voice—baritone deep, had been since eighth grade, she remembered. He'd been big in high school, though—tall,

157

like he still was, but broad shoulders, barrel chest, star halfback on the football team, three years ahead of her. "Jake Javinovich." She shoved her hands deep into the front pockets of her jeans. "Never expected to see you here," she said. She'd expected him to—well, she didn't know—to be a graduate of South Dakota State, to be selling cars or insurance or shares in a gold mine in Rapid City or Omaha. She expected him to want big things and settle for small ones, all the time telling himself that what he had was what *big* was all about.

Jake shrugged. "Yeah. S'a good place here. I always liked cars, you know." He tilted his head. "I was sorry to hear about the fire. On top of . . . well, everything," he said. "You and your dad, though, you're okay, right?"

"Yeah," Hallie said. "It's all fine."

Jake nodded. "There were a bunch of fires like that, oh . . . six, eight months ago. Toby vanDerWal's garage over in Thorsen, that church just north of Old Prairie City, and that old school out past the Seven Mile." He nodded at Boyd. "You remember," he said. "They thought those kids from Box Elder were out here setting things on fire for fun. But they never did prove anything."

"Huh," Hallie said. She looked at Boyd, who seemed intensely interested in the toe of his left boot. "Isn't that interesting?"

"Jake, look," Boyd said. "If you see that truck again, let me know." He said it in the way people said things if they thought the other person had gone on long enough. He said it like saying, *Someone's at the door,* or *My other phone is ringing,* or *My god, look at the time.*

Hallie scowled at him.

"You ready?" he asked. "We should— It's past eight."

Like we have somewhere to be, Hallie thought. Which they didn't, and it was a problem, because it was already day seven. And she still didn't know anything—what had happened to Dell or why. But she could come back and talk to Jake later, without the Boy Deputy around, because maybe she had only a couple of days left, but she was still going to figure this out.

"Yeah," she said to Boyd. "Okay. Where are we going? Should I take my truck or leave it?"

Boyd said. "Garrity? To the Blue Bird. That all right with you?"

"You coming back this way after?" she asked. He nodded. "Then I'll leave it." To Jake, she said, "All right if I leave the truck here another hour or so?"

"Yeah," he said, already sticking his head back underneath the hood of the car he'd been working on. "No problem."

Five minutes later, they were back on the road. Boyd looked straight down the highway as he said, "You don't need to worry about the fire. I'm taking care of it."

Hallie stared at him. "You're taking care of it? What the hell does that mean?"

Boyd rubbed a hand along his chin. "What I'm saying"—he spoke carefully, as if each word had been specially selected—"is that I'm a sworn officer of the law and—"

"My god," Hallie interrupted him. "Are you telling me to be a good little girl? Because *that's* going to work. And, buddy, if you think this is just about fires—"

"How hungry are you?" Boyd interrupted her.

Hallie blinked. "What?"

"Because I am. I'm really hungry. Haven't eaten since noon yesterday. So"—he lifted his hand off the wheel for a second—"if we could hold this conversation until after breakfast—?"

"I didn't actually start this conversation," Hallie pointed out, though she'd been thinking of talking to him about the demo plot and what she'd seen out there. Now? Maybe she'd just figure it out on her own.

Boyd slowed for his turn. He was taking the short route around West Prairie City—two gravel roads and a stretch of hardtop to get to the little hamlet of Garrity and the Blue Bird diner—Best Scrambled Eggs from Here to Montana.

"When we do have this conversation, are you actually going to tell me what you know?" Hallie asked after a moment.

"I'll tell you what I can," Boyd said. He turned left. Dell was in the car, right between Hallie and Boyd. Warmth leached from Hallie's arm and chest. She was wondering how weird it would be to ask Boyd to turn on the heat, when Dell and Sarah Hale and maybe another ghost, she couldn't tell, rushed her, like frightened birds. Like back in the field near Jasper, like they were screaming except with no sound, a flurry of arms and cold and so close and—

Red pain fire fear

Images assaulted her, battering her, like a winter storm against the side of an old barn.

Red red fire black stars Icanseethestars so bright painpain don't hit me please please why

Hallie jammed the heel of her palm against the ridge of her nose as if that would stop the pain. She didn't realize Boyd had stopped the Jeep until she felt the door next to her open. He grabbed her by the elbow and the shoulder.

"Hey. Hey, it's okay. Just . . . hold still. Okay?" There was an edge to his voice—panic reined in tight. Or controlled nerves. She couldn't tell. She was busy breathing.

"Shit." After a long minute, she straightened and shoved Boyd back with a sweep of her hand. She stepped out of the Jeep. Either the ghosts were getting better at communicating or she was getting better at understanding, but she knew what they were telling her now, and she knew what they'd been telling her out where Dell had died.

"Okay," she said.

"Are you—?" Boyd began.

"Do you have a shovel?" Hallie interrupted him because if he asked her if she was okay one more time? She would punch him. Since he was driving, they were in the middle of nowhere, and he was a deputy sheriff, hitting him seemed like a bad idea all around.

"What?"

"A shovel. In your car. Do you have one?"

"I have a spade." He opened the back door of the Cherokee. Hallie heard the sharp ripping sound of Velcro being unfastened. He reappeared with a long-handled, flat-bladed steel garden spade. It was clean, the dark blade winking in the morning sunlight.

Hallie looked at it. "That's a shovel."

"It's a spade."

"Whatever." She reached for it.

He pulled back. "You're not going to hit me with it, are you?"

"Not yet."

He grimaced—or it might have been a half-hearted attempt at a smile. Hallie took a quick step forward, grabbed the shovel, and started across the prairie toward a narrow grove of cottonwood trees down by a dried-up creek.

Boyd watched her, but didn't move to follow right away, and for a moment, she thought he might leave her there. She had both thoughts at the same time—*good* and *don't go*. She shifted the shovel to her left hand; the fingers on her right ached with cold. The new ghost—was it the one she'd seen back at Big Dog's, she couldn't tell—was beside her, going to be here until this was over, Hallie bet.

An old Buick and a dusty Suburban went by up on the road, each of them slowing briefly, then accelerating past Boyd's Jeep Cherokee.

Hallie shoved sideways through a thick cluster of faded wildflowers and a short-thorned bramble. A dozen yards to her left was a mound clustered over with drying grass—an old barn maybe, or a grain bin.

Boyd caught up to her. "What are you doing?" he asked.

Hallie didn't answer. She couldn't stop and talk about this. She didn't want to think about it, didn't want to think about the dark, red-tinged images the ghost had shown her. It wouldn't change anything. If she stopped and talked to him, there would still be ghosts.

She found what she was looking for easily enough—for one thing, the ghost was floating over it, bouncing like she was excited, like she remembered being human. The spot, though, looked pretty much like everyplace else, shorter grass than the big expanse they'd just crossed, evidence of deer and rabbits coming down at night to drink from the creek and bed among the trees.

"Hallie—?" Boyd said, half a question and half something else.

Hallie leaned on the shovel. "What do you know about those fires?" she asked, because if she was going to show him this, was going to be in the middle of *How could you know that?* and *What the hell?* then she wanted some of his cards on the table, too.

"We came out here to talk about fires?" He tried to look confused or . . . he *was* confused, but that wasn't all. He knew something, she could see it clearly by the look in his eyes, something he didn't want her to know.

"You son of a bitch," she said.

There was a snap in the way his gaze turned to hers, as if he'd been a thousand miles away. "What?"

"Dell's death *wasn't* an accident, was it?" And she could see immediately in the way his eyes looked down and away, that she'd guessed right. "You knew and you didn't tell me? You *couldn't say?*"

"I'm a county sheriff's deputy," Boyd finally said, his voice quiet, not as if he was trying to calm her down, more like he was trying to be serious enough, grave enough for the situation at hand—whatever the situation was. "It's my job."

He had one hand in the pocket of his jeans and his shoulder hunched forward, and he looked so . . . young, that it made Hallie blink. She let out her breath, like a sigh. "Look," she said, "just tell me what you know. Tell me why you know it wasn't an accident. Tell me about the fires. About the fire at the ranch— Tell me—" Because she wasn't quite ready herself to tell him about Uku-Weber or the demo plot and what she'd found there. "Jesus Christ, Boyd!"

He didn't speak right away, and she was beginning to recognize that it wasn't because he was the strong, silent type but because he was thinking furiously, trying to figure out what he was going to say. "Look, I've read the police reports on Dell's death and on—" He hesitated. "—a couple of disappearances."

"Shit," Hallie said.

"And the fires. There's . . . Some of it doesn't make sense, okay?" He pulled his hand out of his pocket, took a couple of steps away from her, then turned back, hand in his pocket again. He rubbed his other hand across the back of his neck. "I can tell you what I know," he said. "But—"

"But?" Hallie said. "Oh, no, there's no *but*. You don't set conditions."

"But," he continued, like she hadn't spoken, "I want to know what we're doing here. What's that spade—shovel—for?"

Hallie chewed on her top lip. "Shit," she finally said. "I'll do better than that. I'll show you."

20

She'd expected resistance. But he just shoved both hands deep into the pockets of his jeans, leaned against one of the cotton-wood trees, and frowned, a deep intense frown, like he wished she'd stop, like he anticipated trouble like you wouldn't believe. But he didn't stop her. Didn't offer to help either. And that was fine by Hallie.

On the highest branch of the leafless cottonwood sat a red-tailed hawk, its head jutted forward. Looking for prey, Hallie figured, but it looked remarkably like Boyd—same posture, same stiff motionless watching. She almost pointed it out to him, but decided it wasn't the time.

It took an hour of steady digging before her shovel struck something solid, something that might have been a rock, but wasn't. Hallie dropped the shovel and started brushing away dirt with her hands, surprised that they were shaking. She'd known what was here before she started. She brushed more dirt away, and there it was: the curve of a skull, nearly as brown as the dirt.

"Hell."

It was so long since Boyd had spoken that his voice, uttering that single word, actually set Hallie back on her haunches. She slid her right foot forward to regain her balance. When she looked up, he was gone, striding across the field, not hurrying, but purposeful.

She thought he was leaving only for a second or so before she realized he was calling it in.

"So, one more time, you knew about this because—?"

Three hours later, and Deputy Teedt had asked her that question at least six times. "What did Boyd say?" she asked him.

"Deputy Davies," he said quellingly, "said that you tripped over it."

"Well?" she said.

Probably if he hadn't been wearing his uniform, Teedt would have rolled his eyes. He'd been a friend of her father's until the whole courthouse window incident. For some reason, he'd decided to pick sides—the law or the Michaelses'—and he hadn't come down on the Michaelses' side. "Okay," he finally said. "But don't let me find out—"

"Who is it?" she asked. "How did they die? When?"

Teedt held up his hands. "Whoa, whoa, whoa." And she could hear the *little lady* in his voice, even though he didn't actually say the words. She wished Boyd were here, then thought—wait a minute, she didn't need him. She didn't. "This is police business now," Teedt said. "You don't need to worry about it."

Hallie pinched the bridge of her nose, mostly to keep herself from punching him. "I am worried about it," she said. "I'm worried you're going to—"

"Are we done?"

Hallie wanted to hate Boyd for that way he had of coming up behind her, of talking quietly, of interrupting fights. But she didn't. It bothered her—kind of a lot, actually—but she didn't hate him.

Teedt sucked air through his teeth. "Yeah," he said, drawing the word out. "Ole's going to want to talk to you, though."

"I'm in tomorrow," Boyd said, like it was nothing, finding bodies in the middle of nowhere. To Hallie, he said, "I'll drive you home."

"Back to my truck."

"Back to your truck," he agreed.

Three people stopped them on the way back to Boyd's Jeep. The first, Dr. Ludoc, general practitioner and county coroner, thumping slowly across the field in his old gray Toyota, stopped and asked Boyd what to expect. When he heard it was an old body, mostly bones, he drove on, muttering about dumb-ass deputies who didn't know better than to call him out for something he didn't know anything about and couldn't help with.

The second was Sally Mazzolo, a deputy older than Boyd but newer to the job, who'd been left to direct traffic and was annoyed because there was no traffic and no one had yet come back to relieve her. "They promised I could see this. How am I going to learn? I swear I'm applying to Rapid City tomorrow. First thing, I mean it—"

The last one was some guy from the weekly paper whom Hallie didn't recognize. "Big? Is it big?" he asked Boyd. "I heard a body. I heard—" But Boyd just walked right by him without saying a word and opened the door to the Jeep.

Hallie got back in on the passenger side, fastened her seat belt, and sat there, silent as Boyd turned around and headed back toward Prairie City. She'd been trying to figure out for the last three hours how she was going to tell Boyd about the other body, back where Dell had died. Because she was really very sure there was another body there. Not 100 percent—she'd have to go there, dig it up before she knew for sure. But close enough. She'd considered not telling him—because what did she really know about him—thought about making an anonymous call. But what call was ever really anonymous around here?

"I know where there's another body," she said.

Okay, she'd actually meant to build up to it, ask him what he knew about the toolshed fire, about Dell's death, about the Uku-Weber demo site, get him to talk first.

Huh.

Boyd pulled off the highway abruptly, into a turnout for rig pick-ups. He stopped the Jeep and shifted in his seat so he could look straight at her. He looked . . . scared, which surprised her.

"What?" he said. He didn't sound scared, though. He sounded pissed off and tired, and just like that, she was pissed off, too, because it wasn't her fault she saw ghosts. She sure as shit hadn't asked for this.

"I thought it was pretty clear," she said, biting the words off short. "I know where there's another body."

He stared at her and she couldn't read him. At all. It felt close and hot in the pickup. Too close. Hallie shoved the door open and got out.

Boyd was right there when she got to the front of the vehicle. "You can't—," he started, then shifted gears. "What do you mean, you know where there's another body? What does that mean?" Like he was desperate for her to tell him it had been a guess, that she didn't know anything more than anyone else. That she was just that lucky, and today it had been dead bodies.

But they both knew that wasn't the case.

"I don't—"

He cut her off. "Where?"

She looked at him for a long minute before she answered. She wanted him to know that she was choosing to answer him, not caving to a demand. "Out where Dell died. I can't tell you exactly where. I'd have to show you."

His jaw was clenched so tight, she was surprised she couldn't hear his teeth grinding. She was tired, too, and hungry, and what the hell was his problem, anyway?

They got back in the car, and Boyd pulled onto the road, turning back the way they'd come, then taking the next hard surface road north.

"So, what? Do you think I killed them?" Hallie finally said.

Boyd started, visibly, slowed the Jeep a fraction, and made an effort to ease the grip of his white-knuckled hands on the wheel. He took a breath. "No," he said.

Hallie waited for him to say more, but he didn't. "Do you want to know how I know?" she asked.

"No."

Just that.

No.

You son of a bitch, she thought. Because she'd been going to tell him. She'd been going to tell him about ghosts, about what the ghosts were telling her, about Uku-Weber, about what she'd found out at Bolluyt's—all of it.

Instead, she studied him as they hurtled down the road back toward Jasper and scarred Ponderosa pines. There was a reason he was acting like this, like he wanted her as far away from him as possible. And if there was a reason—

"What is your problem?" she asked him.

"What?" He didn't look at her.

"Maybe it's because you haven't had anything to eat all day," she said. "Maybe you've got a headache. Or your stomach hurts. Because you're not a woman, so you can't be—"

"I don't have a problem," he said.

"Oh, yeah, you do," Hallie told him. "Though I understand that part of the problem is that you don't want to tell me what the problem is."

He looked at her then, as he turned onto the Seven Mile Creek

Road. She could have sworn he almost smiled. Then it was gone, like a cloud passed over the sun.

He didn't speak again as he drove down the old dirt road and parked just about exactly where he parked the last time they'd been here.

As soon as Hallie got out of the car, the ghosts were with her— Dell and Sarah Hale, the unidentified one from the first body, and a new one.

Which she'd been expecting, but still . . . shit. This one looked familiar, too. She hoped to hell they weren't people she'd known at one time. Though the odds were, they would be.

It was one o'clock in the afternoon, and the day was overcast and gloomy. There was a breeze, alternately winter-sharp and rain-heavy, out of the west. In the field in front of her, the hip-high grass had been flattened to knee height by the heavy rains on Sunday. Hallie could see a bundle of barbed wire just off the lane she hadn't noticed the last time she was there. She had no way, with the sun hidden by low clouds, to spot the glint of metal that had attracted her attention before. She figured it didn't matter: the ghosts would show her the way.

And they did.

She was braced for it this time, but it still hurt when they rushed at her, batting their insubstantial hands at her.

See me see me pain blood fear why me whywhywhywhywhy
Shit.

She came back to herself to find Boyd holding her up, her right hand gripping his shirt like an anchor. The feel of his shirt in her hand was soft and cool. For a brief moment, she wanted to bury herself in it, wanted to grab him and hold him, wanted to fuck him in the back of his Jeep right here, right now. Not because she wanted him—god knew, she didn't *want* him, she didn't want anyone—but she wanted to need something, to get something she needed, to feel something that wasn't dying or dead or in pain. He was warm, too, always so warm, like an antidote to ghosts. She let go the handful of shirt she'd grabbed, then paused to smooth the crease her fist had made, realized she was doing it, and stopped.

She pushed him away.

"She's down here," she said, and led him down near the creek by another cottonwood tree, which seemed like it ought to be significant, though she really didn't care. The police would start to say *serial killer*, would say, *Look, he buries them by old creeks underneath cottonwood trees*. Profile that. Because Hallie knew that wasn't the important thing, though she wasn't yet completely certain what the important thing was.

She stopped and marked the spot with her boot. "Right here," she said.

Boyd looked at the ground.

"C'mon," he finally said, "I'll take you back to town."

He started across the field, but stopped about twenty yards in when he realized she wasn't following him.

"Seriously," she said, "what's your problem?"

"I don't want you involved in this," he said.

"Oh, I'm involved," she said, joining him in the field because she wasn't going to yell across twenty yards of prairie. "I'm already pretty damned involved."

"This is now an official investigation, and I can't have you interfering," he said stiffly.

He was lying. Not about it being an official investigation, which it almost certainly was or would be, but about why he wanted her out of it.

The ghost she was pretty sure was the one whose burial site she'd just identified, had been pushing at her elbow as they walked, leaning in when Hallie went straight and relenting when she veered to her right—lean, right, straight, right—directing her. Her boot chinked softly against something in the grass, and she bent down and picked it up, looking at it quick before she slid it into her pocket and pretended she was adjusting her bootlace.

Not metal. Glass. A watch crystal, maybe?

She stood. "The thing is," she said conversationally as she started across the field with him, "I'm not actually in Afghanistan now. I don't take orders from you."

Silence. Hallie could hear the wind rise, could almost hear the ghosts themselves as they floated behind her.

"I know," he finally said, his voice so brittle, she was surprised the words didn't shatter on the ground.

21

She and Boyd drove back to Prairie City in almost complete silence. He dropped her at Big Dog's to pick up her truck and went on to the sheriff's office to get people and equipment before heading back out to Seven Mile Creek Road. What he was going to say about the body, about how he knew where it was, Hallie had no idea.

He looked at her when they stopped, tilted his head as if he was going to say something, but didn't. Just said, "Take care," in a voice so low, she almost didn't hear it.

"Yeah," Hallie said under her breath. Just, "Yeah."

After Boyd drove away, she went looking for Jake Javinovich, but he was gone over to Templeton for parts.

She climbed into her pickup and sat there for a few minutes, studying the piece of glass she'd found in the field earlier.

It was smooth, machined. And it was definitely a watch crystal—or, that's what it looked like to Hallie, at least. It wasn't round but actually hexagonal, not exactly diamond-shaped but with that feel. And it felt old, too, heavy, well-made glass. There was something familiar about it, as if Hallie had seen a watch with just that shape glass, though she supposed there were lots of them out there.

There were three ghosts in the car with her now—Dell, Sarah

172

Hale, and the one from back at the Seven Mile. She still looked familiar to Hallie—shoulder-length hair, a dress with some sort of small print, a narrow belt and low-heeled shoes, dangly earrings and a silver bracelet cuff. Wherever Hallie had seen her before, she'd been laughing. She remembered straight white teeth and laugh lines at her eyes. But she wasn't laughing now.

Hallie shivered, started the truck, and cranked up the heat. She drove west through the middle of Prairie City. It was quiet even for early afternoon, which was usually quiet, though there were cars outside all three bars and the hardware store. Hallie wasn't much for sitting in bars in the daytime, but right now she wished she were doing exactly that, sitting in a booth with her back against the wall. People coming up to her and talking while she drank beer and smiled at them, while she had no cares in the world.

She drove straight to Uku-Weber and parked in the middle of the parking lot. There were only about a dozen other cars in the lot. Hallie, whose experience of the world was mostly ranches, small-town business, and the army, had no idea if this was normal or not. She stared at the building for a long minute. Because this was it, whatever was going on, whatever—whoever—had killed Dell and Sarah Hale and Mystery Ghosts Numbers Three and Four had something to do with lightning bolts, with fake weather machines, with Pete and Martin and Uku-Weber.

She made a quick phone call, then rummaged in the glove box for a pocketknife. She shoved it in her pocket as she got out of the truck. She stood there for a minute, looking at the parking lot and the building and the wide open prairie behind it; then she took the prybar from the back of the pickup truck and walked up the front walk, past the steel and stone fountain where she'd first seen Sarah Hale's ghost, and between the four main pillars.

She thought about following the sidewalk around the side of the building, looking for a side entrance, a way to enter the building quietly. But she'd end up in the atrium anyway, so if she was going in, she might as well go in through the front.

She felt the ghosts—Dell and Sarah and the Seven Mile Ghost—drop away behind her, felt the gritty blast of air as she entered the building—ghost-proofing, she thought, because what else would it be? But why?

As she entered, she shoved the prybar up under her arm and dug the pocketknife out of her pocket.

"Can I help you?" the receptionist called across the open space.

Hallie shook her head. "Nope," she said. "This'll just take a minute." She made a quick slice across her left index finger, waited a moment for the several drops of blood to gather, then let it drip onto the floor.

"Excuse me," the receptionist said. "I don't think—"

The blood hit the floor. There was a brief . . . *something,* like ozone in the air right before a lightning strike, then a brilliant flash as every line in the room—lightning bolt on the floor, symbols on the window strips—lit up like fire.

"You need to leave," the receptionist said.

"Yeah," Hallie said, because she had what she'd come for. "Thanks."

Pete Bolluyt was waiting for her in the parking lot. "Get lost, did you?" he asked.

"Nope." Hallie kept walking.

"This is private property," he said.

"Yeah," she agreed. "It is. I was looking for Martin. Is he around?" She tilted her head and studied him. He looked angry, tight like an overwound steel spring. The fingers on his right hand twitched against his belt buckle.

Pete squinted, like it pained him to even look at her. A drop of rain hit Hallie square on her forehead, followed by a windblown flurry of drops. The sky above them was still clear.

"You need to mind your own goddamned business," Pete said. He stepped toward her. Hallie raised the prybar.

She smiled, though it wasn't funny and she didn't feel like laughing. When she spoke it was slow and deliberate, each word like a punch. "What happened to Dell?"

Pete's right hand clenched into a fist. "You're a fool," he said. His expression was flat—blank—like he wasn't going to hear it, like nothing involving Dell had ever touched him or ever would. Hallie's heart thumped sharply in her chest because this? This was what dangerous looked like.

There was a deep rumble, like thunder, and another burst of rain swept across the parking lot on the wind. She could hear the low sound of a siren, but the way sound carried on the plains, it could be coming from clear back in Prairie City. She took a sharp breath. No going back now. "Maybe I am a fool, Pete. But I've been having a real interesting day," she said. "You want to know what I found?"

Pete cocked his head to the side and said, "Oh, hell, Hallie—I don't care." Which wasn't the reaction she'd expected. She gripped the prybar tighter and backed up two steps. If she had to, she could run, was pretty sure she was faster than he was, could outdistance him on the open prairie, but she didn't want to, had never liked running.

Pete advanced, a grin on his face now, as if he'd been waiting a long time for this. Hallie didn't wait—waiting got you killed—she swung the prybar and hit him hard in the ribs.

An *oof,* a low curse. He stumbled backwards, but recovered quicker than Hallie'd expected. "Little bitch," he muttered.

She thought he'd come after her right then and braced herself for it, but he stopped, straightened, one hand across his abdomen. He shook his head and grinned, like a wolf or something infinitely creepier. "That was kind of a cheap shot," he said slyly. He licked his lips. "Good thing I'm such a bastard, I guess, isn't it?"

Hallie heard the ratchet of a shotgun slide and turned her head to see the man who'd been with Pete at the Bobtail, the one who'd sliced her with his knife, gliding out of the shadows at the side of the building.

Goddamnit.

"You going to shoot me, Pete?" she said. Bitter and angry because there was nothing she could do about it. She'd left herself open.

"Sooner or later, sweetheart," he said. "Sooner or later." He let that hang there for a minute. Hallie didn't look at the other man or his shotgun, kept her eyes focused on Pete, assumed Pete had chosen him for his competence with a shotgun, and she wouldn't do it, wouldn't give him the satisfaction of looking.

Pete cocked his head to the right. The rain was steady now, and both of them were pretty well soaked. The clouds were still scattered and broken; Hallie could see the sun, but she was wet all the same.

"I'm going to stop this, Pete," Hallie said, not bragging, because she wasn't in the position to do that, but because it needed to be said, needed to be laid out plain. Because she *was* going to stop it. Even if she still had to figure out how.

"Not today," Pete said. And without another word, he punched her in the jaw, smooth and quick, like a striking snake. Hallie was as ready for it as she could be, but still, it snapped her head back and bounced the back of her skull painfully off the truck fender. Knocked her to the ground, too, though she didn't realize it for a stark half second.

She was trying to scramble to her feet when Pete grabbed her hard by the elbow and hauled her up. "Martin wants to talk to you," he said.

The sirens, which had been steady background while they were talking, were suddenly loud, were right *there*. Two sheriff's cars pulled fast into the parking lot and stopped, headlights shining on Pete and Hallie.

"Not today, Pete," Hallie said.

The guy with the shotgun had disappeared into the prairie grass when the cars arrived, so it was just her and Pete, looking like quarreling lovers. Pete tried to tell them that Hallie'd been trespassing, but Ole, the sheriff, was disgusted with the both of them.

"I do not need this kind of shit from you," Ole told her when it was just Hallie and him in the little conference room off his office. "Stumbling over bodies? Getting in fights with Pete Bolluyt? Of all people. I always thought you had more sense than your daddy. But maybe I was wrong."

Hallie didn't say anything, figured talking would prolong things, and she was tired and wet and cold. She'd wanted Martin to show his hand, and he had. Unfortunately, she still wasn't sure what that hand was. There was the blood, the lines on the floor and walls at Uku-Weber. But what did it all mean?

She wanted someone to talk to—wanted Boyd to talk to—so badly, it hurt. But that wasn't happening. He made that pretty plain when he'd brought her back to her truck. And she sure wasn't going to beg for it. So, she shoved the thought aside because it wasn't helping.

Ole stopped talking and looked at her. She was trying not to shiver, trying not to look as wet and cold as she felt. Apparently she hadn't been all that successful.

"Oh, get the hell out of here," Ole said.

"Aren't there—I don't know—charges?"

"No, there aren't goddamned charges! But if you're not out of my sight in the next five minutes, there sure as hell will be. If I have to make up a law to charge you with."

It wasn't until Hallie was outside that she remembered that her pickup truck was still sitting in the Uku-Weber parking lot.

Shit.

In the end she called Brett, who was in her car, driving back from Rapid City. She came, though it took her forty-five minutes to get there.

"Why are you all wet? Why is your truck in the Uku-Weber parking lot? And why are you at the sheriff's office?"

"It rained. Because. And I got in a fight."

Brett looked sideways at her. "Well, that last is obvious," Brett said. Hallie figured there was probably a pretty good bruise from where Pete had hit her. It felt like it, anyway. "Do you want to tell me what's going on?"

"Yes."

Silence.

"Now?"

Brett pulled into the long drive to Uku-Weber. Hallie rubbed her temple because she had a headache the size of Texas. "I don't . . . know enough yet," she finally said. "I want it to make sense."

"Don't—," Brett started, stopped, then started again. "It's not your fault Dell died," she said.

Hallie'd been about to say something else, and her teeth clacked together when she closed her mouth. "I know," she finally said.

Brett stopped in front of Hallie's pickup. She turned to look at her, throwing her arm across the back of the seat. "No," she said. "You don't. You don't know. You think you have to do these things yourself. You think you're the only one who can or will or who has to, I guess. But you don't, Hallie. People would help you if you let them."

"Okay," Hallie said, opening the car door. She leaned back in. "Glad to see that psychology degree's doing you so much good."

"Fuck you," Brett said, though there was no heat in it.

"Yeah," Hallie said. "Okay."

22

The sun was shining again, but it had turned cold, little patches of ice along the road as Hallie headed back to the ranch to change her clothes. At least four people were dead—Dell, Sarah Hale, presumably dead six months ago, and the two bodies they'd found today—neither of them Sarah Hale's because, well, because there were two more ghosts turned up where she'd found their bodies.

What the hell?

How had no one noticed?

She stopped the truck, just pulled over to the side of the road because she had to think this out.

She was shivering, but she got out of the truck anyway, stood, and looked at the ghosts, all of them present: Dell, Sarah Hale, and—crap, the other two looked so familiar to her. They were all of a type—except Dell—straight hair and dark, though varied in length, long legged and athletic looking. Dell's tangled mass of hair, the sharpness of her features, her scrappy boots, seemed to set her away from them. And she seemed older than the others, though how could Hallie really tell? Each of them too insubstantial to judge.

But they looked so familiar. And yet . . . not. She'd seen them, or thought she had, somewhere. Damn.

And what about Jennie Vagts? She had the same lightning bolt mark that Dell had had. Had these other women been marked, too? Was Jennie next?

She realized Lorie had never called her back.

She could hear the sound of a car several miles away as she climbed back into the cab and fumbled along the seat until she found Dell's cell phone. She punched in Lorie's number and got voice mail. She left another message: "Lorie, call me. It's important."

She checked her messages. There were three.

The first message was from Boyd. Hallie debated listening to it. "I need to talk to you," it said. "Meet me at Cleary's. Around six. I should be finished with everything by then."

The second message was from Boyd, too. "Please?"

And the third. "I'm sorry about earlier. I can explain. Try to explain. I think. Meet me. Okay?"

It made her laugh, unexpectedly, trying so hard to say what he wanted to say that it took him three messages to do it.

She called Lorie again.

"Did you just call me?"

"I left you a message yesterday," Hallie said.

"Oh." A long pause. "I don't think I ever got it. I mean I didn't get it."

"Do you know Jennie Vagts's phone number?"

"Jennie?" Lorie's voice squeaked, like they had a bad connection.

"I want to get in touch with her."

"You haven't seen her?" Lorie sounded surprised.

"What's going on?"

"I think—no one's seen her since the funeral."

"*What?*"

"No, it's like—I mean, I'm sure it's fine. But her mother was calling around, and what with everything . . . She has a boyfriend up in

Brookings, you know, and her mother doesn't like her to go up there, but she gets away. And she probably just forgot to call because people do. Even her mother's not *worried*. At least that's what she said when I saw her over at Cleary's."

Hallie closed her eyes. Dell and Sarah Hale and Ghost Number Three were in the cab with her, Ghost Number Four having disappeared altogether, air so cold, she should be able to see her breath, though she couldn't. Jennie wasn't here. Wasn't a ghost. So that was good, right?

"Lorie," she said.

"Yeah?" Lorie sounded cautious.

"I need to find her."

"O-okay. Why?"

"You know everyone. Right?"

Silence. "Yeah, I kind of do."

"Would you—? Can you see if you can find her?"

"Sometimes," Lorie said after a brief pause, "I guess sometimes I wish the world was better than it is."

"Is that a yes?"

"I'll do my best."

"Thanks."

Hallie started up the truck, but then had to wait to pull onto the highway for a dusty black Suburban with a long scratch down the passenger side. It pulled into the next drive and sat there until she passed. She watched it in her rearview mirror as it backed around and drove away.

By the time Hallie got back to the ranch, showered and changed and grabbed a peanut butter sandwich, it was five thirty. She went back upstairs to get her wet clothes and throw them in the wash. She fished the watch crystal out of the pocket of her jeans, dumped the clothes in the machine, and went back up to the kitchen.

She set the watch crystal aside for a moment, sat down at the table, and wrote up a new list:

—Blood plus sacrifice plus wall markings
—Lightning bolt
—Same symbols Uku-Weber and demo site fake machine.
—Dell . . . Who killed Dell? Why? Like/not like the others?

Because they hadn't hidden her. Had Dell found out what was going on? Had she tried to stop it?

But what was it? How did it all come together?

It all led to Martin—or seemed to; that much she knew. But what was he doing? Did he seriously have some way to control the weather? And if he did, what did that have to do with Dell and the others?

Shit.

The clock in her head ticked inexorably. Two and a half days to figure this out, not just Dell's death anymore, but to stop it, whatever it was, to keep anyone else from dying.

She picked up the watch crystal, fingering it slowly. She'd seen a watch shaped like that recently. She knew she had. A ghost nudged at her elbow, like a cold dull knife. She shifted away, but it came back again—nudge, nudge, nudge.

Hallie shoved the crystal back into her pocket, and went back to her father's office. She found the key and unlocked the gun cabinet, took out a shotgun and a box of shells. She stood there for a long minute, looking at the shotgun in her hands. This was not a war zone, was not Afghanistan. This was her home. But there was a war going on here, all the same.

She turned to leave, and a ghost was suddenly there, batting at her like back in the field—*fear, fear, red, pain, omgwhywhywhy?*

Hallie drew a sharp breath. She stepped forward; the ghost—it was Ghost Number Four, she saw now—advanced on her again. She stepped back. It stopped. She stepped forward. It batted at her again.

"What? I can't leave the office? The hell? There's no body here." Her voice was snappy, because hadn't it already been a hell of a day? And she was talking to a ghost. She put down the gun, put down the shells. The ghost drifted in the doorway, unmoving.

She took a sideways step to see if there was a gap to the right, and the ghost moved sideways with her. Hallie moved back, thinking she could get through the door. The ghost moved back.

Shit.

She moved another step to her left. The ghost didn't move. Was it actually trying to tell her something? "Oh, for god's sake, just learn to talk," Hallie said. She took two steps to the left. The ghost moved with her. Another step. Still with her. She was in front of the computer desk. In front of the computer. Surely it wasn't telling her to use the computer. The stack of papers she'd printed out the other day when she'd been doing research was to the left of the monitor. She held it out.

"You want to show me which one?"

The ghost bobbed in front of her, like it had no interest whatsoever in anything that Hallie did.

"Yeah," Hallie said. "Okay."

She flipped through the printouts quickly because she didn't have time for this, or maybe this was all she had time for, because if it helped—

Karen Olsen.

In a photo taken in a Colorado library two years ago. *Two years ago.* Her right hand on Martin's arm showed an antique watch with a hexagonal crystal.

Shit. She looked at the ghost. Not exactly the same—longer hair, different style—but close enough.

Well, at least she knew.

There was a sharp rattle on the roof, and Hallie looked out to see tiny pellets of hail pelting down. They came harder, so that it felt like the house was shaking, though it was only the rattle of hundreds of hailstones on the roof. The storm kept up for almost ten minutes, long enough to cover the ground with the tiny pellets. Then it stopped, like someone flipping a switch. Hallie grabbed a jacket, her keys, and the shotgun, but when she walked out the door, the temperature was warm—nearly seventy, she figured—and the hailstones were melting so fast, they looked like they were vaporizing.

If Martin was controlling the weather, Hallie thought, he really wasn't very good at it.

She was hardly out of the long drive, just making the turn from gravel onto hard-surfaced county road, when the cell phone rang. She didn't recognize the number, but she answered it anyway.

"Hallie, so glad you're there."

Martin.

"How did you get this number?" she asked.

"It was your sister's number." Like somehow that made it obvious he would use it to call Hallie.

"Yeah," Hallie said. "How did you know I had it?"

"I don't know." He actually sounded surprised, like it was a mystery even to him. "You didn't tell me, did you? No, of course not. Someone else must have told me," he said. Well, it wasn't like Pete didn't know it, Hallie thought. Martin must have gotten it from him and didn't want to admit it. Which, frankly, if she had anything to do with Pete Bolluyt, let alone was doing business with him in some way, she wouldn't want to admit it either.

"What do you want?" Hallie asked.

"I heard you found a body."

I found two bodies, Hallie thought, *so apparently you don't know everything.* She said, "Word gets around."

"It's a small place," he said, and she thought she could hear the smile in his voice. He was originally from Rapid City, or at least had been from Rapid City when she'd met him for the first time, but he'd certainly embraced Taylor County while she'd been gone. His "spiritual home," wasn't that what he'd called it? "Maybe it's macabre of me," he said, "but do you know who it was? The sheriff isn't saying yet. Pending notification, you know? And I—I knew a girl once who . . . She wasn't, strictly speaking, from around here, but you never know. Well, you always wonder, don't you? And she was from over—"

"Sarah Hale?" Hallie asked.

There was silence. "Well," he said, drawing the word out, "that wasn't—" And his voice seemed flatter to Hallie, though maybe that was her phone, because it was fading out every couple of words, too, as if they were getting farther away from each other. "This was an intrusion, wasn't it?" he said. "You're upset. Finding a body can be an upsetting experience. And after your sister . . . They said you just stumbled across it?"

"Ah . . . yeah." Martin must have pretty good contacts at the sheriff's office, Hallie thought, because he seemed to have all the details.

"And they already—the sheriff's identified the body already? You said the name was Hale, didn't you? Sarah Hale?"

There was a truck behind Hallie on the road, far enough back that she couldn't tell who it was or even exactly what kind of truck it was, grayed to anonymity by the late-afternoon light. She watched it in the rearview mirror—appear, disappear, appear again against the deceptive flatness of the county road.

"No," Hallie said. "I just . . . you know what?" Because she wasn't much for dissembling. "I thought it might be her."

"Oh," Martin said. His voice even flatter, like a knife blade. "That's interesting," he said.

"Yeah, it kind of is," Hallie said, particularly since she knew, and she was damn sure Martin knew, that it wasn't Sarah Hale, though there was a Sarah Hale body out there somewhere, presumably underneath the fountain out at Uku-Weber.

When Hallie'd known Martin before, she'd found him an interesting, attentive person. A little too attentive for her, too much *I hope you're not too tired* and *Are you cold?* and *Here, let me take care of that for you.* But not like he was doing it for what it would get him, more like he actually cared if she was tired or if he was boring her or what she wanted to do that day. This Martin seemed like he wanted to be that Martin, but couldn't pull it off.

"I understand you'll be leaving soon," Martin said.

The abrupt change of subject left Hallie silent for a minute. He was right. Damn him. She would be leaving soon. Leaving in two short days, to be exact. But it would be long enough to figure out what he was doing and to stop him. It had to be.

"The reason I ask," Martin said, filling the silence, "I don't know whether you realize how important Uku-Weber is, Hallie." He laughed. "I know that sounds . . . grandiose, but we really are. And everyone here—I want everyone to be a part of it. You haven't seen how people . . . You haven't seen the struggle."

"What are you talking about?" Hallie said.

"I will make the world a better place," he said. Apparently, *Don't fuck with that* was meant to be understood.

"Are you actually threatening me?" Hallie asked.

"It would be wise," Martin said, "if you remembered that you don't live here anymore."

"Don't count on it," Hallie said. She broke the connection, but where had that come from? That last bit. Because she had a career, would be reupping in a couple of weeks. She wasn't coming back here, not to live.

23

It was close to six fifteen by the time she pulled into Cleary's, having gotten stuck behind three pickup trucks, a Suburban, and a tractor hauling big hay bales for three and a half miles. There were only three cars in the parking lot: two parked by the bar-side door, and Boyd's Jeep Cherokee right up beside the other door.

The restaurant side, distinguished from the bar side by white tablecloths and chairs with padded seats, was practically empty. Boyd, seated at a table halfway along the far wall, looked up when she came in and smiled, quick and fleeting. He was still out of uniform, though he'd changed into a dark red shirt with a button-down collar and faded blue jeans. His face looked tight and thin, as if he hadn't had much sleep lately. Perversely, it made Hallie want to dump everything on him—ghosts and Martin and blood and lightning. She wanted to hit him with impossible things, one right after the other, wanted to see him when he wasn't so controlled, to watch how he reacted. Wanted him to be one thing or the other—on the side of rational and logical or on the side of Hallie.

She could hear faint strains from the jukebox in the bar as she crossed the room. Boyd already had a cup of coffee, but Hallie had had plenty of coffee, and she ordered a beer from the waitress who had followed her across the room to the table.

"I thought you wouldn't come," Boyd said. His hands encircled his stoneware coffee mug.

"You're an ass," Hallie said.

Boyd opened his mouth, started to say something, then stopped. The waitress brought Hallie's beer and left again. "All right," he said, and nodded once. "All right."

They sat like that for a minute, on Hallie's side because she wasn't entirely sure how to go forward if there wasn't going to be an argument.

"I think we should lay our cards on the table," Boyd said, breaking the uncomfortable silence.

"You first," Hallie said quick, like she hadn't even had to think, though she'd thought about it the whole drive in. Who was he? What did he want? How did it help her or Dell or Sarah Hale or Karen Olsen that he was here, that she was talking to him?

"Okay," he said. "Okay." It took him a minute before he actually said anything else. "First, thank you."

Hallie blinked.

An elderly man who looked vaguely familiar to Hallie stopped by the table to thank Boyd for pulling his tractor out of the mud last Thursday. There were already more people in the restaurant than there'd been when Hallie came in. Two tables of gray-haired ranchers who talked to one another across the gap, a table for six that consisted of two women and four kids of varying ages from three to sixteen or so, a solitary man with a grimy gimme cap against the wall by the windows.

"Thank you for coming here," Boyd continued when the man had left their table again. "It was— I'm glad," he finally said simply. He tried a smile, but didn't quite pull it off, like there was a lot more stuff to come and he was afraid it wasn't the right time.

Hallie raised an eyebrow because *I'm glad you came* wasn't going to cut it in the explanation department. There was shoving her out of the way, leaving her behind, there was *This is an ongoing investigation,* there was . . . well, she didn't know what there was, did she? That was the point.

Boyd signaled the waitress for more coffee. "I can explain about this morning," he said. He traced a line on the surface of the table, finishing with a sharp tap. He kept tapping his index finger on the table as he continued, like he was marking off items in his head. "But I need to start, well, at the beginning, I guess."

He sat there for another minute, somehow managing to both look and not look at her at the same time. Maybe thinking. Maybe figuring out how to lie to her. *Don't lie to me,* she thought, and realized just in the thinking how important that was. *Don't lie to me*—because that would be it, the one last thing.

"If I—," he began, his voice low, though it carried clearly. "If I explain things—lay everything out as well as I can—"

"What?" she demanded. "You want, what?"

"I want you to believe me," he said.

Hallie sat back.

Well.

"I can't," she finally said, "until I know what you have to say."

Boyd's shoulders rose and fell in a silent half laugh. "Yeah," he said. He was quiet for another minute, looking into the depths of his coffee mug. Hallie's finger twitched at the loose edge of the paper label on her beer bottle.

"It's complicated," Boyd finally said.

"Everything's complicated," Hallie said. "Just spit it out."

"Okay." Boyd nodded. "All right." But then he didn't say anything else.

"Uhm . . . Boyd?"

"Do you think I'm a Boy Scout?"

"What?"

"Honest, loyal, helpful, friendly."

"Hmmm . . ." Hallie frowned. This was not the direction she'd imagined this conversation taking.

"Yeah, I kind of am. And I'm . . . good with that. I mean, I'm okay being a Boy Scout or whatever you want to call it. But you'd think the payoff to that would be that people—people who know me, would believe what I tell them."

"Okay?" Hallie said, because she didn't know him and if he thought she did, then he had a weird idea of what *knowing* meant.

He leaned forward, intensity coming off him in waves, in the direct stare and the tight muscles underneath his jaw. Hallie wondered if this was what he bottled up in precision haircuts and polished boots and tightly creased khakis. "Because you have to know this before anything else makes sense. Before I can explain earlier today. Which I can. Explain. But this first. Yeah. I think . . ."

"Just spit it out," Hallie said, almost laughing because—wow— the Boy Deputy stumbling over his words was . . . kind of cute, actually—made her willing to listen, at any rate.

He took a breath, rubbed a thumb along his jaw. "When I was . . . I don't know, eleven or twelve, I had this dream," he said. "My parents were arguing, in the dream, about . . . grades, I think. Something about school and keeping up. My brother came in and said the bus was waiting. My mother said, 'No one rides the school bus, you'll have to walk.' My father goes out to talk to the bus driver, and he's standing on the steps up into the bus, and then it—the bus—breaks into a million pieces, like confetti, and my father drops the couple of feet to the street because the bus and the steps he was standing on are gone. Then I woke up."

He looked at Hallie, and his eyes narrowed. "I know," he said, like he'd been through it a thousand times. "Because it was just a dream. But there was a feeling of . . . dread, or doom. My heart was pounding a mile a minute. I just . . . I thought the world had ended. It was just this dream, and I had to wake my brother up to make sure he was still alive, run down to my parents' room to see if they were still breathing."

Hallie didn't know what to say. Because it was just a dream, right? A dream he'd had twelve or fifteen years ago. That was the big deal? The thing he was afraid she wouldn't believe? Well, she believed he had a dream. "I don't—," she began.

"Look—," Boyd said at the same time.

The waitress came back and refilled Boyd's coffee mug, asked Hallie if she was sure she didn't want pie, because the pie was pretty good today. A mother and three boys under the age of ten took a table right behind theirs, bumping Boyd's chair three times as they seated themselves. There was a loud commotion over by the cash register as the man in the gimme cap argued with someone over something.

Hallie raised an eyebrow. "We could go someplace," she said. She wouldn't have, earlier. He still hadn't explained anything, except some weird dream he'd had when he was eleven, but he was—she trusted him. Even after this morning. It was disturbing, actually, but she was going with it.

Boyd picked up the check and walked to the register by the door. Hallie watched him, then crossed to the bar side and picked up a six-pack to go.

Prue Stalking Horse was behind the bar. She brought Hallie her six-pack and change. When Hallie reached over to take the money, Prue leaned across the bar. "Can I tell you something?" she said. There weren't many people on the bar side of Cleary's yet—some ranch hands sitting at the bar, two men toward the back at a round table, and a couple in matching shirts and cowboy hats over by the door.

"Okay," Hallie said.

Prue kept her voice low, though her face was still and calm, pretty much like always. She laid her hand over Hallie's, flat against the bar, and Hallie had to fight to keep from yanking away from her touch.

"How old were you in '94?" she asked.

"What?" Hallie didn't have time for this shit.

"You were, what? Four? Five?"

"Something like that."

Prue stepped back, removed her hand from Hallie's. "Then you don't remember."

"Remember what?"

"The end of Jasper."

Hallie didn't remember, but she knew. Jasper had been hit by a monster tornado in '94, in the fall, after everyone thought tornado season was over.

"I was there," Prue said. "I saw what happened."

"A tornado happened. Right?"

Prue studied her face. Then she said, "Do you believe in magic?"

"What?" Hallie stepped back from the bar. "What are you talking about?" But it wasn't as if she didn't know. Because *something* happened when blood hit the atrium floor at Uku-Weber, because Martin could, or seemed to think he could, control the weather, but she hadn't named it. Because calling it what it clearly was, calling it magic, felt like stepping over the line she'd been avoiding since she started seeing ghosts, felt like never coming back to normal.

Magic.

Yes. Hallie believed in it.

She believed the shit out of it.

She leaned toward Prue. "What—?" she began, but Prue had already stepped back and started wiping down the bar again, as if they hadn't been talking. Hallie straightened, felt an itch between her shoulder blades, like a target. She picked up the six-pack, turned, and practically ran right into Pete Bolluyt.

"Oh, you've got to be kidding me," she said.

Pete grinned at her. He took a half step to his right and picked up a beer that Prue had just put down, anticipating his order. Behind him, was Martin.

Hallie raised an eyebrow. If she hadn't been holding the six-pack of beer, her hands might have already clenched into fists. As it was, the muscles in her arms, across her shoulder blades, and underneath her eyes tightened in anticipation. *Fight or flight,* one of her sergeants had told her, *that's what everything comes down to.*

Hallie didn't run.

"We need to talk," Martin said. He looked smaller than the last time she'd seen him, like, well, like Hallie'd gotten bigger, which she didn't think was right, since Pete still looked the same size to her, or he'd shrunk, which wasn't likely either.

Hallie shook her head. "No."

She took a step to walk around them—Pete and Martin—but Pete moved away from the bar and blocked her.

"Unless," she said, as if she were actually considering it. "Do you want to talk about bodies? Because a lot of them have been turning up. Or—" She snapped her fingers. "—maybe Dell. Do you want to talk about her?"

She stepped up close so that she and Martin were standing nose to nose. No one seemed to notice them—not the cowboys at the bar, not the couple by the door, and definitely not Prue, who was at the far end again, wiping the counter, like her single goal was to make it the shiniest counter in South Dakota. Dell was down there with her, staring at the top-shelf whiskey bottles, though as Hallie looked, she began to drift their way.

Martin shook his head, as if Hallie were just a poor deluded girl in an endless line of deluded girls. "I'm certain I could explain things to your satisfaction. Or, perhaps, show you." He smiled, that smile that Dell and Lorie and even hardheaded Cass used to think was as charming as any man's smile ever and Hallie used to think was "okay," you know, until it wasn't.

"Yeah . . . no," Hallie said. "I wouldn't go anywhere with you."

Martin leaned close; Hallie resisted the urge to step back. "We could insist," he said softly.

"You could try," Hallie retorted. She could feel Dell, cold like a subzero December morning against her shoulder blade, and that was good. At least someone had her back. Martin stepped away from her, setting himself so that Pete's left shoulder formed a half barrier between him and Hallie. Hallie sneered at him. She set the six-pack of beer on the bar.

"We are not going to fight, Hallie," Martin said, like he was talking to a twelve-year-old.

"I don't completely know why yet," Hallie said, "but I know you killed them. Dell and Sarah Hale and Karen Olsen." The last just to see what he would do.

Some of the color drained from Martin's face. But all he said was, "You don't know what you're talking about." He looked at her intently, though, as if he saw something different from what he'd seen before. Dell drifted between them, and Martin took a step back.

Hallie stepped up. "Here's what I know." She ticked points off on her fingers. "I know about the bodies. I knew where they were and how to find them. And I know about the blood. Yeah." She stopped a moment, because Martin had backed up another half step. "I know. I've been to Uku-Weber. I've been in your office. I've seen blood hit that floor. I don't know exactly what it all means or what you think you're doing with it all, but I will. That's what Dell was doing, wasn't she? Figuring it all out. Jesus, Martin. That's why she died, isn't it? Because she knew or was going to know pretty damn soon."

"Hallie—" Martin's voice was sharp enough to get her attention. He stepped away from Pete and seemed to straighten, to draw energy back into himself until he was almost intimidating. "—you don't want to push me."

"Oh, hell, Martin," Hallie said, "you don't know me very well, if that's what you think."

Pete shoved her sideways, one hand wound tight in the sleeve of her shirt. "You better shut up, right now," he said.

Hallie tried to figure out if she should break Pete's foot or his balls. Because he needed to let go of her right now.

"That's enough."

They all turned to look at Boyd. Martin smiled, like he had never threatened anyone, least of all Hallie. Boyd didn't smile back, like he was immune to charm, which Hallie hoped he actually was. Because it would make her like him quite a bit.

Pete dropped her arm and took a step forward. Martin stepped back, projecting sincerity and—yeah—puzzlement, she supposed. Puzzled that he could be so misunderstood. She really hoped she got to hit him someday. "I hope you don't think—," he began.

"Are you ready?" Boyd said to Hallie, like she was the only one in the room.

She deliberately turned her back on Pete and Martin, picked the six-pack up off the bar, and said, "Yeah, I think I am."

24

I didn't need you in there," she said as they crossed the parking
lot.

"I know," he said.

"I could have handled it."

"I know."

"Then what were you doing?"

He stopped, touched her elbow as a car pulled into the lot, and
they both moved sideways out of the way.

"I thought it was time to make it clear where I stood."

Hallie looked at him, but there was nothing to be read in his face.
"Are you saying that—?" She frowned. "I don't understand what
you're saying." Because he couldn't be saying that he knew Pete and
Martin and lightning that wasn't and the things that Hallie knew or
thought she knew or was determined to prove. He couldn't know
about Sarah Hale or Karen Olsen.

He couldn't.

"Hallie!"

Lorie crossed the parking lot toward them. "Are you going in or
out? Because if you're going in, well, I'm going in. But—" She spotted the six-pack of beer under Hallie's arm. "—you're leaving, aren't
you? You don't even have a minute? Two minutes? No, probably not.

You're probably on your way somewhere and I'm keeping you. Well, I won't keep you, but we have to talk." She glanced at Boyd. "That thing we talked about?" She said to Hallie, "I think I might know where sh— I think I might have a line on what you wanted. I'll call you, though, when you're not— I'll call."

And she was gone.

Boyd and Hallie looked at each other.

"Yes, she's always like that," Hallie said, and hoped that Lorie really did have a line on Jennie Vagts, that she would turn out to be up in Brookings or gone on a three-day shopping trip or something that had nothing at all to do with lightning and blood and Martin Weber.

She and Boyd stood there for a minute, as if encountering Lorie had knocked them off stride, as if neither of them quite knew how to go on.

"I meant all our cards," Boyd finally said. "But I have to—I have to start at the beginning."

"With a dream," Hallie said.

Boyd shrugged one shoulder. "Yeah."

This time it was Hallie who said it. "All right." She could be patient for once. She could. Really.

"Mine or yours?" Boyd asked then.

"Oh, mine," she said, and pointed toward her pickup, because she wanted that much control.

Boyd smiled like he understood what she was thinking, but it was a friendly smile, not a mocking or condescending one, and she felt more or less in charity with him as she set the six-pack in the back and opened the driver's-side door. She couldn't say she understood why he wanted to talk about dreams he'd had when he was eleven years old, when they could be talking about what was happening now. Who cared? Who even remembered dreams they'd had back then?

She thought about heading to the old gravel pit down south of Templeton, but it was promising to be a clear night and not too cold, and there were likely to be several different sorts of people there already—target shooters and teenaged couples and people who wanted privacy and weren't likely to get it in a county the size of Taylor. Privacy was all about pretending—that you didn't know or didn't see or weren't there. Sometimes it worked. Sometimes it didn't.

Instead, Hallie headed out past the Sigurdson brothers' ranch and took the turnoff just past Old PC, then turned again and headed east. Another three miles and she turned off onto an old road that saw more horse and cattle traffic than pickup trucks and cars. Ten minutes later, she pulled in behind an old church, the only building for several miles on the big flat open prairie. The building was weathered, some of the windows had been boarded over, and there were gaps in the roof, but for an empty building on the plains, it was in relatively good shape.

On the back door was a sign that read ST. MARY'S. ENTER ALL.

Hallie got out and dropped the tailgate, hopped up, and set the cold six-pack beside her. The sun sat low on the horizon, throwing long shadows across the churchyard. There was the barest hint of the old lawn, everything fading back to short-grass prairie. Even the drive and the gravel parking lot were slowly giving way to the inevitable.

Eighteen miles away on the interstate, Hallie could hear a truck downshifting, the air so crisp and clean that the sound carried. She propped her foot on the tailgate and rested her chin on her knee, a longneck beer held loose in her hand. She wasn't much primed for drinking, but it was the flavor of the thing, of the place that was important. This was a place for truth and secrets, a place where no one could overhear them, interrupt them, second-guess.

Boyd took a beer for himself, twisted the cap, and stuck it in his pocket. He held the beer bottle in his right hand, but didn't drink. Hallie could feel Dell, but she couldn't see her. She wanted all of them here—Dell and Sarah and Karen—because she was going to tell him, she was. Believe her or don't believe her, that part was up to him. Trust him or don't, because suddenly she didn't care about that as much, which she supposed meant that she'd decided to trust him.

"So," she said, "you had a dream."

Boyd opened his mouth, started to say something, then stopped and took a long swallow of beer instead. He rubbed his thumb along his jaw. The light had turned gray, though it wasn't quite dark yet, and it blurred his features. Hallie could see his face, but not his eyes.

"Yeah," he said. "I had this dream." He paused, figuring it all out again, what he was going to say. "For the next three days, I thought something terrible was going to happen."

"Because of the dream? What did you think was going to happen? That you'd disintegrate into confetti?"

Boyd looked at her, and though Hallie couldn't read his expression in the dimming light, she could imagine it. She forgot, sometimes, that not everyone had grown up in her family. "Sorry," she said. "It's your story."

"It didn't make sense when I was eleven, either," he finally said. "But it didn't stop the feeling. Disaster. Somewhere. Somehow. I was so sure of it. I told my parents I wasn't riding the bus anymore."

"How'd that work out for you?"

"Not well. My mother finally agreed that I could stay home until the end of the week, but then, Monday, right back on the bus."

"So, did you have the dream again? What happened?"

"The next week, I had another dream," Boyd said. "This girl I had—well, I had a crush on her—and she was going to Washington, D.C., to the Lincoln Memorial because she'd won some essay contest."

"In your dream?"

"Yes, in my dream. I didn't want her to go. I told her that terrorists had targeted the Lincoln Memorial and she'd be in danger. She went anyway, and when she got there, they put all the kids on a big yellow school bus and took them on a tour of Washington. Just as they were driving past the Lincoln Memorial, the road collapsed and the bus shattered into a million pieces. Same feeling when I woke up, like the world had ended while I was sleeping, like everyone I knew had died." He kicked at a piece of gravel with his foot, held the beer by its neck in his right hand. "Three nights later, I had another dream—six people got on a bus, drove it halfway across the country, and plunged off a bridge in California."

He rubbed a hand across his face. "I tried not sleeping, but that didn't work. I tried sleeping with my light on, with music on. My father told me if he believed in psychiatrists, he'd take me to one."

That surprised a laugh out of Hallie, but Boyd just looked at her like he didn't get the joke. "Because psychiatrists actually exist," she pointed out.

He frowned.

"Yeah, okay. Sorry. Are you still having these dreams? Is that the point?"

"The point," Boyd said, like the point was both what he was trying to reach and trying to avoid. Like he could have just said, *I had dreams, then something else happened*, except he didn't want to say the *something*. Which impressed her, that it was hard for him. "The point," he repeated, "is that two days after I had the fourth dream, a bridge collapsed in the mountains in California near a place called Lincoln, while a school bus was crossing it, and seventeen kids died."

"So . . . what? You read the paper and said, 'Oh my god, that's what my dreams were about'?"

"No." As if he didn't notice her sarcasm. "I didn't figure it out for years. I mean, once I figured out about the dreams, I went back and looked. Because they're never easy. Or clear. And there's never enough time. When—"

Hallie dropped her leg and leaned forward, bracing her hands on the tailgate. "You mean you have these dreams all the time?"

"Not all the time," Boyd said. "Maybe every couple of years. I didn't have any the first two years I was in college, and I thought I'd—Well, it doesn't matter, but yeah, they're dreams about disasters."

Hallie knew the next question. She didn't want to ask it, but she did. "And now? You're having dreams now? About here?"

He nodded. "It started about two years ago. Wide-open prairie and fire and screaming—I mean, different things happened in the dreams, but there was always fire. And storms. Lots of . . . lightning. In the beginning, I don't have them—the dreams—often. It makes it hard to figure things out. And they're like the confetti dream. They don't make sense. They get clearer, more pointed as the disaster gets closer, but the only one that's one hundred percent clear is the one I get when it's too late to change anything."

"How often now?" Hallie asked. "Like every night?"

"Yeah. More."

"More than once a night?"

"Yeah."

Shit.

"It's not very . . . restful," he said.

There was a pause, long enough for Hallie to notice the rustling of dried grass in the rising breeze. Then, "Do you?" he asked.

"Do I what?"

"Believe me."

She reached out and grabbed a fistful of his shirt, pulling him in close. His breath was warm against her cheek. He didn't reach out and touch her in return. He just stood there and waited. "Has anyone believed you before?" she asked.

He huffed out a breath. "I don't tell people."

Hallie believed that. Everything she knew about him said that he desperately wanted the world to be rational and sane, wanted it to count that he did all the right things, made all the right choices. He shined his boots and ironed his shirts and got his hair cut every third Thursday, washed his car and shelved his books in alphabetical order. All that was supposed to mean something, was supposed to guarantee that the world was a logical place with things you could see and taste and smell.

And instead, you got to be Cassandra.

Double shit.

She could feel Boyd's breath, warm and alive, and it made her sad because they were in trouble, really deep trouble, and no one was getting out free.

"I died in Afghanistan and now I see ghosts," she said, said it right out flat, blunt, like a weapon.

He jerked, like a startled horse, and she tightened her grip on his shirt. "Don't you step back," she said. "Don't you dare take one step back, because I believe you. I believe that you have dreams and that they tell you about what's going on here—about why Dell died and about the bodies we found today. I believe you, goddamnit. So don't you walk away from me now."

"Maybe," Boyd said carefully, "you could give me a little more detail."

Hallie's lips twitched, because weren't they a pair? Neither of them wanted to be seers or speakers to the dead or whatever it was they were. Not that Hallie was a constant fan of rational and sane, but a normal world where she didn't see ghosts? Yeah, that'd be awesome on a stick.

"What kind of detail are you thinking would be helpful?" she asked.

"Wait," he said. "You died?"

"Not permanently."

Well, duh.

"I just . . . There was an ambush and I—our Humvee got hit. It went over—down the side of a mountain, and I got thrown clear. I stopped breathing for about seven minutes—that's what they told me. And now I can see ghosts."

"Son of a bitch."

The swearing startled her, out of character for Boyd. He took a step back, and she let him.

"I dreamed that you were dead," he said. He took her wrist, where she'd been wearing Eddie's bracelet before. His fingers circled her wrist. "That's why—that was why—this morning with the second body because I dreamed that, too. Only, I didn't understand until you were standing there that it was you and the bracelet and the body. And I thought—if you would just stay out, it would be all right. I could make it all right. But then—" He made a sound like a laugh, though it probably wasn't. "It couldn't be all right: you were already dead."

"Yeah," Hallie said.

"Are there ghosts here now?" he asked after a moment.

The moon had come up. Stars sparkled brilliantly, the combination enough to turn the sky gray black and cast shadows from the dead tree at the edge of the old church lot. Hallie could see Boyd again, though she still couldn't read his expression.

"Right now," she said, "yes. There's—" She put her hand out, like she would touch each one. "One behind your left shoulder, one about six feet away on my left. And one—" She didn't actually know where Dell was right that second or the still unidentified Ghost

Number Four. Behind her? Disappeared for the moment? "There's usually . . . Sometimes there are more."

"Well, damn," said Boyd.

They stayed like that for a moment. Close, but not quite touching, now that Hallie had loosened her grip on his shirt—Hallie sitting on the tailgate of the pickup truck and Boyd standing in front of her, close enough that she could hear him breathe. A single bolt of lightning flashed across the sky, startling and bright as day. Without thinking, Hallie grabbed Boyd's shirt again and tugged him right up next to her, like it would make them both safe.

Boyd braced himself, his hands just brushing her hips. The flash of lightning didn't repeat itself. She let go of his shirt and smoothed the creases, stopped because she could feel the beating of his heart beneath her hand.

He put a hand on her hip, and her breath caught because it had been—well, it hadn't been that long, but it had been a long time since it had meant something. She put her hand on his face, the faintest hint of stubble, like a rough whisper.

"Sshhh," she said, though he hadn't said a word. He smelled like lime, brown sugar, and vanilla.

"I—"

"No talking," Hallie said. She pulled him toward her and kissed him, hard, like it was the first time in a long time, like it might not come again, like they'd been lost on the same desert island for years, and she'd only just found him.

25

Hallie's eyes were closed, but she saw it anyway, like white phosphorous, like it was so bright, it flashed right through her eyelids. She opened her eyes and she could still see the afterimage, like a great gray block, hanging in the air between her and Boyd.

Boyd's hand was on her arm. "What's wrong?" he asked.

The sky was definitely lighter. Hallie could make out individual leaves on the dying tree at the edge of the parking lot, could see the sharp outline of single blades of grass growing up among the gravel.

"Hallie?"

She rubbed her eyes. "I don't—"

There it was again.

The only thing she'd ever seen remotely like it was the flash of light in the Uku-Weber atrium. But this—this was a hundred, a thousand times brighter. Another flash, then it was gone. Flash! Flash! Flash! Like the flickering projection of an ancient movie camera. Not just a flash, though. A thing. Fifty feet tall, a hundred feet—she couldn't measure it, it was there/not-there too quickly. Shaped like a man—legs, arms, a flat, sharp head.

Like a giant.

Like the sky was on fire.

"Shit!" Hallie jumped from the back of the pickup, almost knocking Boyd in the chest, her heart pounding.

"What is it?" Boyd gripped her arm.

"You can't see that?"

"See what?" There was something in his voice, like he was readying himself. *Have you seen this in your dreams?* she wanted to say.

It looked as if he/it/the fire giant was headed straight for them, looked like it straddled the world, like one stride covered miles.

"Seriously, you can't see that?"

The fire giant moved gradually east, closer to them all the time. As it neared, the trees began to sway, leaves rustling like old paper. Hallie could feel the heat from its passing, dry and furious, still a mile or two north of the old church. A few more strides, becoming smaller and less bright with each one, until it finally vanished completely with a single sharp pop.

"You didn't feel that?" she asked.

"The wind?"

"The fire."

His grip on her arm tightened sharply then released. *What have you dreamed?* Hallie wondered. Before she could ask, Boyd's cell phone went off, a muted buzz. He put a hand on Hallie's shoulder as he answered. "Davies," he said.

The conversation was brief. "Yeah . . . not that far . . . All right."

When he hung up, he said, "We need to go."

"What? Has Martin done something? Has he taken someone? What?"

"You should let me drive."

"Oh, you better just tell me," she said. Because she had no intention of being led by the nose, not by him or anyone.

"On the way."

Only because he made it half a question did she nod and hand him the keys to the pickup.

He headed out fast, the pickup thumping on the rough road. "That was Ole on the phone," he said. "The sheriff," he added unnecessarily. He downshifted and turned west on the next section line road, crunched a tumbleweed underneath the back wheels, and kept on going. "He asked me to find you. He said—"

"Shit, it's another fire, isn't it?"

Boyd looked at her. "How do you know?"

"Is it the house? Is my father all right?"

"He just said there was a fire. To bring you."

"Shit!" She was quiet for a moment, thinking furiously. "Okay. Martin and Pete killed those women. It had to be them. It has something to do with Uku-Weber, with the fact that there's no . . . there, there. The toolshed fire? No one knows what caused it. Even my dad, and he was right there. This fire . . ." She thought about the flickering giant of fire. "Oh god, I know what caused this one."

Boyd didn't look at her, concentrated on the road in front of him. "We need to sit down after this," he said. "To figure out exactly what you know and what I know. And what it all means."

It took half an hour to get back to the ranch on mostly deserted roads, and they could see it as they approached, fire making a bright glow against the horizon. Hallie wanted to get out and run, because why wasn't he faster? Wanted to scream with frustration when Boyd slowed to turn onto the drive. Because it was all so very, very slow.

She had her door open and was already running while Boyd was still slowing to a stop. There were three fire trucks and two sheriff's cars, half a dozen neighbors in pickup trucks and Suburbans. The big equipment shed was on fire, was still burning, was already gone. Firefighters were spraying water on the house and the horse barn and even wetting down the baled hay just off the lane. Hallie couldn't see her father.

Where the hell was he?

Someone grabbed her arm and she whirled, fists raised.

"Whoa," said Hack. "It's—" But she didn't hear what Hack had been going to say, already running for the house.

Cass met her at the door. "Hold on," she said. "He's going to be all right."

Hallie felt as if someone had cut her strings. "All right?" she said.

"He'll be all right," Cass repeated. "Smoke inhalation, pretty bad. And I think his throat's a bit seared, but he isn't burned. They've got him on oxygen."

Hallie pushed past her, her eyes burning. She wasn't going to cry for him. She wasn't. He was stubborn and ornery, and she wouldn't give him the satisfaction. She swiped a hand across her cheek as she entered the living room.

He was lying on the couch with an oxygen mask on his face. Connie and Trevor Solomon were there, EMTs for the local volunteer fire company. Her father looked up when he saw her and started to sit up, but Connie put a hand on his chest and held him back. He tried to say something, but started coughing instead.

"I know, Dad," Hallie said. "It's all right."

Her father shook his head. Gesturing with his hands, like he was angry. And he probably was, losing the big equipment shed meant he'd lost the old Allis and the new Kubota and probably the baler and the sprayer. Though if asked, he would say, *It's just stuff, Hallie.*

Martin, Martin, Martin. The name sang in her head like a litany and a taunt. Was this his idea of a threat? Did he think she was afraid of him? She wasn't.

Cass laid a hand on her shoulder. Hallie jumped; she was that much on edge. "Helicopter's here," Cass said easily. "You going with him?"

"No," Hallie said. She forced a half smile. "It'll make him cranky . . . er. Crankier."

Cass chuckled low. "Oh yeah, that's the truth. And he'll want someone here. You want me to go?"

"Yeah." Hallie licked dry lips. "That'd be good. Thanks."

Cass clapped her shoulder. "No problem. You let people help you," she finished sternly.

"Yeah, I'll be doing that," Hallie said. *Maybe when hell freezes over.*

Her father and Cass were loaded and gone almost before Hallie could comprehend it. The equipment shed was still smoldering, the windows shattered and the roof collapsed. Water ran in tiny rivers down the drive, cutting grooves into the yard.

A dozen men and women, some of them volunteer firefighters, some of them neighbors come to see how they could help, stood under the old tree in the yard, cast in blues and whites by the yard light. Hack approached Hallie. "Listen," he said. "Fire's pretty much out, but we're leaving a truck here. To watch for sparks or flare-ups. Teddy turned the horses out when we got here. They're probably all hell and gone by now. Some of us will come tomorrow and—"

"No," Hallie said. "Don't worry about it. Scout will bring them down in the morning. If he doesn't, I'll get them." She rubbed her eye. "What started it?" she asked, already knowing, but wanting to hear all the same what Hack would say.

He shook his head. "Like the little shed. It just went up. But that ain't right. It ain't what happens. I'm getting an arson investigator out from the state Fire Service in the morning. Already got the call in."

Boyd approached as they talked. He didn't say anything, just put his hand on her arm. She didn't know where he'd been or what he'd been doing, had forgotten him in the intervening moments since they'd arrived, if the truth were told.

"Whatever you think," Hallie said to Hack. It wasn't as if they'd find anything. It wasn't as if she didn't already know. But that was all she knew, that Martin had done it. That he'd done it to threaten her: *This is what I can do,* he was saying, *this is the power I have.* But she still didn't know what that power was. Because maybe she did believe in magic, but she didn't actually know what it was or how it worked. And what about the girls he'd killed? Why had he killed them? What about Uku-Weber? Girls had been killed and companies established for hundreds of years, and the doing of it didn't conjure fire and fire giants to roam the countryside.

"Hallie!"

Both Boyd and Hack were looking at her oddly. "What?" she said, sharp, like they'd interrupted her in the middle of something important.

"Connie says you can stay at their place tonight," Hack said.

"No." Hallie shook her head vehemently. "Shit. No. I'm staying here."

Hack looked at Boyd. Hallie looked at both of them. "Oh, don't even try to talk about me as if I'm not here." She stepped up. "I'm not a little girl. My father has Cass looking out for him. I'll look out for the ranch."

Hack held up his hands. "Okay. Just trying to help. We'll be here another couple hours at least," he said. "And, like I said, we'll leave a truck and a couple of people here until tomorrow." He turned to Boyd. "You got a ride back?"

"Don't worry about it," Boyd said quietly.

Hallie wanted something, but she couldn't figure out what it was. Okay, that wasn't quite true. She wanted to take a shotgun and go shoot Martin in the head. And maybe Pete. Because, sure, it was wrong and would land her in jail or dead herself, but it would stop him. There wouldn't be any more dead girls or fires or disappearances. What if she didn't do it and more people died? Because she could take the heat for it. She could. She didn't have that much to lose.

Someone pressed a bottle of water into her hands. She looked up, surprised that it was Boyd, because hadn't he just been standing right next to her? How had he left and come back and she didn't notice?

"I'm going to check in with Ole," he said, "and then I'll be back."

"You don't have to—," Hallie began, but he was gone before she finished.

She didn't want him here, did she? On the other hand, there would apparently be people here the whole damn night anyway.

And he'd leave if she asked him to.

That was the deciding factor. She hadn't known Boyd long, but she'd noticed that, that he didn't tell her what to do. He just did what he was going to do. Which could be damned irritating, but she sort of liked it.

26

Hallie was surprised that it was only a little after ten when everyone, or as close to everyone as it was likely to get, left. Two firefighters and a small tanker truck stayed down by the ruins of the equipment shed. Hallie left feed for the horses and found the yellow dog and brought him inside. He was still wary of her, but she left the door open until he came in, skirting past her and up the stairs, where he was now lying on her father's bed. Hallie left water for him outside in the hall.

Cass called from the hospital and said they wanted to keep her father overnight, but that he'd be fine.

The phone rang again. Hallie went into the kitchen to answer it.

"What the hell's going on, Hallie?" It was Brett, sounding very un-Brett-like. "Are you all right? Do you want me to come over?"

"It's a long story," Hallie said.

"I'm coming over."

"No. Don't come. It's fine. Don't you have classes tomorrow?"

"I have to be at the hospital around noon."

"Meet me for lunch. I have to come up to see Dad anyway."

"Is he in the hospital? Is he okay? I could stop in in the morning."

"It's my dad, Brett. He wants visitors like the plague." She smiled, there and gone, though Brett couldn't see her. "By which, I mean, he'll be a grumpy bastard, but in his secret heart, he'll appreciate it."

"Ha," Brett said. She yawned. "But you're okay?"

"Yes," Hallie said. "Go away. I'll talk to you tomorrow."

After talking to Cass and Brett, Hallie was wired, like something big was going to happen any minute, like she was on watch. She made coffee and made herself sit at the dining room table and made notes on everything she knew.

Martin was responsible. Hallie felt as if she didn't quite have all the pieces yet, though she had a lot of them. The Uku-Weber building alone. Blood an essential part of it, which might explain the deaths of Karen Olsen and Sarah Hale and Unidentified Ghost Number Four. But why bury Karen Olsen here? Why bring her here? Maybe just because, because he couldn't kill everyone in Taylor County and not have someone suspect?

And then there was Jasper. The whole town. Dell had put it on her list. She'd written *Colorado*—which had to be Karen Olsen. And Jasper. She'd thought it meant where they'd found the second body. But then, Prue had said it, too. And she hadn't been talking about bodies. She'd been talking about the past. About—

"Everything okay?"

Hallie's head came up with a jerk—god!—she hadn't even heard him come in.

Boyd leaned against the kitchen doorjamb. He had a sharp smudge of ash running underneath his cheekbone.

"You don't have to stay," she said, though she was glad he had. She thought she was glad. In the army, people had your back automatically. That was the way the army was put together. But here . . . she wasn't sure what she had, wasn't sure what she could ask.

Boyd didn't answer her directly. "What are you doing?" he asked.

She got up and handed him what she'd written. She started pacing, realized it would take him less time to read it than it had taken her to write it, and turned back to find him staring once more at the sideboard, at the pictures above it, and the vases on display.

"What?" Hallie asked sharply. "What are you looking at?"

Boyd shook his head as if waking. "It's just . . . a decision I have to make," he said. He tapped the paper. About midway down the page, Hallie had written three names: Dell, Sarah Hale, Karen Olsen.

"These names," he said. "You think these others—Sarah Hale and Karen Olsen—they're dead, too?"

Sarah Hale drifted into the room past Boyd's shoulder. "They're dead," Hallie said firmly.

"They're . . . here?"

She nodded.

"I—" He looked drawn and tired. Hallie wondered how much sleep he'd been getting lately. "What do they look like?" he asked.

For a moment, Hallie couldn't remember where she'd put the box of Dell's things she'd taken from Uku-Weber. "Hold on," she said.

She was gone for maybe five minutes, digging up the box and the newspaper with Sarah Hale's picture. It was in a cabinet in her father's office. She grabbed the picture of Karen Olsen from two years ago, still on the desk.

She came back into the dining room to find that Boyd had made a fresh pot of coffee. He handed her a cup. "Thanks," she said with a quick grin. She handed him the pictures. He studied Sarah Hale's face carefully for a full minute.

"I remember," he said. "But it never felt like—I never saw her in my dreams. I thought maybe . . . hoped maybe it was something else." He looked at Hallie. "The bodies you found, these are—?"

"Yes."

He dropped the newspaper with Sarah's picture on the dining room table. "Why do you think—? Shit!"

He didn't say anything more, just stood there quietly and looked at Karen Olsen's grainy photo. After a moment, he started to raise his hand to his face, realized he was still holding his coffee mug. He set it down without looking away from the picture, so that it perched precariously on the very edge of the table.

"Boyd?"

"I tried to find her," he said.

Karen Olsen's ghost had drifted across the room and looked over Boyd's shoulder. She seemed to be staring at her own photograph in the newspaper, which Hallie found a little creepy.

Boyd tossed the printed photo on the table. He rubbed his hand across his face. "I do see women in my dreams," he said. "And sometimes I see their faces. But I never know if what I'm seeing is what happens or what might happen or symbolic of what happens."

"You saw my bracelet," Hallie said.

"I saw that you were dead. Or—" He shook his head. "—I saw that the person wearing that bracelet was dead. I didn't know it was you."

"And you saw her? You saw Karen Olsen in a dream?"

Boyd moved away, then stopped and looked at the posters over the sideboard. His head jerked sharply once to the right, like he was giving himself a hard shake.

"I came here because of her. Because I dreamed that she died outside a two-room house in Prairie City down by the grain elevator. It was detailed and vivid, more like the dreams I get when things are about to happen, not the early dreams that are so hard to figure out. So I came. And I couldn't find the house." He leaned against the sideboard, crossed his arms, then uncrossed them, straightened up and walked back to the dining room table. He leaned both hands flat on the table and looked across at her. "And I couldn't find her. I looked everywhere, but I didn't expect . . . there wasn't any—"

He picked up the photo, stared at it again, then held it out, like evidence of failure.

"This picture's from two years ago," Hallie said. "You came a year ago, right? It was always too late."

There was something that looked like anguish in his eyes; then, as Hallie watched, he put himself back together, his shoulders squared, his face smoothed out. "There were three things about that dream," he said. "It was dark, and the prairie, the whole prairie was burning. She was standing alone in the middle of this circle of fire while everything else burned. She looked—I don't know—she didn't look frightened. She was laughing. She reached out a hand toward—I couldn't see who or what, but I assume a person because something pulled her forward, out of my view. I was just in this dream with an empty circle and fire everywhere.

"The wind began to blow, the flames were going sideways, smoke so it was hard to see anything. She stumbled back, her hand . . ." He put his hand on his throat. "Everything was red."

"Blood?"

He nodded. "Not blood in the sense that it was a dream and not that straightforward, but yes. And there were voices, but I can't tell you what they said, though it sounded like singing or chanting or a prepared speech. Not conversation."

"Lightning? Did you see lightning?"

"What?"

"Pete Bolluyt has a lightning bolt symbol on his belt buckle. There's a mosaic on the floor of the Uku-Weber atrium, a lightning bolt. And Dell had—" She touched the hollow at the base of her throat. "Right there. A mark like a tattoo."

He frowned. "No she didn't," he said.

"It was—" Hallie stopped. But they were laying their cards on the table, right? "I don't think anyone else could see it," she said. "It was only when one of the ghosts touched her."

Boyd frowned. "Draw it for me."

Hallie flipped over Karen Olsen's picture, which Boyd had dropped back down on the table. She quickly sketched a jagged lightning bolt with a heavy cloud overhead. She handed it to Boyd, who studied it carefully. He pinched the bridge of his nose and took a deep breath. "There's another dream I have. It's all fire and blood and prairie," he said. "And I see lightning in that dream. And people. A dozen different ethnic groups, all different clothes. They wander through the dreams, no matter what else is happening. Sometimes two or three, sometimes twenty. They shout at me. Or, it feels like they shout at me, though I can't hear what they're saying. Sometimes if the dream goes on long enough, they start shouting at each other and there's rain and hail and snow and sleet all at the same time and thunder drowns out their voices—which I can't hear anyway.

"Eventually the thunder gets so loud, I wake up."

"So, blood and lightning bolts," Hallie said.

"Karen Olsen died before Martin Weber moved back to Taylor County, right?" Boyd said.

"She died in Colorado," Hallie said. "He brought her back."

"Why?"

"Because it's important that what's happening happens here? Because it's important to him? There's something about Jasper, too," she said. "That town over on the Seven Mile that was destroyed back in '94. Something happened back then. I think. It would have been when Martin was a kid, though. So—"

Hallie thought about Jennie Vagts, about the mark she'd seen on Jennie's neck after the funeral. She wished she'd done a better job of tracking Jennie down. Because if something happened to her on top of everything else—she dug the cell phone out of her pocket and dialed Lorie's number. "Call me," she said when she got Lorie's voice mail, because Lorie ought to have found something out about Jennie by now.

"It all goes back to Uku-Weber," she said, "back to Martin."

"Hallie, you need to let me—"

"Don't say, let me handle it. Don't."

Boyd rubbed a hand across his face again. He stood and walked into the kitchen, leaned against the counter with his coffee mug in his hand, like he'd gone out there to refill it, then forgotten why he'd come.

"I write all my dreams down in a notebook," he said after a minute. "Sometimes I make charts. And I keep hoping that I'm wrong. That my dreams really don't mean anything, that it's all just illusion or delusion or hope or even idiocy, that I'm crazy. I hope, sometimes, that I'm crazy. Because if I am, then there's the chance the dreams will go away or I'll be able to stop, to . . . stop."

While he talked, he opened cupboards and the refrigerator, pulled out bread and cold cuts, lettuce and milk. He found plates and knives and—

"What are you doing?" Hallie asked.

He stopped. "I—"

"Don't be so goddamned helpful," she said, knowing she should be grateful because he took the time and tried to do something and because he was there, but it just pissed her off. "Don't take care of me," she said.

"Look—" There was a snap to his voice that Hallie hadn't heard before. "This is what I do."

Hallie looked at him, *You have no idea, do you?* Then she sat down at the kitchen table, set her coffee mug down, and leaned on her elbows. The tired she was feeling right now went bone deep, like back on long watches, like she'd never come home at all.

Boyd brought the coffeepot over to the table, refilled her mug and then his own, taking a seat himself across the table from her.

Hallie grasped the mug tightly, holding on like if she held on tight enough, the world would turn the way she wanted it. "There's something else," she said.

Boyd looked at the battered surface of the table, which Hallie's mother had painted red years ago. Dirty greenish blue and yellowed ivory showed in nicks and scratches, particularly along the edges and the base of the legs, but no one, not her father or Dell or Hallie herself, had ever offered to repaint it.

He waited.

"There's this symbol on the floor when you come into Uku-Weber," Hallie said. "Like I said, it's a big lightning bolt, all jagged, not a symbol of a lightning bolt, but like a—a portrait of some real lightning bolt. Lots of strands, sharp and jagged. It's like the mark on Dell, like the belt buckle Pete wears. Almost exactly like.

"You can't see it unless you're standing on the second floor looking down. When you're on the ground, on the floor itself, it looks like some abstract, I don't know, weird art or something. But here's the thing, blood hits it, it lights up, the whole thing flashes, like—" She had to think. "—like you're inside lightning.

"So that has to mean something, right? Some kind of power that requires blood and . . . sacrifice. Right?"

"Sacrifice," Boyd said, like he was distracted. "Yeah."

"There are symbols, too," Hallie said. "All along the strips between the windows and the fountain. There's, I don't know—" She tried to remember. It seemed like a lifetime ago that she'd been there. "—there was a buffalo, a stag, a pentacle, something that looked like a fu dog, you know one of those Chinese guardian dogs, an eagle, well, several kinds of birds. There was one . . . it was centered—an ax crossed by a hammer and sword. There was—"

"Wait. Wait." Boyd had straightened, looked sharp and interested again. He pulled a small notebook and a pen out of his back pocket. "Tell me those again," he said. "Everything you remember."

Hallie listed them, added a few more. When she couldn't identify them by name, she described them. Boyd wrote it all down in a neat precise hand. He flipped the page, turned the notebook sideways, and made three quick drawings. He showed them to her. "Like this?" he asked. He'd drawn a stag like a petroglyph, a Celtic knot, and a pentacle.

"Yes." Hallie traced the lines with her finger.

Boyd nodded. "I see these in my dreams. The same symbols. I looked them up. Not just these, but the other ones, too. They represent power or magic in different cultures."

He flipped back to the list, checking symbols off as he spoke. "Lakota. Celtic. Japanese. Germanic. This?" He tapped the page. "It's some kind of Finnish weather god. Uku or Ukko."

"Seriously?" Blood and power and weather. "So the blood binds it together? The different powers or magics?" Magic. Crazy. But then, so were ghosts and invisible tattoos, lightning bolts without storms, and fire giants.

"Do you believe in magic?" he asked.

"I—" No. She wanted to say no. But, holy shit, who were they—the girl who saw ghosts and the Boy Cassandra—to deny magic. Then she stared at him because, "Prue asked me that."

"Who?"

"Prue Stalking Horse," she said impatiently. "Down at Cleary's."

The two of them stared at that little notebook for a moment, like they didn't know what to do next. Which was actually the truth. What did you do about someone who could make fire and control the weather?

The sound of the phone ringing practically knocked Hallie off her chair. Not because it was so loud, but because it was unexpected. She'd forgotten she was sitting in the kitchen at all.

Boyd reached behind him, like he did it all the time, picked up the handset, and handed it to her.

"Hello?" There was no one on the other end. "Goddamnit," she said, sick to death of everything, of ghosts and fire and Martin and people who couldn't be bothered to stay on the line long enough to talk. She got up, slammed the phone back into the cradle. Then she paused, dug out the phone book, and called Cleary's.

"She's not here," a male voice she didn't recognize told her when she asked for Prue. "She had to leave. Like an emergency or something. Said she wouldn't be back until it was over one way or another. Whatever that means."

Hell.

Hallie slammed the phone back into the receiver a second time and crossed to the window.

There were lights everywhere, though it was difficult to see much through the reflection of the overhead fluorescents against the windowpanes. What she could see were lights from the fire truck, from portable spotlights the firefighters had set, from the yard light. People were still coming up the drive and leaving—to see if they could help or to find out what was going on—for most of them, probably both. Hallie was sick of them all, sick of people who helped, who were kind, who were curious, sick of everything.

Dell danced off her right shoulder, cold along her whole right side. She was sick of that, too. Sometimes she thought about when this was finished—and it would be finished—there would be no more Dell, no more ghost, no more reminders.

But there would be justice. There would be an end.

That would have to do.

27

Hallie turned away from the window to find that Boyd had gotten up and left the room. She found him in the dining room, looking at the pictures on the wall again. She put her hand on his back. His shoulder blade twitched underneath her hand, but he didn't look at her.

"Did you ever see a mountain lion?" he asked her. "I saw one in Nebraska a couple of years ago. Not even where you'd expect—it was south of Omaha in this wildlife area just off the interstate. Practically in the city. It was early morning—cold, clear. I don't know. I just—I thought it was a dream, after." He looked at her. Her hand tightened on his shirt. Dell was on his left, staring directly at him, like this one time she could actually see him.

"They say—" Boyd turned and reached a hand toward her face, then stopped. "—that if you hear a cougar's cry, that it's a harbinger of death."

But I already died, Hallie wanted to say.

He took a breath and rubbed his hand across his face. "I don't know," he said. "I mean, you should—" Dell was still looking at him, and Hallie found herself staring at Dell staring at Boyd. Maybe it was a trick of light. Or the angle that made it look like Dell was watching him so intently. *Talk to me,* she thought. And wasn't sure whether she meant Dell's ghost or Boyd.

"Goddamnit," he said. "I don't know how to do this."

The sharp sound of the dog barking from upstairs alerted Hallie to the crunch of heavy tires on gravel. More neighbors, she figured. "Look—," she began, then stopped because she couldn't figure out what to say; nothing in her experience so far had prepared her for Boyd. She wanted to say, *sleep with me* or *thanks for helping* or *go away, don't come back, leave me alone.*

Maybe all of them at once.

Instead she just said, "Shit." And went back into the kitchen to dig out a thermos and fill it with coffee for the firefighters outside.

She walked outside a few minutes later with Boyd behind her and the ghosts behind him. There were three vehicles sitting in the yard—two pickup trucks and a black Suburban with tinted windows and a license plate that read UKUONE.

Martin.

She didn't spot him immediately, which was just as well—laser beams straight out her eyes would have killed him dead.

Boyd grabbed her arm. "Don't—"

She shook off his hand and headed toward the burned-out barn, didn't even realize the moment she started running. The ghosts were right with her as she rounded the corner and saw Martin talking to Tom Hauser with Pete a few paces away, kicking at a pile of burned rubble.

"What the *hell* are you doing here?" Hallie said as she came even with them. "You're not—" She couldn't maintain it, more civil than he deserved. "Get the hell out."

Martin's voice was as smooth and calm as ever, though his eyes glittered behind his glasses. "I'm so sorry," he began.

"Get. Out." Her hand was actually shaking, too much anger with no way to release it. She clenched it into a fist. Pete saw it and moved closer. *Oh yeah,* she thought, *push me.*

Martin ignored her and spoke to Tom, like she was just . . . upset. Or crazy. "Terrible thing," he said. "If there's anything I can do . . ." He looked at Hallie, looked back at Tom. "Anything at all." He spread his hands, like nothing would be too much—future of the community, neighbors helping neighbors.

Jesus.

The ghosts surrounded Hallie in a rough half circle, like armor, like a shield. She welcomed them, welcomed the cold, wanted to reach out and embrace them, what they meant and what they told her. She stepped forward. Martin took a quick step back, frowned at her as if she'd surprised him. "Did you suddenly become hard of hearing?" she asked. "Leave."

Boyd reached them then, and Hallie thought if he stepped in front of her, tried to "protect" her, she would hit him, too. "Hallie—," he said.

Martin stopped him. "No, it's all right. Everyone's upset." He looked at Hallie. "I'll come back tomorrow."

"No, you damn well won't," Hallie said. "Never set foot on my property again."

Martin took a step toward her. If he touched her, she was going to flatten him. He stopped, looked at her intently, like there was something about her he hadn't expected. His face hardened. She could see it in his eyes, dark and shadowed. He was through playing games.

The ghosts maintained their circle around her. She saw Martin through a haze of mist and cold, but she could read him fine, could read the threat in his sharp features and hard eyes.

He reached out his hand, but jerked it back as if he'd been scalded when he seemed to brush against one of the ghosts. He took two quick steps backwards. His voice had an edge that hadn't been there a moment ago, as if he was now, finally, irritated. "You be careful, Hallie," he said.

And that, she understood, was what he'd come to say, to make sure she knew whose fire it was and what he was capable of.

"I am never careful," she said. "Just so you know."

He stared at her hard for another moment or two, and she willed him to start something, wanted him to start something so bad, it was like fire burning underneath her breastbone. He took a knotted handkerchief out of his pocket and said something under his breath. He looked at her like he was waiting for something, looked back at the knotted handkerchief in his hand. He frowned.

"Get out," Hallie said, because enough was enough. He stared for a long moment, as if seeing her for the first time; then he left, like he was just a guy, just stopping by to help, just like everyone else.

"That's what neighbors do," Tom said mildly to Hallie once Pete and Martin had disappeared around the corner, followed a dozen feet behind by Boyd. "Offer to help."

Hallie was still looking in the direction Martin had gone. "I don't like him."

Tom's laugh was low, almost inaudible. "Neither do I."

That made Hallie look.

Tom shrugged. "I know he's popular and he's done a lot of good things for the county. Helped out the Sigurdsons a couple of years back, before he'd even moved back here, when they almost lost the ranch and Aggie Donner over to Templeton when that car of hers burned. And my wife says he listens to people, like he's really listening, not just pretending to because he read in a book somewhere that's how you get ahead. But the thing is, he never gets his hands dirty. It's all money or sending someone to help or buying something, and . . . yeah, maybe it's not right, but I'm a hands-on kind of guy." He looked down at his soot-coated hands and laughed again.

Hallie rubbed a hand along the back of her neck. Martin was so confident, she thought, that she wouldn't, couldn't, had no way to touch him. And yet, if there was nothing she could do, would he have burned the tractor shed? Would he have killed Dell? She didn't think so.

"Hey, you want some coffee?" she asked Tom, holding up the thermos.

"Nah," Tom said. "Got a thermos and some sandwiches in the truck. But Hack wanted me to tell you that the arson investigator'll be here tomorrow afternoon. So, if you can hold off on any cleanup. In fact," he added, "if you can wait for the heavy lifting, Jake and I'll bring the big truck out. Haul the poles and all that sheet metal out of here."

"Sure," Hallie said. "My dad would appreciate that." Because she'd be gone by then, back in Afghanistan. No matter what, that moment was fixed. She had to remember that. Even with her father in the hospital. Even with the barn burned.

"None of us think your daddy did it," Tom said as Hallie turned to go.

"What?"

"No one thinks your daddy set that fire himself. For the insurance or anything. I've known Vance a lot of years. He wouldn't do that."

Hallie wasn't sure what to say. *Thanks for not thinking my father is a criminal?* "Okay," she finally said. Then added, "Thanks for doing this. I mean, I know you volunteer and all, but I—we—appreciate it. Really. Staying all night and all. It's . . . thanks."

Tom put his big hand on her arm. "That's the way it is," he said simply. Then he winked at her. "If you ever come back for good, you know, we can always use new blood."

"I'll think about it," Hallie said. Maybe her ghosts could freeze the fire to death, she thought.

28

Hallie came back around the smoky remains of the barn to find Boyd talking to Jake Javinovich. Unidentified Ghost Number Four floated just off Jake's left shoulder. "So I came out to get the keys from Tom," Jake was saying.

He acknowledged Hallie as she came up beside them. "Because Tom's out here, and that means I'll have to open the garage tomorrow," he said. Like she'd need an explanation. "Anyway, I gotta go. It's getting late, and I bet you're wishing I'd just get out of here already, you know?" He lifted his hand and dropped it, nervous and trying not to be.

The ghost drifted after Jake as he left, drifted back to Hallie, then drifted away again. Jake met Tom halfway up from the barn, they talked for a few minutes, then Jake left, crossing the grass like he had someplace important to be and he was already late. The ghost drifted, alone, halfway up the rise, like it couldn't decide where it wanted to be.

"You gotta understand about Jake," Tom said as he approached Hallie and Boyd. "He hasn't been the same since Jesse."

"Who?" Hallie asked.

"Jesse Luponi?" Tom made it a question. "His fiancée. Or . . . not quite, I guess. She disappeared, hell, I guess it'd be about three and a half years ago now. Jake says it was the day before he was going to ask her to marry him. They thought it was him, of course, at the time. Threw him in jail for two weeks, but they had to let him out because they didn't have any evidence, and no one really knows what happened to her anyway. He got in a bad car wreck soon after. Hasn't been the same since.

"He was—" Tom watched Jake climb into his car, an old Lincoln. "—he was sharp before, ambitious, going places. Now—" He shrugged. "—nobody'll give him a job but me. But he's okay, you know. He's all right." Like Jake was his responsibility, and he didn't want anyone to hurt him or be hurt by him.

"Let me get this straight," Hallie said. "Jesse Luponi disappeared three and a half years ago and Sarah Hale disappeared just this year and no one thought anything about it? No one noticed?"

Tom frowned. "Now, Sarah Hale, she wasn't from here," he said.

"She *disappeared* here," Hallie said. She'd include Karen Olsen in her list, too, except there wasn't any reason anyone would know about her. Except Boyd. And what had he done? When it was all talked out and gone over, what had he really done?

She did not have time for this shit, for people to play games with her.

Tom looked at Boyd. When Boyd didn't say anything, Tom said, "I don't think it's a question of no one did anything. This guy here"—he jerked a thumb at Boyd—"he was asking questions all over the county. Didn't turn up anything, though, did you?" he directed the question at Boyd.

Hallie was so tired, and for once, she didn't know what to say. Well, she knew. But even to her, it seemed a bit unfair to go off on Tom or with Tom right there, because he hadn't done anything, except make sure the house and the horse barn and the rest of the ranch didn't burn to ash.

But, hell. Why were they still talking about this? Why had she let Martin walk away? Because there wasn't evidence? Because he couldn't be arrested for what he'd done? Shit. What had she been thinking? Well, she hadn't been thinking, had she? Not thinking nearly enough.

Boyd and Tom talked a few minutes longer. Hallie didn't pay attention to what they talked about. She was thinking about Jake and about Jesse Luponi and about all the other lives Martin had ruined—was ruining. About what she was going to do about it, about how to stop him. Because he wasn't going to burn anything or put anyone in the hospital or kill anyone or come to her goddamned house anymore.

"Maybe you should let me handle him," Boyd said when they were halfway across the yard back to the house.

Hallie stopped. "Who? Jake?"

"Martin."

Hallie blinked. They were past this. Weren't they? "Don't," she said.

"I'm a law enforcement official. I'm trained for this." Like he hadn't even heard her.

Fuck this. "Fuck you," she said.

A muscle under his left eye twitched.

If he was going to say anything else, he didn't get the chance. Hallie turned away and walked back to the house. She could do this alone if she had to. She could. She wasn't sure she wanted to anymore, which was a startling thing. But she could. That was the important thing.

She was washing out the coffeepot when Boyd came back into the kitchen.

"I'm not—," he began.

Hallie looked at him. He really *was* pretty. Not handsome or rugged, but fine boned, like an overworked marble statue. But that wasn't what was attractive about him to her. It was a little bit his farm-boy hands and his stupid big watch, a lot the way he stood, but mostly because he'd backed her when she hadn't expected it.

She sensed that whatever he was going to say right now? Was not going to make him more attractive.

"I know that this is your fight," he said. He stopped, twisted the cuff of his shirt. His storm-cloud gray eyes were bright and focused—she couldn't have looked away, even if she wanted to. "But, Hallie," he said, "if you go after him now, he'll kill you. He will kill you." He said each word slowly, distinctly. "No one will know. No one will save you. It won't matter. That's what I'm telling you."

It was the way he said *It won't matter* that caught her flat and held her, like the breath had been knocked from her lungs.

It won't matter.

Won't stop Martin, won't save other women, won't bring justice for Dell.

"Is that what your dreams say?" she asked.

"Yes," he said, but he shook his head as he said it, and she couldn't figure out if that meant he was lying to her or he just didn't want to be saying it.

"Okay," Hallie said. Though she didn't agree with him—at all. She didn't see a reason she couldn't take Martin in a fight—split him off from Pete, shoot him when he wasn't prepared. Simple—she could do that.

"We don't have time for this," she said, not giving him an inch, though a part of her wanted to, wanted to say, *You're a good guy and I trust you.* But . . . they didn't have time for that either. "Martin has killed at least four women," she felt compelled to add, "because Jesse Luponi . . ."

"Hallie—," Boyd began.

"But you knew that already, didn't you? You knew about Jesse Luponi."

"I knew she disappeared," he said.

"Jesus Christ! Why haven't you stopped him?"

Boyd took a breath. "There weren't any bodies. I had no proof. I wasn't certain until tonight that it was him." He shoved his right hand into the pocket of his jeans, the strap of his watch catching on the reinforced edge. "There's a system, a legal system. Martin will—"

"A legal system? It's *magic,* Boyd. How does a legal system handle that?"

"He's killed people. It can handle that."

"Well, it hasn't done a very goddamned good job so far, has it? He needs to be stopped, Boyd. No one else is going to die."

"I want Martin to go to jail, Hallie. Not you."

Hallie didn't want to think about what it might feel like to be Boyd, all alone here. The only one who knew what was happening or what was going to happen or, worse, to almost know but never be sure. She didn't want to think about what kinds of decisions she'd make if she were in that situation, about how she'd feel or how she'd cope. She wanted to think about Dell, about how she'd died, because Dell had been all alone, too. And if she'd had anything, anyone—

"Dell died because of you," she said.

"Dell died because Martin killed her." He was so still, like he'd never moved, like he never would.

Hallie wanted to believe he could have stopped this, that he could have known if he'd tried harder, that he could have saved Dell and Sarah Hale. That that was his job. And he'd failed.

After a long moment, Hallie said, "You should go." Because she was too tired for this, too tired to be reasonable.

"Hallie." Like *don't.*

"Do you need a ride back to town?" she asked.

He studied her face. "I'll call someone," he finally said.

"All right," Hallie said. *Go away.*

He turned back at the kitchen door. "I'm on at seven tomorrow—this—morning. If you need anything—"

"I won't," Hallie said.

Boyd left.

29

After, Hallie cleaned up the kitchen and the dining room, scrubbed the counter until it shone. She went back to the computer room and tried to find a home address for Martin, but he wasn't listed. She looked up all the magic systems she could find, their interactions with blood and their interactions with one another. There was nothing on most of it, nothing useful on any of it.

She was too wired to sleep, shouldn't have drunk that coffee, shouldn't have kicked Boyd out or come home or died back in Afghanistan. She had two days left. Two. To find Martin and to stop him.

Because he had to be stopped. Jesus. Maybe if Boyd had been less concerned about doing it "right," maybe Dell would be alive. Maybe Hallie wouldn't be living with ghosts.

She inventoried her father's gun cabinet, pulled out all the boxes of shells, sorted them, and put them away. She filled the printer with paper. She went back out to the kitchen, pulled boots out of the kitchen closet, knocked mud off them, and put them back in three neat rows. She called the hospital to check on her father, then hung up before anyone answered the phone.

She went upstairs, thinking about Martin and what she was going to do tomorrow and how she might get him away from Uku-Weber headquarters and Pete and confront him head-on. She was too wired to sleep, but she needed it anyway.

She fell into bed half-clothed and didn't remember anything until the sound of Dell's phone woke her at quarter to five. Even with the windows closed, she could smell burnt wood and metal in the air. Breathing it was a sharp, thin shock, like someone jabbed a needle through her nose, or like she'd been transported back to a place she thought she'd left behind.

"Hello?"

It was still dark outside, and she fumbled, trying to find the light switch.

"Hello," she said again. "Who is this?"

"Hallie?"

"Lorie?"

Lorie sounded breathless, like she'd run a marathon. And scared. "Oh my god, Hallie," Lorie said, her voice a gasp. "I think we're in trouble."

"Tell me," Hallie said, wide awake now.

"I found Jennie Vagts."

"Okay." She fumbled for her jeans, which were half on the bed and half on the floor, tucking the phone under her chin while she pulled them on. "Good."

"Someone's after us."

"Jennie's with you?"

"Yes! That's what I've been telling you."

"Who's after you? How do you know?"

"They tried to stop us on the road!" Lorie said it like it was the most outrageous thing ever, which in a way, it was. "Look," she said. Hallie could hear the tremble in her voice, but she was working hard to keep it tamped down. "Can you come? I think we lost them. We hid in that big old barn just outside Old PC for, like, three hours. I've been on the section line roads, trying to get to the interstate, but I keep seeing headlights and . . . I'm scared, Hallie."

"Okay, Lorie. It's okay." Which it wasn't. But what else did you say? "Where are you now?"

Lorie told her, and Hallie said, "Do you know St. Mary's? You're, like, five minutes from there."

Lorie took a deep breath. "So, go there, you think?"

"I'll meet you." A short pause. "Lorie, I'll be there."

"Don't hang up, Hallie! Please don't hang up."

Hallie flung on socks and a flannel shirt over her long-sleeved T-shirt. Shit. She thought Jennie would be all right in the short term if Martin caught up to them, because he needed her. But what about Lorie? He didn't need her. *Stupid, Hallie.* It had been stupid to ask for help, because Lorie hadn't known what she was getting into. She'd done it for the reason Lorie always did things—because she wanted people to like her.

The ghosts clustered behind Hallie as she trotted down the stairs, pausing at the bottom to finish tying her boots. She ran a hand through her hair and grabbed her keys and a jacket from the kitchen.

"Are you there?" Lorie said.

"I'm here," Hallie told her. "Tell me when you get to the church." Because that would give her a concrete goal, something to accomplish.

She let the kitchen door slam behind her. It was still dark, but warmer than it had been, and there was ground fog all along the yard and drifting out into the fields. The fire truck was running, generating power for the spotlights. Hallie could see Tom and someone else leaning against the hood. They straightened at the sound of the door. Hallie gave them a high sign and headed for her truck, like she always left in the dark at five in the morning. Like it was normal.

Five minutes later, "We're here," Lorie said, like a sigh. "You're still coming, right? You're hurrying, right?"

"I'm coming," Hallie said. She tried to tuck the cell phone between her shoulder and her ear so she could drive and talk at the same time, but gave that up, turned on the speaker, and threw it onto the seat beside her.

Lorie did most of the talking. "I'm just talking," she said. "Like this is just a conversation." And she proceeded to talk about people Hallie didn't know and things Lorie had done five years ago on vacation. She paused every few sentences so Hallie could say yes, or okay, or *I'm still here.*

"Do you see anything?" Hallie asked her.

Silence. "Oh my god! There are lights! Car lights! Hallie, where are you?"

"Are they headed toward you?" Because you could see headlights for miles out there.

"No," Lorie said after a short pause. "I think they're headed toward Templeton."

"Hang on," Hallie said, which seemed like a singularly stupid thing to say. What else was Lorie going to do? She slid around the next turn, gravel road to gravel road, and pressed hard on the gas. It was wide-open prairie here, horizon to horizon, a few trees near small creeks, their location marked by ground fog glowing silver in the moonlight. Hallie wished she could fly, because St. Mary's was right there. She could almost see it. But there was no shortcut, just section line roads, north, east, and north again.

It was still dark, like dawn would never come when she pulled into the overgrown parking lot. This church and the road leading to it had been where Dell and Hallie and sometimes Brett had come to practice driving, using each other's cars to parallel park, a skill no one ever used in any town in the county, all slant parking and half-empty lots. They'd brought boys here later, started with double-dating because it was "safer," though none of them knew what they actually meant by that.

Dell was beside her now, like she knew that something was happening. She had her hand on Hallie's arm, and Hallie could feel the cold even through her jacket. Sarah Hale was there, too, drifting in, drifting out through the windshield, kind of an unsettling effect. Hallie ignored it.

Lorie's little red Ford Escape was tucked in behind the church, invisible from far enough away, but easy to spot on the approach. Hallie parked next to her, dry grass bending underneath her front bumper. She turned off the engine, but left the headlights on, pointing at the crumbling foundation of the church.

She was hyperaware of every sound as she got out of the truck, the click of the door latch releasing, the tiny, almost inaudible creak of the door as it opened, the grind and scrape of gravel under her boot. Dry grass rustled in the light pre-dawn breeze.

"Lorie?" Hallie's voice was low, not quite willing to shout, though who would hear? She could see miles in any direction. "Lorie?" A little louder.

"Hallie."

Lorie's voice seemed right next to her, and Hallie jumped before she realized that Lorie was standing by the back entrance. "Over here," she said.

Hallie's hand tightened like gripping a phantom shotgun. She forced herself to relax, uncurled her fingers one by one. "Lorie," she said, jogging lightly across the space that separated them. "What's going on?"

Lorie stood there and didn't say a word, which was as unsettling as anything that had happened so far. Because Lorie not talking? That didn't happen very often. "Come on," she finally said, then turned and went inside.

"Shit," said Hallie, because bad things happened in the dark. If she hadn't known that before the army, she'd certainly learned it there.

She trod carefully up the steps, old wood gone dry and rotted through in spots. The top step creaked like a broken door, and she lifted her foot off it quick and stepped through into the back room of the church. St. Mary's consisted of a single large sanctuary with a large finished basement that had served at one time as classroom and meeting room and anything else that was needed. The room Hallie was in was a late addition in the fifties, added on to the back and just big enough for a tiny office, a big storage closet, and an open stairway to the basement. There was no rectory, never had been. Never enough people around to have a full-time minister, not even when, back fifty years ago, there'd been a service there every Sunday.

"Oh my god, Hallie," Lorie said when they were inside.

It was almost pitch dark in the church, except moonlight filtered through two large holes in the roof.

The two of them were standing in a silvery shaft of light from the three-quarter moon. Hallie could see Lorie's hands when they moved. She was wearing a white T-shirt with cap sleeves and something embroidered on the front, jeans and sneakers, and a short little jacket with just one button to hold it closed. Hallie figured she must be cold, because even though it was noticeably warmer than it had been, it wasn't warm.

"I know people, right?" Lorie went on. "You know that about me, that I can read people. Everyone says so. And I thought . . . he was so charming and interested in what I said, which most people aren't.

They just listen to be polite. And the company and the job and everything was so amazing. I thought— God, I was so stupid!"

A chill crept up Hallie's spine and across her shoulder blades. Jesse Luponi drifted past her left shoulder.

"What are you talking about?" Hallie said for what seemed like the five-hundredth time.

Lorie lowered her voice dramatically. "Martin! He's the one who chased us. He put up a roadblock, Hallie!"

"Where's Jennie?"

Something moved in the shadows just below the altar. "It's okay," Lorie said. "You should come out."

When Jennie emerged from the shadows, it was all in a rush. "What's going on?" she asked. "What's happening? Why is this happening?"

She sounded scared and weak and cold. Hallie took off her jacket and approached her slowly, like approaching a skittish colt. She draped the jacket over Jennie's shoulder, and Jennie immediately pulled it tight, hunching her shoulders in so deep, it must have hurt.

"Okay," Hallie said. "Okay. Tell me what happened."

Lorie took a big breath, let it out slow. "So, when Dell came back to town, I was working at Cleary's—"

"Not, like, the birth of the universe, Lorie. Tell me what happened tonight."

There was a pause. "Some of this is important," Lorie said.

"Give me the highlights, then."

"Mr. Weber—Martin—was always really good to me, you know. Because I'm not, you know, anybody. I haven't been to a fancy college and I don't have a degree. I just worked at the elevator and down to Cleary's on weekends, you know. But he always treated me like I was as good as anybody."

Hallie ground her teeth. *Let her talk, just let her talk. It'll get there.*

"And I thought—I wanted to keep that job forever. That's not wrong, right? To want a good job, to want to do a good job? But I didn't— I'm sorry I spied on you, okay?"

"You spied on me?"

"Because Dell killed herself. Or, we thought she did. I mean, I thought—well, everyone thought she did. Except, I think, Martin. Because, Hallie, I think he had something to do with Dell's death."

"But why did he ask you to spy on me?" Hallie refused to be drawn from the main point. "Why did you do it?"

"Well, I didn't do it, not really. I mean I told him about picking you up at the airport and about the funeral and I guess the Bob, but Pete was there and he could have told him, too. But I didn't, like, try to find out what you were thinking or pick your brain or anything. He said he was worried about you. And, well, who wouldn't be—I mean you're tough and everything, but you lost your sister. And I thought—because he said that he was really struggling without Dell and someone needed to step up, and I figured that could be me. Because I can step up. I'm not the smartest or the prettiest or any of that, but I can be there for people."

"How did you find Jennie? How does Martin know?"

"I'm getting there." Lorie's voice lost its edge, sounded snappish. "Just—let me tell it, okay?"

Hallie held up her hands, palms forward, though Lorie probably couldn't see her. "Okay," she said.

"So today—er, last night—I was at Cleary's. You saw me there, remember?"

Hallie nodded, though Lorie probably couldn't see her. She continued anyway.

"I'd been asking everybody about Jennie Vagts. Because no one had seen her, and maybe her mother wasn't worried, but I was starting to get worried because I know everybody. And when I say I asked everyone, you know I mean *everyone*. But nobody'd seen her since, well, since she left with Pete after the funeral."

"I went to Brookings, okay? To see my boyfriend." Jennie sounded defensive, like the visit itself had sparked the trouble they were in now.

"What?" Because that had been the furthest explanation from Hallie's mind.

"I know, right?" Lorie said. "All this time I was looking and getting worried because I couldn't find her, and she was kind of right where people said she was."

Hallie started to say, *Why didn't you check the boyfriend in the first place?* but she could have done that herself. Should have done it herself, because now Lorie was in this as deep as anyone, and no idea how deep that really was.

"So, I went to Cleary's to ask again," Lorie continued. "I mean I'd been there before, but there were a couple of waitresses who hadn't been there then, and I thought I'd be able to catch them. Pete and Martin were there, and they asked me to join them, which I thought was pretty nice of them. One of the waitresses didn't come on until nine, so I figured sure, why not?

"Martin was very charming, fun to talk to, you know? Because he is—charming, I mean. Maybe you don't see it, Hallie, but he's, like, the most charming man, so it's not stupid that people like him. It's not." She paused as if suddenly realizing all on her own that she'd strayed from her point.

"Pete was drinking a lot, though. I thought maybe he was still embarrassed because Jennie had to drive him home that day of the funeral. But Martin seemed kind of pissed at him. They had this little argument while I was sitting there that I couldn't quite hear. It was kind of embarrassing. Martin apologized, though, and said they had to go."

"Lorie, why is this important?" Hallie asked.

"When Martin and Pete were leaving," Lorie spoke slower to emphasize the point, "Jennie walked in."

"I was meeting Sandy Oliver, you know. We were going to have something to eat and then go on out to the Bob." Jennie ended on a half sob, as if she wished the only thing she were worried about anymore was a beer and a good time.

"Yeah, so," Lorie took up the story again. "Jennie came in and I told her you were looking for her and everything. She thought I was . . . kind of weird, actually."

Hallie grinned, though none of this was actually funny.

"But I talked because, you know, I'm a pretty good talker. And eventually I guess it sounded okay or something and we had a beer and something to eat and Sandy Oliver never showed so Jennie and I decided to go to the Bob together. But when we got, like, a mile out of town, they were waiting for us."

"Martin?"

"And Pete."

"Martin was still being really charming," Lorie said. "And, honestly, I didn't realize they'd been waiting for us until later. He said Pete's truck had stalled out and he asked if we could give them a ride back to town, and I said sure, but why not just call. So, I took out my cell phone—"

"And he grabbed me," Jennie said, the fact of it still shocking to her.

"He was kind of mean about it," Lorie said. "Which because it was so surprising, I didn't know what to do. But then Pete grabbed me, and I kicked him."

"Good for you," Hallie said.

"It got kind of crazy because everyone was yelling. But then Martin started trying to do something with this piece of cloth he took out of his pocket and he was saying stuff that didn't make any sense and I kicked Pete again and knocked him over into Martin and we got out of there."

"Why didn't you go back to town?" Hallie asked.

"We tried! A tree crashed in front of us. And then the prairie started on fire. We had to drive through fire, Hallie! When we were through it, it just went out, though. Crazy. I called the sheriff, but it was pretty clear the dispatcher didn't believe me. Plus, she said everyone was out at a fire at your place.

"She said come in, but we couldn't! We hid in that barn for hours; then we tried again. But the phone didn't work, except when I called you."

Hallie stood up. "Except when you called me?"

"Uhm . . . yeah."

"Well, shit."

30

Suddenly, the ghosts scattered like dandelion seeds out the broken windows. Just as quickly, they were back, forming a rough circle around Hallie and Jennie and Lorie.

"What the hell?" Hallie said.

"What?" Lorie said.

There was a sound, getting louder, like the crackle of dry paper or wind through old leaves.

"Shit!" Because she knew what was coming.

"Come on." She grabbed Jennie by the arm and pushed her toward Lorie and both of them to the back of the church. "We're getting out of here."

"What? Why?" Lorie stopped, and Hallie pushed her again. "Go!"

Then they were out the back door and down the steps. Lorie was ahead, already halfway across the parking lot. Jennie stumbled. Hallie caught her under her arm and hauled her up, pushing her forward.

Lorie stopped by the truck. "Hallie," she said. "There isn't anything—"

"Get in the truck!" Hallie shouted because there wasn't time to explain. How could she explain things no one else could see? She snagged the toe of her boot on the uneven bottom step and hit the ground, a jagged piece of gravel jammed painfully into her right knee.

Jennie turned back. "Go!" Hallie shouted. "Keep going!" She still couldn't see it, just a bright glow over the roof of the church, like the rising sun—if only that were actually what it was.

She scrambled to her feet. "Get in the truck!" she shouted at Lorie, who had stopped and was turning back to them.

"I don't— Where are they?" Because Lorie wouldn't see it— couldn't see it—until it killed her. She stood by the truck, unmoving. Everything was too slow—so slow—slow motion, nightmare slow.

Jennie took a step back toward Hallie.

"No!" Hallie shouted, because she'd been wrong about how long they had. Because the fire giant was here, looming over the old church. Hallie turned to face it, shouting, "Go!" one more time over her shoulder, like she could do something, like she could stop fire.

But she had to try, didn't she?

The ghosts—Dell and Sarah Hale and Karen Olsen and Jesse Luponi—surrounded her. She thought—at least we won't be alone.

The roof of the church started to smoke.

Wind rose across the open parking lot, like the sharp edge of a weather front.

Someone screamed.

The fire formed a giant hand and reached down. Hallie ducked. Ghosts surrounded her. She could feel the heat, dry and intense, the kind of heat that could peel her skin to the bone.

She straightened. If she was going out, she'd do it standing.

The hand hovered twenty feet over her head. The church roof burst into flames. Grass growing up through the gravel in the parking lot sparked into a dozen small fires.

There was a hesitation—in the night air, in the land around them, in the rotation of the earth.

The hand descended.

Then it was gone. Like the entire hand snapped out of existence. The thing—the fire giant—was still there, but it was missing its arm. Hallie started to turn, opened her mouth to tell Jennie and Lorie to get into the truck, was pulling her arm back to toss Lorie the keys. Fire snapped and crackled within the thing's body, a thick orange tendril of flame ran along its back, across the shoulder and down, forming a new arm, a new elbow, a new hand, like burnoff from a blast furnace.

It reached down again—no pause, no hesitation. But it didn't reach for Hallie.

Hallie dived forward and knocked Jennie down, covered her with her body. The heat again, a rush of wind like a rising summer storm. Hallie kept her head down, kept Jennie covered beneath her until the heat diminished.

And Lorie screamed.

Hallie scrambled to her feet and ran. But she was so late, days and months and eons too late. Lorie had tried to get away, was maybe twenty yards out into the prairie when the fire came down.

It seemed to take forever, but was really only seconds. Hallie couldn't get close. The heat dropped her to her knees, and all she could do was watch, made herself watch. Told herself that it wasn't like other times when people burned, that it was quick—instant—just that one initial scream and Lorie was gone. That's what Hallie told herself.

Because she had to tell herself something.

The church was still burning when the sun came up fifteen minutes later.

The grass in the parking lot and the adjacent field smoldered, and

Lorie . . . there was no Lorie any longer, not even a charred and blackened body, just ash and bone, already scattering in the wind. The fire giant, its task completed or the power that held it gone, had disappeared—took three strides back out into the prairie and then vanished with a loud pop, like air rushing into a sudden vacuum.

Hallie's face stretched tight and aching, from the heat or from not screaming, she wasn't sure which. She made a wide circle around the spot where Lorie had died, then turned back to the parking lot.

"Jennie?"

No answer.

Hallie put her hand on the hood of Lorie's car, then yanked it back. The metal was hot like it had been in the noonday sun.

"Jennie!"

She heard someone coughing and rounded the car. Jennie lay on the ground. She was talking to herself.

"Oh my god! Oh my god! She burned up. She just—she burned!" She turned wide eyes to Hallie. "My god!" she said.

Hallie reached a hand down to help her to her feet. Jennie scrabbled backwards, out of reach. "What was that?" she said, like Hallie would have—*must* have—an answer.

Hallie reached down again, as if Jennie hadn't just pushed her away, grabbed her by the arm just above the elbow, and pulled her to her feet. Halfway up, Jennie yanked back hard, like she wanted to pull Hallie to the ground with her. Then she was on her feet, staring at the smoldering grass and swearing, "Oh my god. Oh my god. Oh my *god*!"

"Jennie," Hallie said, surprised at how calm she sounded, because inside, she wasn't calm at all. "Can you—?" Dell's ghost put her hand on Hallie's wrist, and for once Hallie didn't notice the cold. Because it wasn't cold anymore, all the cold in the universe had been burned away.

"Jennie."

Hallie wanted to be gentle, realized that Jennie needed her to be gentle, but that had been burned out, too. "You need to stay," she said. "With . . . with . . . someone should stay."

"I could— I—" Jennie's eyes were full of fear and sorrow and horror. "I'm so sorry. I'm—" She looked at Hallie as if she were suddenly registering her. "Are you going?"

Hallie thought of a hundred things to say—*I have to stop him. It's my fault Lorie was here, that she was looking for you, that she died. Martin did this. Martin. Did this. Martin.* But she had no more words. There was no room for words. For anything now, except ending this. For ending Martin.

She turned her back on Jennie, who was standing at the edge of the parking lot, shivering. She jumped into the bed of her pickup truck and unlocked the saddle box. When she'd taken a shotgun and a box of shells from the locked cabinet in her father's office, she'd thought of it as a safety precaution. In case she had trouble at the Bob or someone ran her off the road.

She hadn't thought of this.

She loaded the shotgun, hopped out of the pickup bed, and slid the gun behind the front seat.

She returned to Jennie. "It'll be okay," she said, a hand on Jennie's arm.

"How?" Jennie asked. "How will it be okay?"

"It will stop," Hallie said.

When she left, she didn't look at the place where Lorie died.

31

Hallie hit the gravel road out of the church parking lot already doing forty. The truck slewed left. She yanked the steering wheel hard to the right, recovered, and kept right on, jamming harder on the gas until the pickup flew across the shallow dips in the road as if it were, finally, capable of flight.

She had as good an idea as any where Martin was—the company, Uku-Weber, with its lightning bolt mosaics and magic symbols on the wall.

She had wound her little truck up about as far as it could go by the time she hit the county road. At the intersection, she stepped hard on the brakes and spun the steering wheel wildly to the left. It was possible she went briefly up on two wheels as she rounded the corner. The tires slid, gripped, and held. The next twenty miles, the highway was paved and straight. She wound the truck up almost to 110 and passed an old Buick on the straight like it was standing still.

She felt like a ghost herself, cold and frigid and not entirely whole, felt like she could drive this fast forever and never touch a thing.

She had no idea what time it was, let that go, too—let go of family and friends and the future, of the army and the ranch. In this moment, on this road, there was Hallie and her ghosts, morning fog, and the whine of the truck engine.

That was all.

Her phone rang and she answered it, like an automaton, without even thinking.

"Hello, Hallie."

Martin.

"You son of a bitch."

"It's time for you to leave," Martin said. His voice had a brittle edge.

"Dell tried to stop you, didn't she? She found out what you were doing." Dell the ghost floated next to Hallie in the cab. Hallie wanted to say, *See, this is what you did, you killed her.*

"Dell loved the concept, the idea that we could make the world a better place, but she wasn't willing to do what needed to be done."

"Wasn't willing to kill people, you mean?"

Lightning struck directly in front of the truck. Hallie slammed on the brakes. How did he know where she was? It occurred to her that he had known before, too, at St. Mary's. She put her foot back on the gas, not driving slowly, because what did lightning care if she drove thirty-five or ninety? But more cautiously.

She looked at her phone. Dell's phone. That's what her father had said. The phone Lorie could call when she couldn't reach anyone else. The phone she'd had with her since she got home. She flipped it over and thrust it straight into Dell's ghostly side. She felt a short, sharp shock, the cold like a jolt of pure electricity. But it was there, the lightning bolt seared into the plastic case, like the one on Dell's neck, on Jennie's jaw, on Pete's belt. Hallie put the phone back to her ear.

"Listen to me." She said each word deliberately and distinctly. "I am coming after you, and I'm going to stop you."

She flipped the phone closed, tossed it out the window, and turned down the next section line road she came to. It would take a little longer. She'd have to travel a more circuitous path than she'd planned. But she would get there. And she would stop him.

She didn't know how long the siren had been wailing behind her before it finally registered, the pitch so perfectly in tune with her own thoughts that it could have been forever and she wouldn't have noticed, might never have noticed, that was how much her world had narrowed, except now she could see the crossbar lights—red and blue—strobing in her rearview mirror. Diffuse and pale in the early morning light, like they were underwater, like they were drowning.

She ignored them. What were sirens and flashing lights to her? They had nothing to do with fire giants or Lorie Bixby burned to death or what Hallie meant to do. The siren persisted. The red and blue lights flashed at the periphery of her vision like an approaching storm.

When she slowed for the last turn before Uku-Weber, the car sped past her. A flash of white and gold, then it turned into her, angled her truck toward the side of the road. Hallie accelerated. If she were fast enough, she could slip past in the narrow space between the car and the ditch. The other car matched her.

She slammed on her brakes, thought she'd swing left behind the other car, but she hit a patch of loose gravel that had been run up onto the pavement from the shoulder. The back end of the pickup skidded sideways. She turned into it and braked hard to avoid the ditch. By the time she straightened the pickup out again, the sheriff's car was sitting across the road in front of her.

Hallie jumped down from the cab, grabbing the shotgun from behind the seat. She didn't wait for him to come to her. Because she knew who it was. Because it was always him.

Boyd.

"Don't you stop me," she said. She held the shotgun loose in her hands.

Dell floated halfway between the two of them, like she couldn't choose.

Choose, Hallie thought. *Now is the goddamned time to choose.*

"Jennie called the station," Boyd said as he approached. His voice was low and calm, familiar and irritating, but Hallie swore that his hand shook in the particulate light of the headlights when he reached out to her. He looked angry and scared.

Welcome to my world, Hallie thought, because she was both—angry and scared—herself.

A chill wind cut across the prairie, brown grass along the road bending over like tired soldiers. Hallie smelled horses and cattle and, faintly, the sharp scent of death, of some animal that had crawled in the ditch to die. The ghosts—except Dell—were ranked behind her, her own personal phalanx, like Boyd was the enemy.

And maybe he was.

The sun was up, but hidden by cloud cover, the air damp, fog still clinging to everything so that they seemed cut off, the two of them, from the world and its concerns. The flashing lights on Boyd's car reflected back at them against the pervasive gloom. Everything was both sharp edged and flat, as if watching Lorie die had dropped her into a world with limited dimension.

"Jennie told me what happened."

"She doesn't know what happened."

"I do," he said. His headlights cast his face in planes and angles, and for once, he looked his age.

"You're not going to stop me," Hallie said.

"Let me help you."

Neither of them saying what it was that he couldn't stop and that she intended to do. The shotgun in her hand spoke her intentions loud and clear.

She cocked her head. "It's not going to take both of us to shoot him," she said. "Not that you would." She let her anger flare, because if she could make him take one step backwards—just one—she would know that she was right, that this was the right path. "Because you've already told me where you stand. And it's all about the rules, isn't it? Because you know what's coming—you've known what was happening for a while now. You could have stopped it before Lorie died, before *Dell* died. But no. It has to be legal. It has to be right. And we'll pretend the world is all—pretend there's hope and justice and the sun coming up every morning and everything will be okay if we just really really want it to be."

The skin around her eyes was tight as a drum. Her words were tight, too, as spare and mean as an old dog left to die on a battlefield.

They stood like that for a long moment, like it was a standoff, which it wasn't. Hallie had a loaded shotgun in her hands. Boyd had a pistol in a holster with the flap still snapped closed. But she wanted him to push her, wanted it to be on him, wanted him to force her to shoot out his tires or threaten him or even punch him. She wanted him to do it because he was kind or concerned or something—just goddamned *something*.

"Hallie . . ." Boyd struggled with what he wanted to say. "This—" He gestured with his right hand, attempting to encompass the prairie. He was wearing that same bulky black watch, and Hallie thought the top of her head might blow off from the fury, from looking at that watch. Something about it—the watch against bone, made him human—individual—to her. Made him Boyd. And she didn't want him to be human, didn't want to remember a moment when they'd wanted the same thing or seemed to understand each other. She wanted him to be Teedt or Sally Mazzolo or even Ole.

If one of them had stopped her, she would have blown a hole in their radiator and gone right on, like she was the Terminator back from the future, put together from scrap and a clockwork heart.

"I'm going to leave now," she said. *Stop talking to me. Go away.* "You're going to let me."

Boyd spoke slowly, as if he knew he had to choose his words carefully. "I'm not asking you to let me take care of this. Or saying that you shouldn't be angry. Because you should be, you should be really angry." He took a step toward her. "But it's not going to work, Hallie. I can *see* that it's not. Martin is— He gets more powerful. With every sacrifice. Every ritual."

Hallie considered the fire giant, how it had snuffed out Lorie like she was nothing. They cremated bodies at, like, two thousand degrees, and it took hours. Martin's power, what was required to reduce someone to bone and ash, took seconds, was way beyond funeral parlors and cremations. Hallie didn't care.

She didn't care.

If Boyd couldn't understand that. Maybe he couldn't understand anything.

"I don't care," she told him.

Boyd's hands clenched into fists. "I do," he said.

When Hallie'd been a kid out on the middle of the prairie in the middle of the night, she had sworn she could hear traffic in downtown Rapid City. Her father would tell her she was crazy, and the two of them would walk clear out away from the house, lie on their backs in the prairie grass, and listen. And maybe she hadn't really been able to hear downtown Rapid City traffic, but she could hear cars on the road six miles from the ranch, hear the whine of a semi changing gears out on the interstate.

And right now, she heard the deep rumble of cars or pickup trucks. The sound half-hidden by the muffling fog and the undercurrent of the early-morning prairie waking up, by their conversation and their own idling vehicles. Maybe they were several miles away, maybe it was someone's family car, or a couple of pickup trucks on the way to town for breakfast or the paper.

But Hallie knew it wasn't.

Boyd unsnapped the flap on his holster. Clearly he knew, too.

"You have a plan for this?" Hallie asked.

Boyd stepped up next to her. "There's something I need to tell you," he said. "About what I've been dreaming."

"Yeah? Now's not really a good time." She stepped up and turned so that they were not quite back to back. She raised her shotgun. The fog wasn't all that thick, but it obscured things so she couldn't see more than thirty or forty feet in any direction. And it was starting to rain.

Dell nudged Hallie's elbow, kept nudging it, like she was trying to push her somewhere—closer to Boyd, farther away, Hallie couldn't tell. Her elbow was numb and cold, and she didn't need that right now. She moved away from Dell, a step closer to Boyd.

A flash, blue white like lightning but everywhere at once, blinded her. She stepped forward. Boyd grabbed the back of her shirt and hauled her backwards. She heard them, felt them, the rush of something big inches in front of her, the roar of pickup engines revving high and hot. She blinked furiously against the afterflash from the lightning. When she could finally see again, Pete's truck was three-quarters across the road directly in front of them, stray bits of gravel plinking against the fender of Boyd's car from its spinning stop.

Two men slid out the passenger door, both of them armed. Pete appeared from the other side, a grin plastered on his face, his eyes wide—Hallie could see a rim of white around the edges. Dell drifted across the gap toward him. Sarah Hale chose that moment to drift right through Hallie's right shoulder. She almost dropped her shotgun.

"You are really starting to piss me off, Hallie."

Martin strode around the back of Hallie's pickup truck. Hallie had to move sharply to the right to watch him and Pete and the other men all at once. Boyd had already moved, as if he'd known where Martin was before he even announced himself. The truck Martin had arrived in lurked behind Hallie's pickup, like a rumbling black shadow, cutting off their escape.

Hallie tried to smile at him, pretend this was all a game and she knew it. But she couldn't do it, could only twitch her lips. She pointed her shotgun straight at his chest instead, got some small satisfaction out of the gesture.

Martin looked at the shotgun, looked at her.

Then he smiled.

32

Hallie's grip tightened on the shotgun. She could do it—that's what she told herself—she could shoot him right now, while he stood there and smiled. She could. She counted up everything he'd done, all the people he'd already killed. He needed to die, right?

"Hallie, don't," Boyd's voice practically in her ear. She'd forgotten how close he was, surprised she hadn't felt his breath against the back of her neck.

"No." Not sure whether she was talking to Boyd or Martin. She took a step—toward Martin—away from Boyd.

Martin held up his hand. "I've tried to explain to you," he said.

"How many women have you killed?" She didn't have to listen to this.

Thunder rumbled ominously above them. A flash of lightning bright enough to irradiate bones momentarily scattered the mist and half-blinded Hallie. She blinked. Blinked again. Afterimages danced like ghosts before her eyes.

Martin held out his hand, palm upward. Just above this outstretched palm was a small irregularly shaped ball of blue white fire. "This is the power I have," he said. "I can bring rain to people who have none. I can stop a downpour, prevent a flood. As my power continues to grow, I'll be able to change the paths of hurricanes, to reroute hailstorms away from precious crops, to fill lakes and streams. The world will be a better place."

"You've got to be fucking kidding me," Hallie said.

Martin frowned.

"You kill people." Hallie couldn't believe she actually had to explain this.

"For the greater good."

Pete stepped forward and stood behind Martin's left shoulder. His pistol was nickel plated with a leather grip and fancy scrollwork on the barrel. Hallie wondered if he'd ever used it before.

"I won't let you kill anyone else," Hallie said.

"Stop me."

With no more warning than that, he flung the fireball at her. Before it left his hand—before Hallie even realized it was going to leave his hand—Boyd grabbed her around the waist and dived for the ground. The fireball slammed into the hood of Boyd's car and exploded with a shriek like a wounded cougar. Hallie rolled, bright pain where her hip had hit the ground, and fetched up behind her pickup truck, leaning against the fender.

She could hear crackling fire, the acrid smell of plastic burning. "Boyd?" she called in a loud half whisper.

"Right here."

His voice came from three feet directly behind her. She almost shot him, so surprised/relieved/pissed off to hear his voice.

"Shit," she said.

"Stay here," Boyd said in a tight hard voice.

"Wait—fuck!" Because he was up and walking around the edge of the truck while Hallie scrambled, cursing, to her feet. She slammed herself tight against the pickup cab and pointed her shotgun across the hood of the truck to cover him. Because what the *hell* did he think he was doing?

Then—fuck. Fuck! Because suddenly she got it—she did. What he'd been saying earlier, what he'd been trying to tell her, what his dreams had no doubt been telling him for days.

He thought he would die here.

Well, fuck him.

Not if she could help it.

"Stop!" she yelled. By which she meant everyone.

Boyd's hands were out to the side, away from his pistol, which he had holstered once more, though Hallie noticed that the flap was still unsnapped.

Martin's hands were half-raised, too, and Hallie'd be damned if he was going to have the chance to make another one of those fire-balls. She fired her shotgun over his head. Everyone, except Boyd, looked at her.

"I said stop."

"We need to talk," Boyd said.

"Enough talking," Hallie said.

Boyd continued as if Hallie hadn't spoken. "You're in a bind," he said to Martin. "I get that. I do. Even if you've covered your tracks perfectly, even if you kill us." He gestured in a way that encompassed him and Hallie both. "Even if you save the world." He took a step forward. "Someone will be looking. Hallie's dad? He's going to notice that she's gone. Ole? Even if he thinks I'm a pain in the ass—which he doesn't—he's going to come looking."

He took another step forward.

Hallie wished she knew what in hell he was doing.

"What are you saying?" Martin asked.

"I'm saying we can make a deal."

"No, we can't," said Hallie.

"Fuck that," said Pete. He waved his gun at Boyd. "He doesn't want to make a deal," he said to Martin. "What kind of deal is he going to make? Neither one of them is going to keep their mouths shut. Hallie—hell—you know she's never shut her mouth her whole life. And this guy?" He waved the gun again, actually waggled it, like he'd forgotten he was even holding it. "Hell, he's the goddamned Boy Scout of the fucking century, this one. You think he'll walk away? It ain't gonna happen."

Pete's voice rose, but the more agitated he became, perversely, the more rock steady he held the gun in his hand. When he finished, he was pointing it directly at Boyd's head, though he was looking straight across the road at Hallie.

"Come on out from behind that truck," he said to her. "I want to see you."

Boyd half turned without taking his eyes off Martin. "Stay right where you are."

"Boyd . . ."

"It's all right," he said. "Don't worry about it."

Hallie took a half step to her right, still partly concealed by the bumper and the gloomy morning mist. "Don't *worry* about it?"

Boyd looked pale but determined, and Hallie realized she was every bit as pissed at him as she was at Pete and Martin—for playing his hand, whatever it was, without her.

Pete took a step closer to Boyd. "I'll shoot him. Goddamnit, Hallie, I mean it."

"You shoot him," Hallie said, "I shoot you. Simple."

Pete grinned. "Damn, Hallie," he said. "You're something else, you know that? Martin here, he wanted you to be the first sacrifice, you know. Way back. But you left too soon. He had to find someone else. But it should have been you."

A chill ran down Hallie's spine, and she knew it wasn't from a ghost. Dell drifted toward Pete, like she was drawn on a string. She reached out and touched his face. He shifted his head against his shoulder, like brushing away a pesky fly.

Hallie was so angry, she was surprised she could still function. So amazingly pissed at everyone: at Martin for every single woman he had killed, at Pete for helping him, at Boyd for playing out a hand he hadn't let her in on. She was even—maybe most—pissed at Dell for dying and leaving this mess behind.

"Did you kill her?" Hallie asked. The wind rose sharp and dry, eating away the mist like it had never existed. Green-black lightning, like the glow of a black light, cracked a dozen yards above their heads.

"I don't—," Martin began.

"Not you," Hallie said. She nodded at Pete. "You. Did you kill her? Because she wasn't a sacrifice. It wasn't about the 'greater good' or making the world a better place. She didn't disappear. She was killed. Because she found out something. She tried to tell the sheriff, maybe she tried to tell me, I don't know. She had to be stopped. So, I want to know, Pete.

"Were you the one who killed her?

"Because she liked you, you know. I always thought you were an ass. But Dell actually liked you."

"Hallie." Boyd's voice was full of warning.

She ignored him.

"Seriously, Pete," she said. "Dell liked you." Each word like a pistol shot, satisfaction in the way Pete flinched like he'd been hit.

"Shut up," he said, his growl like a wounded wolf.

"Enough," Martin said.

"It had to be you, Pete," Hallie continued relentlessly. "Did you get right up close to her? Did you kiss her? Did you tell her everything would be okay?" She moved to the front of the pickup as she spoke, could feel the rumble of the idling engine in her forearm as it rested on the hood.

Pete's hand trembled, the gun shaking. Lightning and thunder above them, the rumble rattling so deep in Hallie's chest that it felt as if the ground were shaking, as if they were on a badly lit carnival fun ride.

"I didn't kill her," Pete said, his eyes wide and white rimmed. "I didn't. I wouldn't have killed her."

"I said stop!" Martin shouted, and raised his hand, filled with fire.

Hallie shot him full in the chest. The impact knocked him backwards off his feet.

Pete roared. "I did not *kill* her!" He fired wildly, not caring whom he hit. His men dropped their guns and crawled behind Pete's pickup.

Boyd winged Pete in his gun arm, but not before Pete got off a final shot, hitting Boyd in the leg. He collapsed to the ground like a puppet whose strings had been cut.

Shit.

Boyd's hands were on his leg, blood seeping through his fingers, spreading across the crisp fabric of his khaki pants. Hallie crossed the short distance between them, grabbed him by the collar, and dragged him backwards—no conversation, no ceremony—get it done.

Out of the corner of her eye, she saw Martin struggle to his feet, and she realized with horror that although his shirt was shredded, he wasn't bleeding.

"You can't shoot him," Boyd said through gritted teeth.

"Jesus Christ!" Hallie said. "You might have mentioned that earlier."

"That was a mistake, Hallie," said Martin.

"Can you get in the truck if I cover you?" Hallie asked Boyd.

"Leave me," Boyd said. "It's the only way you'll get out of here."

"I'm not leaving you, you stupid ass," Hallie said.

Martin took a step toward them.

"Fuck!" Hallie yelled. She rose and stood between Boyd and Martin.

Boyd levered himself to his feet, leaning heavily against the door of the pickup. "Hallie—"

"Shut up."

She raised her shotgun. Maybe it couldn't hurt him, but it would buy them a minute, maybe two. Maybe it would be enough. Though she knew that it wouldn't.

Behind her, Boyd's breathing was sharp and quick. Dell had left Pete, was beside her again, like they were finally in this together, finally standing against Martin. Together.

Then, the rest of them were there, too, all her ghosts in front of her, like the first wave, like Hallie's own ghostly suicide squad, which would be funny under other circumstances—a suicide squad of the dead. The ghosts didn't look at Martin or Pete, who was still on the ground swearing. They looked dead-on, straight at Hallie, like they'd never looked at her before, like she was the only interesting thing on the whole empty prairie, like she was the world.

Martin closed the gap between them, his hands working intricately, drawing a symbol in the air. Hallie raised her shotgun. The ghosts stared at Hallie. Boyd put his hand on her shoulder. It trembled from shock.

"Just go," he said.

"No."

The fireball formed in Martin's hand. He made a pass with his other hand, and it grew. It flickered, burst frantically forth like a miniature sun flare, and died. He looked from his hand to Hallie, puzzlement writ large across his face. He stepped forward. The ghosts widened their semicircle around Hallie until they floated exactly halfway between Hallie and Martin. Dell put her hand on Hallie's arm, a white-hot shock but comforting in a way.

Martin took another step forward and stumbled before catching himself up sharp, his face pale. He raised his hand and—Hallie assumed this wasn't by design—thrust it into the center of the ghosts.

It felt as if a needle had been plunged into her brain, like she was burning from the inside out and freezing at the same time, all of them connected in that moment, like a chain—Hallie to Dell to the other ghosts to Martin. Hallie's knees buckled. She caught herself and looked up in time to see Martin stumble backwards with a look of shock and pain on his face.

He shook his head, like a dog shaking off river water. He raised his hand again, the ball of fire re-formed, but this time it was sputtery and tiny, more pale pink and orange than bright blue white. He lifted his arm to throw it. It fizzled and went out.

Hallie didn't hesitate. She shot him again, then turned and wrenched open the door of the pickup and wrestled Boyd inside. She turned back, thinking to shoot out the tires on Pete's pickup. Martin was already back up on his knees. He held a dark cloth—soaked in blood? His hands wove a quick intricate pattern. Sparks, little more than the snap of static electricity spit from his fingertips.

Hallie raised her shotgun. If she shot him now—

The window next to her head shattered. Dull thump of a bullet right into the seat cushion. Pete was on his feet again, as likely to shoot one of his own men as Hallie or Boyd, but dangerous all the same.

Hallie reluctantly put up her gun, dived into the cab, and got them the hell out of there.

33

Hallie didn't stop until she was five miles, three section line roads, and a dry creek bed away. Her hands were shaking, which pissed her off. Pissed her off *more*. And she was actually all right with that. Pissed off was better than scared or helpless.

They were on a long stretch of county road, heading west. Hallie scanned the highway east and west, scanned the surrounding fields, too, because you never knew—maybe Martin could fly. Seeing nothing, not a single vehicle, not even a few head of cattle, she pulled onto the first faintly outlined lane she came to, down to a tiny creek with an old barn that leaned at least thirty degrees in the direction of the prevailing winds and dead brown grass that came halfway up the windows of the truck.

Boyd's hands were still clamped tight around his upper leg, his breathing harsh in the closed space of the pickup cab.

Hallie dug behind the seat and came up with a couple of T-shirts, old but clean. She ripped his pant leg open and laid the T-shirts over the bleeding bullet wound like two thick pads, then put his hands back so he could continue to apply pressure. There was no exit wound, which made things both more and less complicated. He needed a hospital, and the nearest one was over thirty miles away.

When she finally spoke, Hallie's voice sounded odd and echoey. "How does his magic work?" she asked. "Do you know?"

"What?"

"When we left, he didn't have any magic. He couldn't make those fireballs. Do you know—have you dreamed about that? Does using the magic drain him for a while? How long before he follows us?"

"Uhm." He licked his lips. "Fifteen—I don't know—twenty minutes, maybe."

"How sure are you?" Hallie asked. She knew she sounded like she didn't care that he was injured, like she didn't care that they were in trouble like you wouldn't believe, like she wasn't worried. Eddie Serrano would have known—maybe her father, too—when she sounded like that, like everyday business as usual, when she didn't say, *Are you all right?* or *I'll take care of things,* or *Don't worry, it'll be fine*—that was when she was crazy with worry, so much worry, she couldn't talk about it, because if she talked about it, she couldn't go on. "How sure?" she asked again.

"Not very," he said. "Look, I don't think . . . I wasn't supposed to be here." He looked around the cab of the truck, half-amazed, like maybe he really wasn't there at all, like maybe he was in a dream and he'd lost track.

"You're an ass," Hallie said. "You thought you would die back there? You *dreamed* it? And you didn't think to mention it to me? Or stay the hell out of the way? Or, you know, not die?"

Boyd huffed a short laugh. "Well, I didn't," he pointed out. He shifted in the seat and pushed the heel of his hand down hard on the folded T-shirts, which made him grunt and slide sideways an inch or two before he caught himself and leaned tiredly against the window.

"You need help," she said.

He nodded. He pulled out his radio, but the antenna and the front panel had gotten smashed all to hell. He dug in his pocket for his cell phone and retrieved it with a grimace. "We can call it in," he said. "You can leave me here. It—I would be all right."

"I'm not going to leave you here," Hallie said.

Dell was up against the dashboard and the windshield, and for the first time, Hallie wanted to reach out and take her hand, to say, *We're in this together, right?*

Right.

She just needed a plan.

"When Lorie died," she said. She leaned across the seat and slowly moved Boyd's hands so she could check his gunshot wound. "It was the fire giant/thing/whatever again."

"The one no one sees?"

"No one but me," she agreed. The bleeding, she was pleased to see, had slowed though the wound was still seeping blood sluggishly. Boyd looked even paler than he had a few moments ago, and when she put her hand on his arm it was shaking. She turned sideways so she could see him and still take in a good 360 degrees around the truck. So she could be ready. "It came and we tried to run. And, I don't know, stupid, the only choice, I'm not sure. But it was *there*. The church was already burning.

"It reached down." Hallie still remembered the descent of that hand, just above her head. "It reached down for me. Then it stopped. That's when it killed Lorie."

"Because it couldn't kill you?" Boyd struggled to sit up straighter. "Is that what you're saying?"

"I don't know," Hallie admitted. "Is it? How does his magic work? What do you know?"

Boyd shook his head. "Blood. Sacrifice. Power from the blood and from forcing the different cultural magics together. Like a . . . like a forced melding. But beyond that, I don't know."

"Are ghosts magic?" she said.

Boyd frowned. "What?"

"Yeah, sorry, never mind." This was a stupid conversation. Or a conversation she shouldn't be inflicting on him. Which made it stupid. She opened the pickup door and got out, retrieving her shotgun from under her feet and the box of shells from behind the seat. She reloaded the shotgun. It was a pump-action Remington and held four shells plus one in the chamber if she wanted. There were still two shells left, but Hallie'd learned the hard way that it paid to be prepared for the worst.

The ghosts had done something to Martin when he'd touched them. She was pretty sure, though trying to remember exactly what was tougher. She remembered his hand coming up, the blue white ball of flame. She remembered the needle-sharp pain in her head, down her spine. Dell floating beside her. It was unfair that she wasn't here for real, that Hallie couldn't talk to her. She was never going to be able to ask Dell why she'd gotten involved with Martin in the first place, what she'd known and when, never going to sit down across the table from her and share experiences neither of them would ever tell anyone else.

Hallie shook her head sharply, finished reloading the shotgun, and tossed the box of shells back behind the seat.

She climbed back into the cab, and when she shut the door, Boyd said, "Supernatural."

"What?"

"Ghosts," he said. "Ghosts are supernatural."

Hallie looked at him. He had his back angled against the door and his bad leg propped half across the seat. He was a mess, his face pale as porcelain, his pants shredded, at least the one leg, and his shirt crumpled, dirt ground deep into the creases. And there was something about his eyes, like he wasn't quite seeing her, even when he was looking directly at her. "Are you delusional?" she said.

He laughed.

Okay, yeah, not the smartest thing she'd ever said. And he'd been shot, so if he was delusional, it wasn't a surprise. She humored him—sort of. "Supernatural is magic, right?"

"I don't know," he admitted. "I don't . . . think so."

"Magic is supernatural?"

He thought about that, then nodded. "Yeah," he said. "Yeah, okay."

She thought about that herself, then nodded sharply and started the truck again. "Ghosts and magic," she said as she backed the truck around. "Okay."

When they were back on the county road, Hallie said, "Can I use your phone?"

Boyd looked at the phone on the seat like he'd forgotten he had it. "Yeah," he said. "Sure. What happened to yours?"

"I lost it," Hallie said, picking up Boyd's phone, and tried to figure out the buttons without actually taking her eyes off the road.

A minute later, "Brett?"

"Jesus, Hallie! Where are you?" Brett sounded both angry and scared and not remotely calm.

"Where are *you?*"

"Where am I? Where do you think I am? I'm at the church. We're all—"

"Is Ole there?"

"Yeah. *Everyone,* Hallie."

"Is the ambulance there?"

"No." Boyd's voice was unexpectedly strong, though when Hallie looked at him, he was still slumped against the door.

"Yes," Hallie said. "I can drop you off there. You can get—"

"Don't go after him alone."

"I think—" Hallie kept picturing that last moment over and

over—Martin and the ghosts and her. "Yeah, I think I can. Plus," she couldn't help adding, "you're not in any shape to help me."

"Hallie?" Brett's voice sounded tinny and far away.

"Yeah," Hallie said to her, "listen, I'm—"

"No. *Listen*." Boyd's voice might be weaker, but there was a thread of determination running through it that demanded Hallie's attention. "I—I'm not sure I can explain this," he said.

"Hold on," Hallie told Brett. She slowed to turn west onto another old gravel road.

Boyd wiped the back of his hand across his face and left a streak of blood along his jaw. Hallie bit her lip. "Something's—," Boyd began. "Something's happening to me. Blood loss. Shock. I don't know. But I can see—I keep seeing." He stopped, frustrated. "It's like when I'm asleep, but I'm not. Right now, I'm not asleep." He stopped again, like he'd meant to explain everything to her in a logical, coherent way, only the words came out all wrong.

"What, like you're having visions right now?" Hallie asked him. "What are you seeing? How?"

"I think . . . I think it's important for me to be there."

"Where?" Hallie demanded, and part of it was a test. Because he couldn't possibly know what she had in mind.

"The Seven Mile," he said. "I need to be with you when you lure Martin to Seven Mile Creek."

Or maybe he could. Shit.

"Brett," Hallie said into the phone. "There's been a change of plans."

34

Hallie could see the strobe of crossbar lights at St. Mary's church from a mile away despite the persistent gloom. The fire appeared to be mostly out, but there were cars lining the road for at least a quarter mile, a good half dozen sets of flashing lights in the church parking lot itself; sheriff's cars, an ambulance, and, Hallie guessed by now, a state trooper or two.

Hallie pulled up just short of the long line of cars and pickup trucks, backed into a grassed-over lane. She put the truck in neutral but kept the engine idling. She checked Boyd's wound. He said something to her that she couldn't understand and so ignored.

"Boyd," she said.

"No," he said, sharp and hard in a way she hadn't heard before. "This is my decision, not yours."

"I could make you—," she began, then couldn't go on with it, because he was supposed to be dead, had *expected* to die, and he hadn't. It was all, suddenly, a huge pile of *shouldn't happen* and *didn't exist* and *couldn't be*—ghosts and sorcery and prophetic dreams and fire. And Lorie, dead up there when she shouldn't be, didn't deserve to be.

Her hip ached from hitting the ground earlier. She wiped a hand across her face. "You know what?" she said. "Fine. You do what you want." *But you can't make me care.* Like telling herself that would make it true. She didn't look at him as she scrounged greasy old rags from under the seat and wiped up some of the blood on the seat beside him.

"Hallie," Boyd said.

"Shut up."

"Damnit, Hallie. I robbed an ambulance for you!" Brett's voice directly outside Hallie's window startled her so bad, she slammed her left elbow hard against the doorframe. Then, before Brett could see Boyd, could register the bullet wound and the blood on the seat, Hallie hopped out of the pickup truck and shut the door behind her.

"Tell me what's going on, Hallie," Brett said. She pulled pressure bandages, gauze, and a couple of bottles whose contents Hallie couldn't identify from underneath her coat.

"Did you bring water?" Hallie asked.

"Hallie—"

"Do you remember much from that first aid course we took in high school?"

"I'm six hours away from my EMT certification," Brett said after a pause.

Hallie blinked. "You are?"

"You've been gone, Hallie. Things happen."

A sharp flash of lightning, ten miles or so to the east, lit bright against the clouds.

Shit.

"Do you trust me?" Hallie asked.

Brett looked at her. A pickup truck and a car following drove slowly up the road. Another bright flash of lightning, closer, and Brett's face looked like flint or steel, hard planes and edges. The pickup truck went on up the road, but the car slowed. The passenger window rolled down.

"Everything all right?" It was Jake Javinovich.

"Yeah," Hallie said. "We're all good." By which, she meant no.

"What's going on up there?" Jake asked, leaning forward, his arm laid along the back of the seat.

"Fire, I guess," Hallie said. "Figured we'd stay out of it."

"Yeah." Jake's head bobbed up and down. "Okay, yeah." He rolled up his window and drove on.

Brett let out a deep breath, like she'd been holding it. "All right, Hallie," she said. "But this had better be good."

"Jesus Christ!" Brett said a minute later, when they were around on the passenger side of the truck and she got a look at Boyd's leg. The swearing was an indicator, because Brett didn't swear that often, not like Hallie. "I can't fix this!" she said.

"Just . . ." Boyd spoke before Hallie could, like he needed to retain something, some small bit of control. "The bleeding's stopped. Mostly. You can wrap it, right?"

"Hallie," Brett said, like reason was still on the table. "We've got to get him up. . . ." She gestured with her chin toward St. Mary's and the ambulance.

"Yeah. That's what I said." Hallie helped Boyd slide over to the middle of the pickup's bench seat. "I'm sorry," she said to Brett. "We don't have time." Brett looked at her for a long, uncomfortable moment; then she sighed and climbed into the cab.

Lightning flashed again, nearly overhead, the sharp crack of thunder immediate.

Hallie drove them back out onto the county road for a mile and a half, then turned west along a well-traveled gravel road. When she came back out onto pavement again, about five miles altogether from the church, she pulled into a small layby and got out of the truck. She left the driver's door open.

She held Boyd's gaze as she took out his phone again and called Martin.

"Hallie," Martin said, smooth as silk, like she hadn't shot him twice in the chest an hour ago.

"Let's finish this," she said.

"It doesn't have to be like this," Martin said. "You could join me. We could do this together."

Hallie gripped the phone so tight, she was surprised it didn't break. Martin didn't wait for her to respond, but kept right on talking about saving the world, about how it would be worth the cost, about the sacrifices that had to be made.

You *sacrifice, you son of a bitch,* Hallie thought, boggled that he was that self-centered, that he actually couldn't understand why anyone couldn't be talked around to his way of seeing things.

"Martin," she broke in as he was in the middle of a long convoluted sentence about drought conditions in southern Florida. "I wouldn't kill for power."

"You shot me," Martin pointed out. "Twice."

"You threw a fireball at me."

"I don't have to talk to you, Hallie," Martin said.

"Because—what? You can kill me anytime you want? We both know that's not true."

A short silence on the other end of the line. "What do you want?" This time his voice was sharp edged and dark.

"I'm at Seven Mile Creek, Martin. You remember? That's where Dell died. Where you killed her. You want me? Come and get me."

She broke the connection before he had the chance to reply.

35

Hallie got back into the pickup. Brett had used the time to replace the bloody T-shirts with a pressure bandage. Boyd looked better, less pale. Or, she hoped he did, hoped she wasn't just fooling herself, hadn't made a grim and terrible mistake when she didn't insist on getting him in that ambulance and headed to the hospital.

"Tell me," Boyd said. He sounded rough, like he'd just come off a twenty-four-hour shift. Hallie put her hand on his good leg, because she was so tired of being in this alone. And even though she was still alone—what was he going to do to help her, after all, he couldn't even walk—it made her feel calmer, more centered. He laid his hand over hers and squeezed. It was warm, his hand, and so . . . human, like no one had ever touched her before.

"He'll come," she said.

"Hallie . . ."

She shook her head. There was nothing he could say. It had to happen. Martin would keep killing people. He would burn the ranch and hurt people she knew and maybe destroy a whole town because he could, he could do that. They'd talk about freak storms and tragic acts of God, about the horrible magnificence of nature and the destruction it wreaks, but it would be Martin.

She would face him, win or lose. Her only choice was whether she faced him alone. Or with Boyd.

"What exactly is going on?"

Both Boyd and Hallie turned to look at Brett. Hallie assessed her—the Brett she'd always known, the Brett she'd become, was becoming, would someday become. She wanted Brett to come with them, to take care of Boyd, make sure the bandages stayed in place, that he had water, that she could drive the truck, and Boyd, out of there if things went bad.

On the other hand, Brett didn't know anything about . . . well, anything. And she needed to know. Hallie figured she had about fifteen minutes to fill her in.

"Everything I'm going to tell you," Hallie said to Brett as she pulled back onto the road, "is fantastic. Okay? And I don't mean fantastic, like, *awesome*. But fantastic, like fantasy, like things you wouldn't believe in a million years. But you have to believe it because it's the truth, because it's bad, because it's going to get worse, and because I'm sorry—I really am—but you're going to be right in the middle of it."

Boyd leaned his head against the back of the seat, his injured leg stretched so that Brett had to pull her own legs in and to the side to accommodate him. His breath came quick and shallow, but Hallie knew he was listening to every word she said.

She took a deep breath.

"Martin Weber kills women so he can use their blood to control the weather. He burned my father's barn as a threat to me. He burned St. Mary's church because he was trying to kill me. To stop me from trying to stop him. He killed Lorie. He killed Dell. He's killed at least three other women, too."

Silence.

"I—" Hallie stopped. This was harder than telling Boyd. This was Brett, practical, rational Brett, who wouldn't even pretend to believe in the Tooth Fairy when she was seven. "I see ghosts, Brett," she said, because even if it was hard, there was no other way to say it—not for Hallie—other than straight out.

"I see Dell's ghost."

She looked over, and she could actually see Dell right then, floating just in front of Brett, as if for once she knew what the conversation was about, as if she knew they were talking about her. "I can see the ghosts of the girls that Martin's killed."

"Martin hasn't—," Brett began, latching on to the one comprehensible fact.

"Martin shot Boyd, Brett," Hallie said tightly.

"Technically, Pete shot me," Boyd offered.

"Shut up," Hallie said.

Brett shifted so she could look at Boyd's face. "Martin *shot* you?"

"Pete—"

"Yes! Martin kills people, Brett!"

Brett chewed on her lower lip. "These—" She coughed. "These 'ghosts' . . . they haunt you?"

"Yeah," Hallie said after a moment. "I guess you could call it that. They want something, want me to do something for them. And they show me . . . things."

"Is this, like, posttraumatic stress?"

"No! It's not posttraumatic stress. It's I-actually-died-in-Afghanistan-then-came-back and now I see ghosts. Look, I don't care if you believe me. This is the way it is."

"And Martin controls the weather," Brett said, as if saying it in that way, flat, like a fact, would force Hallie to see how ridiculous it was.

"Yes," Hallie said. "I think he draws the energy from storm lightning. I think he's pulling too much, and I think it's starting to backfire on him. That's why this." She waved her hand at the pervasive gloom outside the truck cab. It had to be at least noon by now, maybe later, but it felt like five o'clock in the morning all dark gray clouds and knee-high ground fog and spattering rain. "Martin blew up Boyd's car tonight with a fireball. He burned Lorie to ash and bone at St. Mary's church. Didn't Jennie tell you?"

"Jennie," Brett said heavily, "was not exactly coherent."

"You mean, you didn't believe her."

"No one believed her! They gave her a sedative to calm her down."

"I can let you out," Hallie said.

"What?"

"I can stop the truck, and I can drop you off right here. There should be a cell phone signal. Someone can pick you up. You'll be fine."

Brett was quiet for a long moment. She looked at Boyd, whose eyes were half-closed as he tried to brace himself against the vibration of the truck as it traveled down the highway. "Do you believe this?" she finally asked him.

Boyd seemed to consider his answer. "Everything she's telling you is true."

More silence.

Hallie slowed for the turn onto 54 South. She was sure she would reach Seven Mile Creek before Martin, but there were things to do once they were there, and she needed to know whether Brett was on board with this or not. From here until the end, everything had to work as planned—there would be no second chances.

"Look," Brett said, "what you're telling me is not possible. It's not. I'm studying psychiatry, for Christ's sake, Hallie! The mind—

people believe things all the time that just aren't true. And there's help. We help people."

"Someone shot Boyd," Hallie pointed out. "Someone killed Dell."

Brett worried at her lower lip some more. "Yeah," she said, sat up straighter in the seat. "Okay. *Okay*. Look, what you're telling me, it's not possible. It's not." She held up her hand. "I don't even want to talk about it. But—" She leaned forward to look around Boyd, looked *at* him, too, taking in his pale face and wounded leg. "—but you need me to help you? Yes. Absolutely. I will do that." Her voice was brisk and firm. Hallie knew she wouldn't waver either, no matter what happened, because once Brett decided, it was done.

Hallie turned onto Seven Mile Creek Road and drove slowly into the abandoned town of Jasper. The old Jasper church sat on the edge of town, roof completely collapsed and sagging into itself so the walls were only five or six feet high, all shattered gray wood and old framing. Everything else had been mostly flattened, and it was an eerie place to be today, with ground fog weaving in and around the uneven landscape. There was another half wall a block-length or so past the church and a crumbling chimney. Hallie turned and headed toward the creek, back to the place where Dell had died.

Boyd put his hand over hers again. She'd forgotten her own hand was still on his knee. He lifted her hand off his leg and held it. She wanted to squeeze his hand so tight, it would crush the bones in his fingers to dust, felt like that was the only way the feelings inside her—love and fear and hate—could be acknowledged and understood. She wanted something from him so desperately that it scared her—wanted him to stand with her, to believe in her—she didn't even know what it was that she wanted, but she wanted it bad.

Right now, though, he was the ticking clock, the thing that was saying, *This is how much time you have.* Not much. Because he needed more than a pressure bandage and a couple of ratty old T-shirts.

Finish this.

The words echoed in Hallie's head. For the first time, she actually, maybe, thought that she could.

She pulled off the old lane halfway down the quarter-mile stretch between Jasper and the old farmhouse. There were traces of gravel underneath the grass, everything, including the road itself, grown in since the tornado had destroyed the town, way back. She turned the pickup so it faced back the way they'd come, left it running with the headlights on.

It wasn't as if she didn't want Martin to find her.

She got out and stood, taking in the landscape around her. She was certain she was right. Really pretty certain she could stop Martin. But what if she couldn't? She wasn't alone. If she didn't stop him, if she failed, Boyd and Brett would die with her. She should have dumped Boyd at the church, left Brett behind with him. She shouldn't . . . she should have done this on her own.

"I need to be here." Boyd's words echoed her thoughts almost exactly, like he had seen inside her head.

"You were wrong before, about what was going to happen," she said. She didn't look at him when she spoke.

"I wasn't wrong," he told her. "Things changed."

"You're not . . ." Her voice was a half whisper, and she still wasn't looking at him, though she'd taken a step back, her legs tight up against the running board, because this wasn't a real conversation, they weren't really talking about life and death and dreams that foretold the future. They weren't.

"I thought you only saw these things in dreams."

"These are dreams," he said. "Because I'm—"

"Okay," she said quickly. "But you don't *know*. About whether they're *really* dreams and about whether—you're guessing."

"I'm not guessing," he said. "And neither are you."

She finally looked at him. "Brett can drive you out of here right now," she said. Her voice had gotten even softer, and she wasn't entirely sure why. "You need a doctor."

"Brett can drive herself out of here," Boyd said. He drew his pistol and handed it to Hallie. "But I'm staying." He made a gesture with his right hand. "Give me your shotgun," he said.

She studied his face, as if she could memorize each specific feature, as if she needed to. "I know what I'm doing," she said.

"So do I."

She tucked the gun into the waistband of her jeans, which seemed awkward and, frankly, dangerous, but there wasn't anything else to do with it, and Boyd was probably right. She would probably need it. She took a moment to scout the immediate area. Ghosts followed her as she circled the truck and assured herself that it was solidly right out in the open. There was Dell and Sarah and Karen and Jesse and—oh crap—Lorie. Which stopped her, like she couldn't breathe anymore.

Goddamnit.

Then there were two more ghosts, women she'd never seen before, but, hell—they were welcome. It was going to be a party.

Close to where Hallie had parked were two small outbuildings, like toolsheds or gatehouses. One was mostly collapsed in a heap of soft gray lumber. The other leaned strongly, like a gentle breeze might topple it. Hallie kicked in the door. In the distance, she heard a truck engine, not close, but out there.

She returned to the truck, and without a word between them, she helped Boyd out and over to the shed. He could barely put any weight on his right leg, and before he'd gone a half dozen steps, he was leaning nearly his whole weight on her.

This was a mistake. Her mistake.

But it was too late to argue about it now.

He stopped her when they reached the shed. "Not inside," he said.

She looked at him. "You can't—" *Run. Hide. Save yourself.* "They'll see you."

"It will be Martin and Pete," Boyd said. He looked at her, but his eyes were unfocused, like he wasn't quite seeing her. "And I want them to see me," he said. "I want them to know you're not alone."

Hallie looked at him for a long moment. "All right," she said with a sharp nod. She found an old wooden chair with no seat and one leg an inch shorter and a flat piece of board to lay across it. She helped him lower himself and handed him the shotgun, which he managed to hold in surprisingly steady hands.

"What you're seeing," she asked him after a moment. "It seems more—" She wasn't sure what word she wanted. "—accurate? Because I thought your dreams were symbolic. I thought you had to figure them out. You don't seem to be guessing here."

He shook his head, winced, and wiped a hand up across his cheekbone. "Right now?" he said. "It's like a movie. Not constant. It still comes and goes, but sometimes I can see you, for example. And it's just you. Right here. Right now. But at the same time, I see you thirty minutes from now. Or an hour. Or whenever."

"Jesus," Hallie said.

She left Boyd and walked farther into the open. There was a row of trees twenty yards or so from the old outbuildings. Not the farmhouse windbreak but a boundary for the town of Jasper. On this side, once, there had been groomed grass and monuments and flowers. On the other side, it would have been winter wheat or grazing cattle or bromegrass for hay. It took her a minute or two with the ground fog and the general gloominess of the day to find what she was looking for. She literally tripped over it, or over a broken fence post, sticking up about six inches, but obscured by the tall prairie grass.

She tested things a few times—two steps forward, a step back, several steps directly to the side, then forward again.

All right, she thought. She could do this. She knew where the line was, knew she could find it again when she needed to. She could make this work. She could.

She returned to the truck, where Brett was standing with her arms crossed, hunched against the damp. Hallie handed her the keys. "You should leave," she said.

"No," said Brett. "I told you I was in and I'm in. I'm not leaving."

"Well, here's the thing," Hallie said. "I don't know what you can do. I don't have a weapon for you. And I'm not sure I can protect you."

Brett looked at her thoughtfully. "The way I see it, you need two things."

"I do?"

"You need an observer. Someone who can—if everything goes completely to hell—if you don't . . . succeed. You need someone who can tell people what happened."

"And that'd be you?"

Brett shrugged. "It could be me," she agreed.

"What's the second thing?"

"Don't you think it's remotely possible, you might need an almost-EMT when this is over?"

For quite some time, Hallie had been hearing a vehicle. She'd assumed that whole time that it was Martin, and she'd been expecting him. Now she could see the filtered gray of headlights through the gloom turning onto the old road. They stopped. She could hear the idling engine as clear as if it were right in front of her, pulled up next to her own pickup.

"You know what?" Hallie said. "Let's hope those are good reasons, because it's now officially too late." She put her hand on Brett's arm. "Sorry," she said, because she really was. "Don't let them see you." Her grip on Brett's arm tightened. "I mean it."

Brett threw her cowboy hat through the open window of Hallie's truck and disappeared, down into the open field and the all-consuming ground fog.

36

Hallie stood alone in the dim pool of light cast against the curling fog by her headlights as Pete's big Ford pickup drove slowly into view. Ghosts—Dell, Sarah, Lorie, Karen—ranged behind her. She welcomed the cold they brought. She felt as if she had finally become as cold as they were, as if she finally belonged.

Dell drifted forward as the truck rolled to a stop less than ten feet in front of Hallie. She looked translucent, almost the color of the fog herself. Distant thunder rumbled overhead.

The truck's doors opened. In the glow of the dome light, Pete reached back and plucked a rifle off the rack. Martin's hands were empty. He stepped in front of Pete and stopped a foot or so away from where Dell was floating. She didn't look at him, but appeared to be studying Pete intently.

Pete was still wearing the same shirt, ripped and bloody along the left sleeve. He held the rifle rock steady in his hands, though, and he seemed calmer and more focused than the last time Hallie'd seen him.

"What are you so afraid of, Martin?" Hallie asked him, indicating Pete and his rifle with a sharp nod of her head. "It's not like I can shoot you."

He frowned. "I can shoot *you*, though. Have you shot. We could end this right now."

"Then do it," she said. Because it was still games to him; he still thought he controlled the field.

"I want you to understand," he said, shifting the ground slightly.

"No, you don't, you tried to kill me."

Martin didn't reply immediately. "I was . . . intemperate."

"Jesus, is that what you call it? Lorie *died*."

"But you didn't," he said. "*You* didn't."

"So what? You think I'm like you? I'm not like you."

"No," he said. "But you're not ordinary either, are you? If I could make you understand—"

"Why? Why? Because you think you're the hero? You think you're going to save the world? Because you think if you can just convince me, maybe you can convince other people, too. Maybe someday they'll understand. And all your awesome won't have to be a secret anymore? Is that what you think?"

"I've tried to explain, Hallie," he said in that patient-kind voice that turned out to be neither.

"There's a few things I have a little trouble getting past," Hallie continued. Sarah Hale bumped steadily against her left shoulder; Karen Olsen against her spine.

Another ghost flickered into view to Hallie's left. Shit. Who else had Martin buried here? This one wore low-slung jeans with huge bell-bottoms that covered her feet, heeled boots with squared-off toes. Her pale hair flat and straight, a long-collared shirt like something out of a movie from the seventies.

"How do you know all this?" Hallie asked him. "About magic and blood, about combining them?"

Martin smiled. Pete stalked between them and over to Hallie's truck. Hallie stepped to the side as he approached so he couldn't get behind her. He grinned at her and poked his gun into the pickup's cab then stood there, staring into the creeping gloom.

"My grandmother," Martin said, "lived in that farmhouse over there . . . oh, a long time before I was born. She moved in with us when I was five, but we used to drive out here, she and I. We'd sit in the car and look at where her old house had been and she'd tell me stories. She'd tell me how important it was to have power. How power could be had. I loved to listen to her, but I never thought they were anything more than stories.

"Then she showed me," he said. "What real power was and how to get it."

"Jesus Christ, Martin," Hallie said. "That's really pretty creepy."

"No," Martin was insistent. "No. It was . . . wonderful. Special. No one understood. They took her away from me. But I promised her. I promised."

Pete crossed between the trucks again—was he trying to distract her?

"Quit moving," she told him.

He kept on walking. She fired. The bullet hit the ground just in front of his right foot. He stumbled back a step and glared at her. "Stop it," she said. "I may not be able to shoot him," she indicated Martin with her chin, "but I can sure as hell shoot you."

Martin held a knotted cloth in his hands. She hadn't seen him produce it, but it was there, all the same. "They call what I do perversion magic, as if I'm perverted, but the truth is I'm the only one, the only one doing real magic. The others, they cling to their little colloquial rituals, because they're not willing to take the step, to—"

A flash of lightning so bright and close, the concussion knocked Hallie down. She scrambled to her knees, for her gun, for cover. Afterflash danced in front of her eyes, and everything seemed eerily silent, thunder still ringing in her ears. A second bolt struck, even closer than the first. Hallie rolled under her pickup. Where was Boyd? Brett? Were they all right?

She couldn't see anything, clouds so low and the sky as dark as midnight, though it was early afternoon still. She counted to ten, too quick, like the rhythm of her heart, scrambled out from under the truck and into the tall grass just beyond the old track she and Pete were parked on.

Shit.

She had to assume Brett was okay, hidden and safe. Because there was nothing Hallie could do right now if she wasn't. That left Boyd. And Pete and Martin.

She still couldn't see anything. The afterflash had faded but the fog was thicker, serious fog now, not just wispy ground-clinging stuff. Like pea soup, like fog never was in South Dakota in the fall. She could barely see her own pickup. *That's the way you want to play,* she thought grimly. *Works for me.*

I just want you to understand sure hadn't lasted very long.

She rose to a half crouch and circled to the back of her pickup. She couldn't see anything, but conversely, no one could see her. She slid across the narrow gap between her truck and Pete's and used her pocketknife to slash his two front tires.

No one was leaving until this was done. One way or another.

She used her own truck as a touchstone and circled wide, hoping she was judging correctly, that she would come to where Boyd was and that she wouldn't surprise him, that he wouldn't shoot her. Presumably he would know she was coming—because didn't he know the future?—but she'd pushed her luck enough already.

She stopped when she figured she'd crossed half the distance to take her bearings. Thunder still rumbled overhead. She could hear nothing on the ground, no rustle of dry grass, no cocking of guns. The ghosts were with her. Though she could barely see them in the fog, she could feel them with her like arctic winter breath against her skin.

She moved forward again. It felt . . . not at all like Afghanistan, actually, the fog and the damp and the land, all different. And she didn't have an army at her back. That was different, too.

"Hallie! Down!"

She dropped. Boyd's shotgun boomed. Once. Twice. A sharp cry behind her, then silence.

She rose, but stayed low, gun ready. She couldn't see Boyd. She couldn't see who he'd fired at.

Then she heard him coming toward her, his injured leg dragging.

"How the hell are you walking on that leg?" she asked quietly when Boyd emerged from the fog.

He shrugged. "Because I had to." He was pale, but not noticeably worse than the last time she'd seen him. She offered him her hand, but he waved her off. She moved in the direction of the cry she'd heard, and he covered her back. Just like that—no need for words.

She found Pete not five yards from where she'd been standing. He was still alive, still scrabbling for his gun. And crying. Which Hallie couldn't even blame him for, because he'd been shot in the gut and it must have hurt like hell.

"I'm sorry." Boyd looked shaken, though Hallie didn't know whether it was from shooting Pete or from his own wound. "I couldn't— He would have shot you."

She crouched beside Pete. He grabbed her shirt. "I never meant for her to die. You have to believe me. Believe that. Martin said I killed her, but I didn't. I *didn't*. I would have remembered if I'd killed her. Right? *Right*? I'd have remembered. . . ." He drifted off into incoherent mumbling.

Hallie unwound his fist from her shirt and rose. "Stay here," she said to Boyd. She put her hand on his arm, held it tight like she would never let him go. "You'll stay here, right?"

He looked at her. *Looked* at her. "I'll stay," he said.

When she released his arm, he grabbed her shirt and pulled her a half step back so she had to look at him again. He cupped her chin, looked at her for a moment without speaking, then gently turned her head thirty degrees to her right. "He's forty-five yards that way," he said. "He was headed almost straight north." He made an intersection, one hand over the other—the path she would follow, the one Martin was on. "That's all I can tell you."

She gave him a sharp nod, but she didn't say another word. She didn't think she could.

She'd gone about ten yards when she stopped and looked back, expected to find that he'd disappeared, that she was alone again, but she could still see him. The fog had lifted without her noticing, not completely, but she could see maybe twenty, thirty yards ahead now. To her left was the old storage building and the chair where Boyd had been sitting.

All right, she thought, oriented now. *All right.*

She found Martin not ten yards farther on, headed straight for her.

"Hallie." His face was completely emotionless, like he had been wiped clean. "I heard gunshots. I thought—"

"Thought maybe it was all over?" Hallie said. "Thought maybe Pete had saved you the trouble?"

"I never wanted it to come to this," he said.

"You *always* wanted it to come to this." The fog continued to lift, though it was still gray and overcast, low clouds with occasional flashes of lightning so high, they looked like distant explosions. Hallie wasn't sure why the fog was lifting, and she didn't care, assumed there were limits to his power even now, to how long he could sustain things, how much blood was required.

She was hyperaware of where they stood, so close. She moved a few paces to her left. Martin turned with her, but he didn't move.

Move, goddamnit.

She paced back to her right. Dell and the other ghosts were at her back. She wanted them in front of her. Why could they not just this once do what she wanted?

"You can't defeat me," Martin said.

"It's so easy," Hallie told him, pacing back and forth, coming a little closer to him all the time. "Ole has bodies. I gave him bodies."

"You think a jail can hold me?" He took a step back, away from Hallie.

Yes, thank you.

"I don't know," she said. The grass was taller just beyond the two of them, clustering in shadowed mounds and low spots, like tiny limestone sinks. "But you sure won't be able to pretend you're doing this for charity anymore."

"I could rule the entire world," Martin said. Dell drifted in front of Hallie. Martin took two more steps away from her. "I control the weather. I'm immune to guns." He looked pointedly at the pistol in her hands.

"And yet, you're backing up, Martin," Hallie said. "Why is that?"

He stopped. "I'm not afraid of you," he said.

"You should be."

She dropped her gun, took two quick steps forward, and hit him as hard as she could in the chest with her fists. He stumbled three quick steps back but didn't fall.

Hallie grinned at him without humor and stepped toward him, into the old Jasper cemetery.

Cold descended like a blizzard off Mount McKinley. Ghosts rose from every old grave. Ghosts everywhere—Hallie's ghosts and strangers, surrounding her and Martin.

Ghosts.

So cold.

Martin staggered again, but he still didn't fall. The ghosts alone were not enough. Hallie had known they wouldn't be, had known since back on the road when Boyd got shot. She'd known. She took a deep breath and grabbed Dell, which immediately started a chain—Dell to Sarah to Lorie to all the ghosts in the cemetery . . .

To Martin.

Pain stabbed through Hallie's head so sharp and sudden that she fell to her knees. She struggled to rise. She could see Martin as if through a film. On his knees. Falling onto his side. Something passing from him to the ghosts so that they were bright, more solid, the effect moving rapidly from one to the next, straight to Hallie. The pain in Hallie's head grew until it was a white-hot rail spike straight through her skull and down her spine. Her vision blackened. She couldn't see Martin at all anymore.

Then Dell drifted away from her. The pain receded. She could breathe.

She staggered to her feet. She swayed, blinking fiercely. Six feet away, Martin had already climbed to his knees. In another moment, he, too, would be back on his feet.

Just out of Hallie's reach, Dell drifted. Drifted, and looked at her. Actually looked at her.

"I know what I'm doing," Hallie said.

She said it out loud, said it like Dell could hear her, like she'd understand. She reached out her hand one more time. Dell reached out and took it.

Good-bye.

Martin screamed.

"Hallie."

Hallie was cold. And her ass was wet.

And oh my god, her head hurt like fire. She groaned.

"Hallie."

She opened her eyes. At least she thought she did, but there was something wrong with them. Because she appeared to be looking at the world through a waterfall. Or a rainbow. Yellow and blue and green like prisms and raindrops.

"Can you sit up?"

"I—yeah—oh crap." The stabbing white-hot railroad spike was back. Right through her skull, right down her spine. She tried sitting up again. The second time was easier. Not because the pain had lessened. Because she was getting better at pushing it away. "What happened?" she asked.

"It was like—wow!"

That couldn't be Brett, though it sounded like her. Brett didn't say *wow*.

And besides if that was Brett, then—

"Are you all right?"

Boyd.

"You shouldn't be walking around," she said, still blinking furiously because she needed to see, damnit! And not tiny fucking rainbows either.

Boyd touched her arm, and she almost recoiled because he felt as if he were on fire. Then she realized that it was her, that she was so cold, he felt like a furnace.

"What have you done to me?"

Hallie struggled to turn her head. She could barely make out Martin on the ground, sobbing. His hands covered his face, as if he was trying to hide. "My god, what have you done?"

A siren echoed in the distance, though it sounded in Hallie's head like a giant Chinese gong.

"It was—" Hallie heard something in Boyd's voice she hadn't heard before. Wonder? Fear? A combination of the two? "We could see it, Hallie. It was as if, while the magic ran through them, the ghosts were all alive. Visible."

"Dell?"

"I don't know," Boyd said. "I can't see them anymore. I can't see her. I'm sorry."

Hallie closed her eyes. With them open, her head hurt worse, which she wouldn't have believed possible. It felt as if she'd forgotten how to see, as if she were seeing the world from outside.

She could hear Martin talking behind her. "I was a god," he said. "I was a god. And you—you destroyed me."

Hallie turned toward the sound of his voice.

"No," she said. "The dead collect their own price, you sorry son of a bitch."

37

Hallie hadn't seen a ghost for three weeks.

They'd been gone by the time Ole and the others had arrived. Martin had confessed right there, in the middle of the cemetery in a rambling long monologue that included his grandmother's entire history including two husbands and three dead children, every woman he'd killed, everyone he'd thought of killing, every detail of his magic and the rituals behind them.

Ole had looked at Hallie like somehow he suspected the whole thing was her fault, but he'd let her go in the ambulance with Boyd, long drive to Rapid City while the EMTs told Hallie how she should have done things, and Hallie blinked and shivered, wrapped in three blankets, and held Boyd's hand. And breathed.

They kept her overnight at the hospital, but they couldn't tell her what was wrong with her eyes. By morning, her eyesight was more or less back to normal and her headache was gone. Until she walked out the front door of the hospital, and it slammed into her like a pile driver and knocked her to her knees.

She finally got back to the ranch three days later, days that had involved intense back-and-forth conversations between Hallie, her doctors, and the army, who wanted her back, but not if she couldn't stand up. They extended her leave five more days and told her to report to Fort Leonard Wood at the end of that time for a complete physical.

There were no ghosts when she'd come back to the ranch, her father out of the hospital and coming home with her. Brett came over an hour after she got home, like she'd had a trip wire installed on the drive. They sat together on the back porch, and Brett made Hallie tell her from the beginning about ghosts and Martin and weather magic and how Lorie had died.

"It seems so . . . unlikely," she said when Hallie finished.

"That doesn't mean it isn't so," Hallie said.

Brett shook her head. "I don't like it," she said.

"I don't think events care whether you like them or not," Hallie said.

"Huh. Yeah." A pause as they looked across the prairie. The sky was cold and gray. It would snow soon. Brett looked over at Hallie, gave a quick dazzling grin. "Maybe I'll just remember it differently," she said. And if anyone could do that, it'd be Brett.

Hallie had tried to visit Dell's grave a couple of days later. Because if the ghosts were gone, she should be able to do it, right? But the minute she'd stepped across the boundary, they'd begun to rise, ghost upon ghost upon ghost. Not *her* ghosts, maybe, but still there, reminders of a past Hallie didn't even know and had no part of. She'd stood in the parking lot for a long time, wanting to go in, to stand in front of Dell's grave like she would if the world were normal.

She thought of the time her father'd been gone to Brookings for some continuing education thing and a fierce blizzard had swept in out of Canada. She and Dell had spent three hours getting the horses into the barn and finding the dog, who was trying to shelter in the lee of the equipment shed. Between the equipment shed and the house, Hallie'd lost Dell and crawled on her hands and knees back to the shed, knew she'd never find her and headed back to the house to find Dell on the back porch with a rope ready to head out after her.

"What were you thinking, you dumb ass?" Dell had said. "You know I'm always fine."

I'll always be here, she'd written in Hallie's yearbook.

And she always would.

But not the way she'd meant it. Or Hallie'd always figured.

She made one more attempt to enter the cemetery, but the old ghosts were still there. They weren't malicious, didn't know they were stopping her. They just wanted someone to remember.

Jennie had come to the ranch two days after Hallie and her father had come back. Hallie met her in the front yard where Jennie hugged her tight, which made Hallie uncomfortable as hell, though Jennie didn't notice.

"Because you saved me, Hallie," she said. "And if you ever need anything. Anything. You tell me. I'll do it. Anything." Then she went away, which Hallie couldn't help but think was somewhat of a relief.

After that, she packed up her things and left her father standing on the porch and drove herself to the airport. Not that he wouldn't have done it or Brett. But she was afraid and she didn't like being afraid and she didn't want to talk to anyone about it or even tell them why. But the headaches weren't going away. They were like being hit in the head with a sledgehammer, and she was getting them, still, two or three times a day. They didn't last more than a couple of minutes, but she was down. Out. Nonfunctional for the entire two minutes, like someone threw a lightning bolt into her brain.

She was pretty sure she and the army were finished. And she didn't want anyone to tell her they were sorry.

She got back to the ranch on a Tuesday. She wasn't entirely finished with the army yet—or they weren't finished with her—because cutting someone loose took reams of paperwork and weeks of time. But they had nothing for her to do and nothing to do for her, and someone decided she was due thirty days' leave anyway and signed the papers and tossed her back.

She found her father down behind the horse barn, pulling the wheel off an old ATV. He dropped it when he saw her. "Got it at auction last week," he said with a wave at the four-wheeler. "Better than nothing."

Hallie thought of all the things he'd lost—at least three tractors, half his field equipment, twenty years' worth of tools.

"I'm sorry you got dragged into this mess," she said.

"What mess? That bastard Weber? The only thing I'm pissed about is you didn't ask me to help."

He folded his arms across his chest, and Hallie could see that he really was pissed. Which, he probably had a right, because it was his daughter who'd died and he cared about things like that, cared like hell, no matter what anyone else saw or thought.

"So, you going to be here for a while?" he asked.

"I don't know," she said honestly.

"Plenty of work." He turned back to the ATV, shoved a crowbar into the gap between the tire and the wheel. "If you stay."

Hallie knew he would never actually say one way or the other, would never act as if he wanted her to stay, even if he did.

She'd visited Boyd a couple of times at the hospital up in Rapid City that first week before she left, but in the meantime, he'd been released and she didn't know where he'd gone. She actually called the sheriff's office.

Patty, the backup dispatcher and an old friend of Hallie's mother, answered the phone.

"He's on leave. Ole told him not to come back for at least three weeks. And then he'll be on desk duty for a while, which, in this county is boring, let me tell you. Plus he blew up a car. Ole was plenty mad about that."

"He didn't blow up a—"

"He calls in every couple of days," Patty said. "I can tell him you were asking."

"Don't worry about it," Hallie said.

Tom Hauser and Jake Javinovich and half a dozen others came out two Saturdays in a row with a couple of big trucks to haul away the remains of the equipment shed. The insurance agent and a claims adjuster had been there two days after the fire and promised Hallie's father a check was coming.

"I'll believe that when I see it," he'd said.

Before Hallie left for Fort Leonard Wood, she'd been hauling old equipment out of the wreckage when Jake came over to work beside her. For a good while, they'd worked in silence. Then, pretty much right out of the blue, Jake said, "Sometimes, you know, some-times . . . I see things that people tell me aren't there." He stopped as if he had to think for a minute about what those things were. "Not people, okay? But . . . fog in graveyards and—once in Rapid City, I saw a dog, a dead dog, get up and walk around. I mean, the dog was still lying there. I could see that. But then, there was this . . . other, all just walking around. It's been since . . . after Karen, since the car accident." He looked at Hallie then. "I almost died, you know. Not like I stopped breathing or nothing. But I saw the Reaper. I talked to him. And you don't come back from that like nothing happened."

A sharp pain, like a needle, skewered Hallie through her left eye when Jake said *Reaper*. Another headache. Because that wasn't what happened to her. She'd remember that.

"Why are you telling me this?" she asked, though it even hurt to talk.

"People talk," Jake said. "About what they think happened between you and Pete and Martin. Not that anyone knows what happened. Or believes it if they do know. Or even really knows . . . or even think they know." He stopped, wound up in his own tangled words. He inhaled sharply. "I'm saying that maybe I know a little what it's like. If you ever wanted to talk. If . . . that would help."

"Yeah," Hallie said, didn't even add *okay*, because when had anything ever been helped by talking?

She didn't miss the ghosts.

She didn't.

Besides, she had to figure out what she was going to do now. Stay and ranch with her father? Go to college? Sitting in a classroom was as unappealing as ever, but she was going to have to do something. Brett had been talking up psychology yesterday, and Tom Hauser was trying to convince her to get EMT certified and join the ambulance crew.

"That doesn't actually pay anything, Tom," Hallie said.

"Yeah." He'd laughed. "Welcome to the prairie."

On her third day back, down by the horse barns, unsaddling Scout, because now that there were no ghosts around her, the horses let her near them again, she saw Boyd coming down the lane. He looked pale and thin, and every bit as young as she remembered. He had an aluminum cane with a black rubber base, and he was limping, though not badly. She thunked the saddle down on the fence rail, slipped the bridle off Scout's head, and waited for Boyd to reach her.

He was dressed as only Boyd would dress: loose-fitting jeans with a crease down each leg, boots that looked like he'd taken them new out of the box that morning, a red denim shirt all crisp with knifelike edges.

"How are you?" she said, leaning against the top fence rail.

"You never gave me my gun back," he said in lieu of greeting, "Ole's mad."

"Ole's always mad," she said. "What else does he have to do?"

She couldn't stop smiling, and she didn't know why. He looked tired, but better than the last time she'd seen him, lying in that hospital bed in Rapid City.

He reached up and put his hand over hers, where it rested on the top fence rail. They stood like that for a moment or two, not talking.

Like idiots, Hallie thought, because did they really have nothing to talk about anymore?

"I was going to buy you breakfast once," Boyd finally said.

"It's a little late now," Hallie told him. She hopped the fence and picked up the saddle and bridle.

Boyd laid a hand on the sleeve of her shirt. "I could buy you dinner," he said.

"You're on."

She let him make his own way back up the lane, while she went ahead of him into the horse barn to put her tack up. When she came back out to meet him, there was a moment when the low-slanting sun flashed brilliant against an old aluminum horse trough tipped up against the barn. Hallie looked away. When she looked back, Boyd had nearly reached her.

And behind him was another ghost.

"Goddamnit," Hallie said.

She was pretty sure she'd seen that ghost before, forgotten in the scramble of Dell and Lorie and all the women Martin had killed. She was young, maybe younger than Hallie, maybe the same age, with short blond hair. She was dressed in black and staring right at Hallie, like she saw her, like Dell had at the end, like Hallie was the Thing that kept her anchored here on Earth.

"Are you all right?" Boyd asked when he finally reached her.

Goddamnit, Hallie thought, *why can't you just leave me alone.*

"I'm fine," she said to Boyd. "Let's go."

They walked up the lane toward the house together.

The ghost followed behind.